Karen Haden

Karen H
x

Copyright © Karen Haden 2024.

The right of Karen Haden to be identified as the author of this work has been asserted by her in accordance with the Copyright, Designs and Patents Act, 1988.

First published in 2024 by Sharpe Books.

For Simon, Ben and Zoe

Truth is fallen in the street and equity cannot enter

Geneva Bible, Isaiah Chapter 59 Verse 14

PAYING IN BLOOD

Prologue

January 1613

Dear Geoffrey,

I am writing to let you know that I have found two suitable candidates. Both appear scared, but otherwise of healthy body and mind. They will be delivered after nightfall on Saturday as you instructed.

The two were arrested on minor charges. We can keep them for two or three weeks, as no-one is interested in trying them before the royal wedding.

When we meet on Thursday, I would like to discuss the latest draft of the itinerary, to ensure we have adequate security arrangements in place. As members of the team remind me, the Catholic threat did not die with Guy Fawkes. I am equally concerned by the growing number of London's citizens disillusioned with King James' rule.

Your faithful servant,

Leonard Redfern

KAREN HADEN

Monday

Nieuwpoort, Low Countries 1600

1

When we had dealt with the first line of casualties, I spotted John Crackleton's black foot. The wiry soldier had rolled off his stretcher near the entrance, but could not crawl from the tent. As I turned him over and looked into his bloodshot eyes, Crackleton blinked, still alive.

"Here's another one for the table," I shouted across to the stretcher-bearer Gwyn, "We must have missed him earlier. Where is Lupton now?"

"He went outside, saying he felt ill. It's the smell."

"What's a surgeon doing in a battle if he can't stomach the stench?"

Gwyn apologised, "I've been with Lupton for many years, Baxby. He's not usually like this."

I sympathised more than I admitted. Cadiz had been more fun, four years before. An exciting expedition, as my patron Geoffrey had foretold. After capturing the port and watching their fleet catch light, we drank the Spaniards' sweet wine whilst others cleared the dead.

Nieuwpoort was heavier on our side. Musket shot tore through flesh and bones alike, with casualties continually arriving at the tent door. Boy-soldiers gasped their last breaths along each side, obstructing Lupton's efforts to save those who might live to fight again. I was an additional hindrance because the surgeon tried to teach me as he worked. Lupton was a kindly bald veteran with a steady hand and saintly patience, but no-one could train a novice during a battle like Nieuwpoort.

A pike-man had bled to death that morning. I failed disastrously, unable to tie the ligature tight enough or hear Lupton's instructions over the patient's screams. I remember little else, except that he died in agony before Lupton severed his arm.

"Let's hope for better luck next time," the surgeon had said, "We can't save them all."

"There won't be a next time," I spat, as I wiped the table down, "I shouldn't have accepted this post."

Despite his stoic words, Lupton was clearly upset. He was affected by all the deaths, which was not surprising, it was gut-wrenching work. The pike-man's corpse lay in the pit behind the tent, evidence of my previous ineptitude. Why had Lupton not returned? His precious instruments lay on the table where he had left them, so he was unlikely to have gone far.

Crackleton twisted on his stretcher, clearly in pain.

"Can you hear me?" I asked, bending down.

"Tell Catherine I love her," he whispered in reply.

Assuming he was going to die, his thoughts were for his wife. I knew he loved her and his children deeply. We had chatted on the ship, and again when we crossed the border from the Dutch Republic states.

The soldier was a little older than me, from a village in north Lincolnshire, whereas I was raised near Boston to the south. I had found him cheery company on the march, although not particularly quick-witted. Despite talking at length about his family and comrades, he knew little about the campaign itself. Contributing jealously guarded funds, Queen Elizabeth clearly understood the risk. If we did not destroy the Dunkirker pirate bases in the Spanish-held states, the Narrow Sea would never be safe for Dutch and English ships.

Despite his lack of knowledge, the former strip-farmer had appeared brave and ready to fight.

"I obey orders," he had said, "Others are paid to take charge."

Regardless of his salary, Lupton needed to take charge now. With years of experience as a surgeon, he had the skills to save Crackleton's life.

"I'll go and search outside," I offered, eager for fresh air,

"Lupton can't have gone far."

"You'd better hurry, Baxby. Crackleton won't last long."

Another line of casualties was forming by the entrance. No-one knew where Lupton was.

The breeze had strengthened during the morning, bringing grey clouds from the sea. The canons still fired in the distance but the roar of the fighting had moved further away.

A familiar Boston militiaman was limping towards me from the dunes, carrying a bundle of booty he had collected there.

"Baxby!" he greeted me, ruffling my hair, "I thought I recognised your gawping eyes under that dark mop. This isn't a place for boys."

I pulled away, repulsed. Could he not see my thick beard? I was clearly an adult.

"I'm eighteen years old or thereabouts."

"At least you've grown," he grinned through missing teeth.

I shouted, remembering the old man was deaf in one ear, "Have you seen the surgeon Lupton? He's disappeared."

The militiaman stooped to retrieve a buckle he had dropped, cursing King Philip and his papist army for the inconvenience, before pointing in the direction of a dry stream bed.

"I saw him heading down towards the sea, when I was robbing the Spanish pigs."

"But Lupton's the only one who can operate on Crackleton's leg."

"God help us all. You'd better find him soon. We can't rely on you."

I could have punched him despite his age, but did not want to waste precious time.

What had possessed Lupton? Why had he wandered so far? The dry channel was eerily quiet, with steep sides limiting my view ahead. As I picked my way through the blood-stuck bodies, I could be ambushed at any time. Spanish and allied soldiers lay in equal number, proving no divine favour for Roman or

PAYING IN BLOOD

Protestant sides. The flies showed no preference either. Sweat made it hard to grip my sword.

Penetrating deeper into the dunes, I heard faint English cries ahead. Quickening my pace, I turned a corner, discovering the source of the screams. Not Lupton, but an English lad in mortal danger, half-way up the bank. He was trying to escape from the fat Spaniard beneath him by grasping at rye-grass tufts. The brute kept slipping back but was perilously close.

Struggling to gain a foothold myself, I watched in horror as the Spaniard chased the lad higher, swiping at his doublet, one, two, three, until close enough to make the fatal cut. It was distressing to witness, but intent on his prey, the Spaniard did not notice me. The wind direction meant he did not hear me either. I crept up behind while he searched the corpse. Plunged my sword in his side, as he twisted to pull a small chain from his victim's neck. A straight-forward kill, which gave me brief pleasure, knowing he would take no more English lives, but saving Crackleton remained my priority.

The beach stretched in either direction, as far as I could see, rippled by the retreating tide. Clumps of familiar seaweed littered my route. However, when I reached the water's edge, I discovered a gruesome truth. My former comrades' bodies washed back and forth in the froth, as if refusing to leave the scene of their slaughter or let me forget their fate.

Wading in to look for signs of life, I recognised the tortured face of a Stamford man as his head brushed against my leg. He told me he was the first to join when the muster lieutenant came to his town, Dunkirker pirates having sunk his uncles' ship. Now the former blacksmith would never march south to take his revenge.

"Lupton!" I called out, although it was futile, "Lupton, where are you?"

So many bodies, men who would be missed by those who loved them back home.

Up to my knees in the cold Narrow Sea, I checked each bald

head in turn, until I found Lupton's bloated corpse, wrapped in bladder wrack. There was no doubt, the surgeon would never operate again, on Crackleton or anyone else.

Spray soaked my clothes when I shut his eyes, but I did not care at the time. Salt mixed with tears, hurting mine when I rubbed them. A believer would have prayed, instead I yelled at the sky, "Geoffrey! This is all your fault."

I never wanted to see my patron's smile or hear his silver tongue again. Crackleton's death would be his responsibility not mine. If a seasoned surgeon could not cope in the tent, how could anyone expect me to work there? I was also angry with myself for being duped by Geoffrey's charm.

A herring gull circled overhead. There was no one else to hear my cries.

PAYING IN BLOOD

2

Cold and numb, I stumbled back up the beach, cursing Geoffrey again. I imagined him sitting by the fire in a warm London inn, enticing other boys with tales of adventure and generous pay. He organised training and Spanish lessons before Cadiz, and I was excited to sail there with him.

Since Cadiz, in truth, I had been bored, accompanying merchants and their crates across the Bay of Biscay, with the occasional opportunity to translate a sentence of Spanish.

I made my displeasure clear to Geoffrey whenever we met. He knew I wanted to work at court, and only informed me about the Low Countries assignment two days before I sailed, having come to a private agreement with our regimental commander.

"Sir Francis Vere is an old friend. He will appreciate your help. I'll give you some ointment jars to take. A bright young man like you could rise to prominence in his service, after the fighting is done."

Geoffrey refused to answer my questions when he accompanied me to the ship. He just smiled and stroked his moustache. What a ghastly shock when I discovered what I was expected to do.

"My surgeon Lupton needs a dresser," Sir Francis greeted me.

My face must have betrayed my ignorance and surprise. I had never met a man of such standing before, and did not know how to respond.

"His stretcher bearer Gwyn is a sturdy Welshman, who is good at holding patients down. Lupton needs someone with nimbler fingers and a sharper mind, to bandage wounds and perform various procedures he will explain."

"Geoffrey never mentioned ...."

"Lupton's getting older, so tires more easily. Please help him in any way you can. My servant will take you to his tent."

What a ridiculous plan! Sir Francis thanked me for the ointment jars, before dismissing me.

When the gull flew down to peck a corpse, I threw a pebble to scare it away, then hurled another, as far as I could out to sea. It started to rain as I began the journey back. Where else could I go? The gull cawed overhead, mocking each step.

In the dunes I saw the Boston militiaman again, laughing with a friend. I recognised the little chain in his hand. It was the one the Spaniard had pulled from the boy. The thief was showing it to his accomplice.

"Can't you find Lupton?" he laughed, "Shall we tell the wounded to dig their own graves?"

This time I punched him, not something I am proud of now but I felt better afterwards. Both men were rude to my mother, shortly before her death. She never forgave their cruelty, so why should I?

As I watched the pair scavenge in the sand, searching for buttons and buckles which had scattered from their sack, I realised they were as stupid as they were coarse. Although the odds were against me, it was not *inevitable* that I would fail. Sir Francis appreciated my help. Lupton had been impressed by how quickly I learnt. "You'll make a good surgeon one day, Baxby. You just need to practise."

I made my decision quickly, fearful and defiant in equal measure. However terrified I felt, I would prove my detractors wrong by amputating Crackleton's foot. He might live to see his wife and family again. Without my intervention he would certainly die.

More casualties were waiting outside the tent when I returned.

"Where's Lupton?" one called out.

"Tidy up the line," I shouted back, sounding braver than I felt, "Lupton won't be joining us, I will operate instead."

Muttering their misgivings, the men shuffled into a more orderly queue. Having stated my intention, I realised the enormity of what I proposed. Gwyn appeared in the doorway, looking across expectantly.

I shook my head, "Lupton won't be joining us. I will remove

PAYING IN BLOOD

Crackleton's foot."

He put an arm on my shoulder and steered me inside, then found a new apron, even larger than the one I had worn that morning. The smell threatened to overwhelm me. How could I do this?

Crackleton was on the table, circled by friends who had come to help. I had not anticipated an audience, and wanted to send them out. Gwyn assured me they would prove useful. One could hold each limb, leaving him free to stem the flow of blood as best he could. Reluctantly, I agreed.

"Let's get started. Crackleton has waited long enough."

"You're so young," one friend protested, "Have you done this before?"

Gwyn came to my aid, "Of course Baxby has. Do whatever he says."

"Keep quiet throughout the procedure, to help me concentrate. The quicker I make the cut, the better for everyone.

"Tell Catherine I love her," Crackleton sobbed, "I shouldn't have left without saying a proper good-bye."

"Stay still. There's nothing to worry about," Gwyn lied.

"Tell my children I love them too. I never meant to leave like that."

His life and his family's future were in my hands.

As Gwyn passed me Lupton's favourite saw, the colour drained from Crackleton's face.

"Hold firmer," I ordered his friends.

Only the lower part of the leg was rotten, meaning I could cut below the knee. Crackleton screamed as I made the incision, tried to turn away as the pike-man had done before. Blood seeped over the edge of the table, mostly missing the bowls.

I hesitated, then admonished myself, remembering what Lupton had taught me. Ignore the screams, the agony and blood. Speed is essential. There is a job to be done.

The others watched in trepidation. Gwyn whispered a short prayer. Mercifully, Crackleton passed out while I was sawing. The cannons went quiet outside. My comrades cheered when a boy rushed in to announce our allied victory. I kept my eye on my patient, drawing the saw back and forth, back and forth.

Time seemed to pass slowly. Why was it taking so long? Crackleton's bone was tougher than it looked. I shivered, still damp from the sea, but kept on sawing. Cutting my way through, many times, until the foot fell to the floor. After hitting the rim of a bowl, it came to rest against my own.

I staggered backwards, overcome with relief. Someone helped me to a stool, scarcely able to breathe. The others clapped and shook my hands. I felt like I was in a dream, watching myself, not participating in the celebrations. What had I done?

Eventually, Gwyn passed me some ale and I started to recover.

"Well done, Baxby. Lupton would be proud."

I could not move for some time afterwards, utterly exhausted. Crackleton woke as Gwyn bandaged his stump, then screeched in pain trying to sit.

"Keep still while we find a stretcher."

"Catherine!" he cried for his wife again.

"Don't worry. You'll see her and your children again."

He closed his eyes as they carried him out.

Crackleton had survived his operation and I had atoned for my previous failure. I did not know then whether he would live for hours or days or years, or how his life would entangle with my own. I drank his health regardless, at least he had a chance.

PAYING IN BLOOD

3

Sir Francis Vere's servant found me in Crackleton's tent in the morning. After attending to other casualties, I had kept vigil by his blanket, until falling asleep myself.

"Wake up, Baxby. The commander wants to see you, immediately. Bring some of those ointment jars."

"Does he know that Lupton has died?"

"I believe so. Hurry up."

Pleased to be summoned thus, I ran back to my tent and packed my bag. If Sir Francis knew how I had saved soldiers' lives, he might recognise my efforts, even increase my pay.

"Believe me, he won't want to lose you, Baxby," Geoffrey had promised, "He will probably take you to court."

The servant led me to the large farmhouse which had been appropriated for the Vere brothers' use. Their cook had roasted the farm's chickens in the fireplace overnight. The chamber smelt delicious, but no-one offered me breakfast. The commander rose from his seat at the end of a long table, where he and his brother had been drafting letters with secretaries.

"I was sorry to hear about Lupton's passing but you did well yesterday. Thank you for your hard work."

Even without his breastplate, Sir Francis looked imposing in his padded leather jerkin. His nose was chiselled to a point like his brother's, unlike any commoner's I had seen.

"Congratulations on your great triumph, Sir. I am honoured to serve in your army, and look forward to reaching Dunkirk."

Following our resounding Nieuwpoort victory, like all the men, I assumed we would slaughter the pirates by the end of the week. After thanking me again and requesting more ointment jars, Sir Francis told me the cruel news. Instead of pressing on to Dunkirk, the Dutch had ordered our retreat. I did not believe him at first.

"We can't stop now, Sir. The Spanish are on the run. Couldn't we fight on without them?"

"Having seen the strength of the Spanish forces, the Dutch have made a wise choice. Bad weather saved us from the Armada. Sand jammed their muskets yesterday. Regardless of the relative merits of our religions, our small impecunious island cannot hope to expel mighty Spain from her territories. It's time for us to go home."

There would be no handsome salary from captured pirate gold. The campaign was over. Sir Francis was saying good-bye.

"You've shown great talent here, Baxby. I will send a letter of commendation to Geoffrey, to help him find another role, commensurate with your skills."

It was no consolation at the time. What a waste of a summer! All that blood, the bodies in the ocean and the pit behind the tent. Lives lost for no gain on the ground. From now on, the Dunkirker pirates would laugh at us for being cowards too.

The black stallions in the yard increased my sense of despair, looking better fed than most of our men. Would I ever earn a reliable salary, or be able to afford a horse of my own?

We sailed back with the ragged remnants of the Lincolnshire militia, on the *Mary-Anne*. The Red Lion landlord Edmund Sibsey had introduced me to her captain Atherton when I was a boy. With a billowing beard, untamed like the waters he crossed, Atherton had ferried goods across the Narrow Sea for years. The hold was full of serge cloth, so we had to sleep under canvas on the deck.

Crackleton seemed small as he took his first steps, leaning on his friends' arms. Unusually for a soldier, he never grew a beard. There were plenty of matted curls on top of his head, but little hair on his face. Battling with crutches later, I realised how determined he was, his lack of stature countered by a stubborn single-mindedness.

As we watched a Dutchman timidly cross the deck, Crackleton laughed, "I'll soon be quicker than him."

A woman told us that the well-dressed foreigner was looking to buy cheap Lincolnshire land. However, when I suggested asking him for work, she caught my arm.

"Be careful. He's an Anabaptist heretic. They don't baptise their babies. They let them go to hell."

I did not understand what she meant, but avoided the Dutchman throughout the voyage as a precaution. Crackleton did the same, similarly ignorant.

Remarkably, he did not catch a fever on the voyage home. His colour improved and he became more talkative again.

"Thank you for removing my foot, Baxby. I would have died without you."

"The stump may take weeks, or even months, to heal. Then you need to find a carpenter who can fit a wooden leg."

His attempts to improve my mood on the ship were less agreeable, suggesting I become a barber-surgeon, without understanding the cost, then chastising me for being too negative.

"If Geoffrey helped you before, he could help you again."

"But he's a lying snake. I can't trust anything he says."

"I don't know why you complain so much. I just want to get back on dry land, to see Catherine and the children again. I want to work my field-strips and provide for my family."

He told me that the couple had married young, after a memorable evening in the local churchyard. Their daughter Anna was born first and then John Junior.

"The trees were in blossom on our wedding day. The sun shone, and Catherine looked beautiful."

Memories of my own childhood cracked open, when he described their two rooms and dirt floor. My mother also carried firewood and piled it by the stove. I never wanted to live like that again. Crackleton was happy with his lot, but I wanted to earn considerably more, and live in a water-tight house.

Realising how few coins I had left, I descended into even deeper gloom.

I did not recognise the Boston Deeps as we came close to the shore in the fog. It was even hard to see the *Mary-Anne*'s drooping flag above our heads. Lincolnshire has a dangerous coastline, with shifting banks and silted flats which constantly split and re-shape. We all knew that without clear sight of St. Botolph's church, we could miss the Haven entrance and run aground. Atherton held the tiller with both hands, listening for the look-out's cry, as the ship sailed on blindly.

Crackleton moaned, "I don't want to drown without seeing Catherine and the children again."

It would seem particularly cruel, if he survived the amputation only to perish at sea. Neither of us could swim.

The Dutchman dropped to his knees in prayer, "God have mercy on our souls."

Atherton ordered him below, insisting on silence, but before the crew could bundle him down the ladder, we heard a strange new sound. Quiet at first, then growing louder and more regular with time.

"What's that?"

"St. Botolph's bell. We're nearly home."

The Dutchman whispered quieter prayers. The rest of us spread along the starboard side, looking for signs of land. As the mist curled and lifted slightly, we heard a cry from above.

"The Stump."

The look-out had spotted the top of the church's distinctive tower, rising through the fog. Atherton turned the ship, sufficiently to clear the Haven entrance. The Dutchman cried, the militia cheered, whilst Crackleton waved a crutch in the air. The *Mary-Anne* and all on-board were safe. Thank you, Atherton.

Hopefully, I could navigate my career with similar skill once ashore. There must be a way to escape Geoffrey's hold. I needed to consider my options, as calmly as I could, and free myself from his preposterous schemes.

PAYING IN BLOOD

London 1613

4

Baxby leans back against the stone wall of the cell, wondering how he could have been so naïve in his youth. Geoffrey would not loosen his grip so easily. He was too useful a resource.

Could he have done anything differently? Would he have left for London if his mother were alive? Without parents, the young Baxby had been particularly easy prey, dependent on Geoffrey from their first meeting, as if bound by a loathsome cord.

Dozens arrive in the capital each month, from hungry villages in the north and west. Some hope for riches, others enough food to survive. They enter the gates exhausted and desperate for work, ready for patrons and sundry agents to exploit.

Baxby's cell-mates urge him to continue. They want to learn more about Catherine. He has called her name in his sleep.

KAREN HADEN

Boston, Lincolnshire 1600

5

I returned to a colder climate than I expected. Battling through the wet Low Country summer, I had imagined more warmth and sunshine back home. Lincolnshire's weather was worse. As the *Mary-Anne* slipped upstream, the mist cleared to reveal the flat landscape. Flooded fields shared the same depressing shade as the sea and sky, with one darker line of smoke drifting upwards from the Sailors' Inn. There would be famine again that winter.

Geoffrey was not waiting on the mud bank quay at the Haven. Two other figures attracted my attention there. Drawing nearer, I recognised the Muster Lieutenant, waiting to take the militia inland. His slightly shorter companion's back was turned towards me, slicing the air with his rapier blade for the older man to admire. The garish blue cape, hanging from his shoulder, might be fashionable at Richmond Palace, but looked conceited in Lincolnshire.

"Do you know the man with the Muster Lieutenant?" I asked the militiaman, standing beside me on the deck.

"That's his ambitious deputy Julian Felde. Be careful. He'll scratch anyone who gets in his way."

I laughed, "He will need to buy a more sensible cloak if he has ambitions here."

Sleepy oarsmen emerged from the cottages to ferry passengers from the ship. Hawkers filed along the broken causeway from Fishtoft to sell their wares. I had no intention of obstructing Felde or anyone else's efforts to gain prosperity. Finding work for myself was my priority, as my money would not last long.

Stepping ashore, I missed my footing, and fell back in the mud. The lad who helped me up, darted out of reach, then pointed at a letter, protruding from my pocket.

"Careful Sir! Don't lose that!"

PAYING IN BLOOD

The rat had tripped me up and deposited the letter, in one well-rehearsed movement. I could have caught him if I had been quicker, made him squeak.

Looking down, I recognised the curling *Baxby*, written in Geoffrey's stylish hand. When I turned the letter over, I was surprised to see that it was sealed with the Bishop of Lincoln's mark, a strange addition for my godless patron. Why would a bishop endorse his handiwork?

Slitting open the seal, the handwriting was beautiful, as always, but the contents disappointingly brief. Geoffrey instructed me to meet him in Lincoln cathedral in three days' time, at Secretary Sculthorpe's office in the north-east transept. There were no clues as to what he expected me to do or why he had arranged to meet me there. Also, three days was a long time to wait without pay.

More passengers were coming ashore from the *Mary-Anne*, their raucous shouts distracting me as I made my way up the bank. A woman, who had lost her bonnet, fell in the water while remonstrating with the oarsman who refused to fish it out. Whilst laughing at her mud-streaked antics in the shallows, Crackleton received a letter of his own.

"Baxby, will you read this to me? A kind boy stopped it falling from my pocket when I slipped in the mud."

Crackleton was more credulous than me, but how strange that he should receive a letter in the same manner as my own! His carried the Bishop of Lincoln's seal too. Although addressed in a tidier hand, there must be a connection between the two.

"I'll read it in the Sailors'. Let me help you up the bank."

Already busy, we found a table with some warmth from the inn fire. Crackleton sat stroking the seal on his letter while I bought drinks. The shutters were closed, for protection from the weather, but the innkeeper passed me a candle to use.

I struggled to make myself heard at first, until a whore led the loudest militiaman upstairs.

"This is from the Bishop of Lincoln's secretary," I started.

As my comrade watched me scan the page, I feared my expression would betray my dread. Why had I agreed to read this? I had already removed his foot, now I had to tell Crackleton that his beloved wife was dead.

Catherine died in Lincoln in July. No cause was given in the letter, which informed him that the Diocese paid for carriage to her home parish, and burial in the churchyard there. Writing on the Bishop's behalf, his secretary Sculthorpe emphasised that all the procedures had been performed correctly, in 'full accordance with the order given by Her Majesty Queen Elizabeth in the Book of Common Prayer'. This might give some Church assurance of eternal rest in heaven, but I could not convey such sentiments. Omitting the pious quotation, I found the only words that could give comfort in my opinion.

"Your wife rests in peace."

Catherine was free from this dark world, which some would envy.

The pitiful one-legged soldier held his head in his hands and wept. He had been longing to see his wife again, but would never do so.

After recovering some composure, he scowled, "I can't read but I'm not stupid. Why did the secretary write this to me?"

"Had Catherine met the Bishop before?"

"Of course not. She rarely left home. Our village is nearer Gainsborough than Lincoln."

Such a woman would be particularly vulnerable, alone in the city.

"This is a terrible shock for you. Would you prefer me to leave?"

"Please fetch me another drink."

By the time I returned to the table, some friends had gathered round to offer sympathy.

Someone asked, "Why did Catherine travel to Lincoln? Why did she die there?"

Crackleton shook his head, "I don't know. She must have walked, because we could never afford a cart."

PAYING IN BLOOD

Incensed on my friend's behalf, and craving more details myself, I scanned the page again. How did Catherine die? Why did the Church pay for her body to be taken back? The Secretary should have omitted the religious ramblings in his letter, and provided a few simple facts instead. This was a contemptible way to break appalling news. The Lincoln clerics must be as heartless as our drunkard near Boston.

I retrieved my own letter, intending to show Crackleton the identical seal, but was interrupted by the Muster Lieutenant striding in to order stragglers to assemble for the ferry upstream. His deputy followed behind, clearing tables as he went. When a whore protested that she had not been paid, he found a coin on the soldier's behalf. Those women knew all the tricks.

Unfortunately, Crackleton was not as astute. Forgetting his missing leg, he tried to stand, and hit his head on the table as he crashed to the floor.

"My children!" he wailed, "The poor law patrol will presume I'm dead. They will carry them away as orphans. I'll never see them again."

Felde came towards us whilst I was wiping the gash on Crackleton's head.

"Take pity," I implored, "This soldier has just learnt that his wife has died."

He stopped when he saw the letters on the table, drew his rapier blade and pointed the tip at my face.

"Keep away, Baxby! This has nothing to do with you."

Felde wore powder on his cheeks and slightly crooked nose. His perfume irritated my nose, a cloying mix of musk and lemons. However, his behaviour towards Crackleton annoyed me the most. Instead of showing respect to the wounded soldier, Felde kicked him towards the door, causing him to yelp in pain.

"I'll let you know if I find out more about Catherine," I cried out.

Crackleton did not reply.

As I watched Felde drag him to the boat, I wondered whether the deputy was Secretary Sculthorpe's messenger boy. Felde could have brought the two letters from Lincoln, paid the boy who tripped us up. He seemed mean enough to employ such a tactic.

Standing outside the Sailors' in the rain, I was overcome by a deep-founded desire to discover how Catherine died. Crackleton deserved to know the truth. I suspected foul-play, and wanted to know more, on behalf of my grieving friend and also for myself.

I caught the last ferry up the Witham to Boston. Two soldiers were sick over the sodden side. I was home.

PAYING IN BLOOD

6

Apart from the drunken militiamen rampaging through the town, Boston had changed little while I had been away. Fords and puddles filled familiar dips, where water could not drain away. No-one had repaired a section of jetty, which washed away some years before.

Turning off the High Street, I paused outside a barber's shop. Could I become a barber-surgeon as Crackleton believed? Here was an opportunity to find out more.

"I don't cut soldiers' hair," the barber greeted me.

"I'm not a soldier."

"Good Lord! It's Baxby under there. You look like one with that dreadful beard. Take a seat. Edmund Sibsey will die of shock if you walk into the Red Lion yard looking like that. I'll shave you for his sake."

The pincers, scissors and blades on the shelf seemed inconsequential compared with Lupton's tools. If I could amputate a foot at Nieuwpoort, I must be able to do this job.

As the barber started to chop my hair, I asked, "Do you perform surgery here?"

"I pull teeth and excise warts, a barber in Stamford removes fingers and toes. Why do you want to know?"

"I'm interested in becoming a barber-surgeon myself. What would you advise I do?"

"You might find one who needs an apprentice, but how will you afford the fees? It takes seven years to train. My father found this position for me."

The barber's comment was uncharitable. He knew my background like others in the town. If I had a father to help me, I would not be asking him.

When he finished, he found a mirror to show me his results.

"Now you can visit the Red Lion without scaring Sibsey's guests."

How strange I looked. My eyes seemed ridiculously large

beneath the short fringe, but the pencil beard was charming.

"Keep it like that," the barber instructed, "Your hair's too thick to grow long."

I had fewer coins in my pocket, and was no closer to finding work, but at least I looked more presentable. It is a shame the beard has grown now.

I found Crackleton asleep in the Loggerheads porch. His friends were drinking inside, whilst Felde argued with the landlord demanding compensation for the damage they had caused. My friend's head wound had dried, but his stump was bleeding again. He woke as I retied his bandages.

"Baxby, is that you? I didn't recognise you without your beard."

He clasped my arm, and held it fast. I glimpsed tears in his eyes.

"Catherine died in July," he sputtered, clearly drunk, "When I was looking forward to seeing her again, she was already dead. My wife died before you removed my leg."

If he had known at the time, he might not have recovered so well.

"Don't give up, Crackleton. I won't give up on you."

"She was angry when I enlisted with my uncle. She didn't want me to leave. I don't know how I will live without her now."

I pressed his letter in his hand, "Look after this. I'll do my best to find out what happened to Catherine when I'm in Lincoln. I promise."

"I'll go back to my village and find my children. You'll always be welcome there."

Felde was finishing his conversation inside. I left quickly, not wanting to encounter him. When I looked back, Crackleton was asleep again.

The Red Lion yard was busy as usual. I paused outside the gate. With three galleried sides and a stable block, it was still an impressive sight. The inn was special to me, previously a refuge of sorts. Hopefully, Edmund Sibsey would be able to help me again.

The landlord emerged from a doorway, wearing his faded pink jacket which matched his cheeks. A strong man, with broad shoulders and large hands, he carried a bundle of hay across the yard with ease, before turning to reassure a gentlewoman who was complaining about the privy smell.

When I opened the gate, he beckoned me in with customary warmth.

"Baxby! Come in! How wonderful to see you again. You look handsome with that little beard. All the girls will want to marry you now."

Sibsey raised his voice for more guests to hear, "This young man's a hero. Those big brown eyes were always staring out to sea. I knew Baxby would go far in life, but even I didn't expect him to capture Cadiz with Essex."

"You served with the Earl?" even the gentlewoman sounded impressed.

I tried to explain that I never met the renowned commander on the expedition, but Sibsey ignored my protests, beckoning more guests across. He took great pride in repeating favourite stories about my achievements overseas, despite knowing little about my role. His tales of Spanish slaughter were as popular as his beef and beer.

Fortunately, given the state of my finances, my old friend would not let me pay for my board. He led me up to one of his best rooms, on the top floor, next to the wealthy Dutchman from the *Mary-Anne*. It was the room where he let me stay after my mother died, reminding me of her.

For the first twelve or so years of my life, she did her best to compensate for my missing father. When she went, I was bereft, overwhelmed by a sense of emptiness I had never known before. Sibsey let me stay until the following spring, then recommended a few weeks in London, with his cousin. How did he know that would be the tonic I needed?

After marvelling at the Bridge, the Tower and St. Paul's in the sunshine, his cousin introduced me to an old acquaintance from his journeyman days in the Boar's Head. That is how I met Geoffrey, a fortuitous coincidence at the time. I stayed away much longer than I had intended, and subsequently only returned for short stays.

"It's good to be back," I smiled.

"It's always good to see you, son. My home is your own."

Sibsey had no children, and never mentioned his wife. Once his ostler told me that she had ran away long ago, with a suitor who did not expect her to work so hard.

"When can we talk?" I asked.

"Come down to the kitchen after the evening meal. We can chat while I'm clearing up."

In addition to the ostler, the landlord employed a cook and two servants, but there were always jobs to be done.

All the Red Lion rooms had glass and comfortable beds. I must have fallen asleep. The Dutchman woke me with his snoring next door. Listening to his irritating rattles in the dark, I considered my options again. Even if I found a barber-surgeon who needed an apprentice, how would I pay the fees? Sibsey was generous, but clearly could not afford new clothes for himself. If I asked him for work at the Red Lion, he would recommend speaking to Geoffrey instead.

Where was my letter? I fell over the piss-pot searching, and cursed in anger and pain. Geoffrey had snared me like a stupid animal. I needed his help again, however much I resented it.

PAYING IN BLOOD

7

When I descended the stairs, Sibsey was talking with the *Mary-Anne*'s captain in the kitchen, their voices audible over the crackle of the fire.

"I've stored the cloth in the loft," Atherton said, "Your store is too damp, like most in this town."

"What else have you brought this time?"

"Eye-glasses and pocket Geneva Bibles."

Atherton emptied the contents of his bag on the table. Through the hinge gap, I saw the intriguing instruments and tiny books. Lincolnshire lacks natural harbours and predictable rivers, so monopoly companies prefer dependable ports further south. Smuggling is profitable for those with local knowledge like Atherton.

"The Genevas have more pictures than the previous edition, but are still the same price."

"I'll take them all. Some editions are on the official list, but the Church limits the print-runs."

"I can bring more next time."

That was not the end of their business.

"I've got two more for you," Sibsey said, "A girl in the cellar who's on the run for stealing peas. Her godfather will pay the usual price to get her out."

"Good, that will supplement my income on the crossing back. And the other?"

"My young servant confronted his vicar on Sunday. He told him his grandfather died in 36 along with 'many good Catholics'. Why can't he just sit in church like everyone else, let the prayer book words wash through his empty skull?"

"That vicar's an affront to all religion."

"That may be so, but the lad has a papist problem in his head. He thinks a Spanish princess should succeed Queen Elizabeth. What if he tells the vicar that?"

"That's ridiculous. England will never be Catholic again. The pope excommunicated Queen Elizabeth, and we'll never forgive the Spanish Armada."

"My servant must keep his mouth shut. If not they'll lock him up, or worse, and remove my licence."

"I'll hide him in the beak head like the poacher last year, where the shit-stench should bring him to his senses. Where is he now?"

"In a safe house."

"Get him to the ship by dawn. We'll sail on the morning tide. I'll take the girl now."

A common thief could hang if caught, whilst Sibsey's servant might burn as a heretic. I was more fortunate than those fleeing the country to save their lives, whatever Geoffrey planned next.

After Atherton had left, Sibsey fed me fish and cheeses, while he scrubbed the trenchers and bowls.

"Geoffrey lied to me," I moaned, "He knows I want to work at court.

"He has good contacts, but can't know everything."

"He never warned me about that tent."

My old friend turned to face me, "Baxby, you know how much I care about you, but you must meet with Geoffrey next. I can't afford to employ you here. You're better off with him. He's been like a father to you, and will reward your loyal service. Just wait and see"

Obviously, Geoffrey was not my father, given his blue eyes and fine hair, but there was no point arguing more with Sibsey, who had a higher opinion of him than me.

However, the landlord found Crackleton's letter harder to believe.

"Are you certain Secretary Sculthorpe didn't say how Catherine died? Or why she travelled there?"

"He just gave a list of religious rites that had been performed."

"That's strange. Perhaps she took produce to sell."

"The Crackletons' land scarcely grew enough to feed the family. She couldn't afford a cart or market taxes. It's a long way for a woman to travel alone."

PAYING IN BLOOD

"I saw Secretary Sculthorpe once, when the Bishop visited our deanery court. He seemed well organised then. Could you ask him what happened to Catherine, when you visit the cathedral? After he's explained everything, you can tell Crackleton."

I put my arms around Sibsey's neck, as I did when I was a boy. Where would I be without his support? He taught me to read, using inventories and books his wife had left at the inn.

"What are you doing, son? You're as soft as your mother. You need to get back to your room, so I can clean this place."

"Do you know Julian Felde?" I asked instead.

"Why are you interested in him? Has he been writing letters too, or is he a rival for a pretty girl?"

"He hurt Crackleton in the Sailors' Inn."

"The Muster Lieutenant told me Felde's established a reputation since inheriting land to the north. His name's been linked with candidates for our vacant Lord Lieutenant position."

"I've seen the type before, decorated donkeys who will rope their necks to any noble or knight who can pull them to higher office."

"That's unkind and foolish Baxby. Felde could be influential one day. Anyway, women like men with good prospects."

"This isn't about a girl."

"Very sensible to wait until you've settled into your next position. There'll be plenty of time for women later. That little beard and new haircut may attract attention though."

KAREN HADEN

London 1613

8

Baxby pauses, picturing the Red Lion again. Although he cannot remember how long he has been imprisoned, Sibsey's kitchen remains clear in his mind. He longs to drink beer at that table again, but it is impossible. His ankle is chained to the wall.

Daydreaming, he swaps the cell walls for wide Lincolnshire skies, and follows the path from his old cottage to the coast. He jumps the ditches, and follows the furrows as he did as a boy. The waves lap the shore-line, he can almost smell the salt-air.

Neither of his listeners, a vicar and printer, has visited Lincolnshire. Born and raised in the capital, they have not seen the need to venture north, but the faraway story provides relief from the shock of their arrest. Where once they had homes, professions, families and shoes, now they possess the clothes they were wearing a week ago, and a rough blanket.

PAYING IN BLOOD

Lincolnshire 1600

9

The weather and my poor finances forced me to take the Witham ferry, rather than hire a horse. Families came on board after Tattershall, taking shovelers and teal to market. Although I would have liked more space, their conversation provided a temporary distraction from my concerns and the drab landscape.

A comely woman told me how she lured ducks through decoy tunnels, which seemed an effective method, given the number in the boat. Sibsey was right about my beard and hair-cut. Women paid me more attention. Her daughter wanted to talk at length, but was too young and silly for me. It was a relief when her mother recognised a bend in the river, and instructed us to look up.

The city of Lincoln rose like an island, above the flooded Witham and Trent. The main spire of St. Hugh's cathedral had fallen down some years before, leaving only the tower and the other two smaller spires, but it still looked magnificent.

We disembarked, in the first rays of sunshine since my return from Nieuwpoort. Brayford Pool was even busier than usual, due to the floods. The route which Catherine would have taken earlier, lay underwater that day.

On my previous visit, I had sufficient funds to bribe my way through Stonebow Gate. Now, I had to queue with the duck-sellers, waiting to pay their market taxes. Absent-mindedly swinging bird-bundles behind them, the feathers made me sneeze.

Lincoln was divided into three jurisdictions, governed by the Mayor, Sheriff and Dean. The City, which skirted the lower slopes, was connected to the drier Bail and Minster above by the aptly named Steep Hill, a long climb.

Growing increasingly worried the higher I went, I considered

Catherine's fateful visit again. Was she nervous when she tackled that incline too? Did she know she was nearing the end of her life? Even Lupton was unlikely to have guessed his breakfast would be his last.

An old woman paused beside me, when I stopped to catch my breath.

"Why do you need to rest? A young man should race up Steep Hill."

Clearly local, I asked, "What is the Minster district like? I'm due to meet someone there."

She crossed herself, "Blessed Mother of God! Be careful son. Stay silent if they trick you with questions. Pretend you don't understand. They caught a Catholic priest last year. No-one saw him again."

Anxious and confused, I headed on up to Castle Square. Why could Geoffrey not meet me in the White Hart, which looked more inviting than the vast arch of Exchequer Gate?

Cathedral guards stood to attention on either side, then kept me waiting while they checked my papers. Was there a problem? They would not say. I sat in their guard room, fuming in silence.

When I eventually passed through the Gate, my anger dissipated, confounded by the sight. A contrast to the noisy City and Bail outside, Minster Yard was empty, but I felt I was being watched. Hundreds of stone saints and sinners stared down from ledges, high above on the cathedral's great west wall. I crossed the flagstones, and stood transfixed beneath rows of disapproving eyes, grotesque features and strange animals.

Tiptoeing in through a side door, the cathedral seemed even bigger than when viewed from outside in the Yard. The building was cross-shaped, like the church back home, but monstrously proportioned. Vast arches and stained-glass windows spoke of unattainable wealth, and mysteries beyond my comprehension.

The scene in Sculthorpe's north-east transept office was beyond my comprehension too. The Secretary was instructing another cleric to move fanciful robes between rails. They both wore black cassocks, his fastened with a multi-coloured cord.

"Pusey, this chasuble needs cleaning. You should have checked before. I will suggest His Lordship wears the purple one instead, with the embroidered stole or the plain."

Neither saw me at first, their view obscured by an enormous desk in the centre of the cramped room, stacked high with pyramids of books. When I coughed, the chastised Pusey negotiated his way past similar piles of silver-ware and candles on the floor, to confront me.

"Who are you? What are you doing here?"

"I'm Baxby. Geoffrey sent a letter telling me to meet him here."

The Secretary rose to his full height, knocking against the nearest books on the desk. He was considerably taller than Pusey, but his most striking feature was his prominent nose. It was large and bulbous, not distinguished like Sir Francis Vere's.

"Wait in the nave until Geoffrey arrives. Don't touch anything," he instructed, straightening the books back into line.

The Secretary seemed organised, but not in the way Sibsey had led me to believe. How could anyone spend so long arranging all the ecclesiastical impediments in the room?

"Mister Sculthorpe, would it be possible to speak about another matter? I'm interested to learn more about a letter that you wrote to my friend John Crackleton."

"*Reverend* Sculthorpe," he corrected, "Geoffrey said you were intelligent. He was obviously wrong. Wait in the nave until he arrives."

"But Crackleton ..."

"Can't you see I'm busy sorting the Bishop's robes? We need someone who will do what they are told."

I stood there, indignant. Why would he not let me speak? Pusey rotated his eyes towards the door, indicating I should leave.

"What are you waiting for?" Sculthorpe bellowed, losing patience.

It must be difficult to work for such a demanding master, one who lost his temper so easily.

Through a poorly mended split, I could hear them arguing inside.

"Geoffrey told me this one was intelligent and pliant. We can't make another mistake. When we introduce him to our honoured guest, he mustn't let us down. Our visitor will not tolerate defiance."

"That boy wouldn't dare. He's harmless and scared."

"You know how demanding our guest can be. I've hired extra staff to wait on him. You're too slow. We should have finished sorting these robes by now."

Neither man gave any clues about their visitor's identity, but he was obviously important.

Momentarily thinking I had disturbed a ghost, I was startled by a movement beside me. A buxom woman appeared suddenly, with a broom and bucket of cloths.

"Excuse me, I need to speak with Secretary Sculthorpe," she said, heading for the office.

"I wouldn't recommend you go in there. He's in a terrible mood."

Heeding my advice, she put her bucket down, revealing some plump white flesh beneath her bodice.

"Who are you, Sir? What are you doing here?"

"I'm Baxby. I've just arrived from Boston."

She looked at me, up and down, leaning on her broom, some chestnut hair escaping from beneath her cap.

"Have you upset Secretary Sculthorpe? You seem very young."

"Young for what?" I retaliated.

"For loitering outside the Reverend's lair," she smiled, tilting her head towards the door, "I'll come back to see him later."

"Are you a cleaner here?"

"No, I'm the Archbishop of Canterbury, and this is my crook," she laughed, poking my ribs with the broom.

What impudence! She caught me off guard. I expected such behaviour in an alehouse, but not in a cathedral.

PAYING IN BLOOD

"The Secretary said an important guest was arriving today," I managed.

"He's here already, with his escorts who are eating in the Dean's kitchen. You look hungry yourself."

She tossed an apple towards me, before picking up her bucket and marching off.

I called out, "What's your name?"

"Agnes. We'll meet again," she laughed, waving her broom in the air.

10

Agnes' apple was delicious but small. I ate it while watching choristers process down the central aisle. They disappeared behind a huge wooden screen, practised tuneless chants, and then processed back again. I counted woodworm holes, until a fluttering pigeon upset my tally. Stained-glass window light flickered from pillar to pillar as the afternoon progressed, but Geoffrey did not appear.

As the sun went down, the high pulpit proved too tempting to resist. I climbed the spiral staircase, and tried to imagine the cathedral full. There was a bible on the lectern, as heavy and conspicuous as Atherton's were surreptitiously small. Keeping my arm in the open page, I found a sumptuous frontispiece with a portrait of Queen Elizabeth. This was a 'Bishops' Bible', not one for ordinary people like me. Intrigued, I turned the stiff pages until the weight hurt my arm.

When I descended the stairs, I realised that Geoffrey had been sitting on a pew, watching me from below.

"Alexander, it's good to see you again. What's happened to your hair? Where has it gone?"

He persisted in calling me by my first name, even though no-one else did. His own sleek hair curled perfectly about his handsome face. Mine was too thick to stay in place like that.

"I gave my last coins to a barber in Boston. I've run out of money."

"Did you see Edmund Sibsey while you were there? How is he keeping? I'd love to visit the Red Lion one day."

Geoffrey licked his lips when he lied, a surprising habit for one so guarded otherwise.

"Your hair and beard look much smarter. The barber did a good job."

It was time to confront him, "Geoffrey, I'm not happy with the way I was treated. You never warned me about Lupton's tent. How can I trust you again?"

PAYING IN BLOOD

"Sir Francis sent a letter of commendation. I know you worked hard. You've proved yourself. Just do what you're told."

"That's what Secretary Sculthorpe said. I don't trust him either."

"Please be patient a little longer."

He made me sit down on a pew beside him, and spoke more quietly, "These are dangerous times. Queen Elizabeth is growing old, and still hasn't named her successor."

"Will she die? Sir Francis Vere needs her to fund another campaign to capture Dunkirk."

"Please listen carefully. I want to talk honestly with you. England's enemies will exploit any weakness or uncertainty, for their own advantage. Some may seem like friends. We must be careful."

"Sir Francis isn't a pretender to the throne. You'll waste your money wagering on him," I laughed, as much at the thought of Geoffrey being honest as the Vere family's ambitions.

"I never waste my money, or that of my clients. Come with me. I will show you something."

As he led me towards the screen, behind which the choristers had sung, I looked back at the galleried walkways, high above the central arches on either side of the nave. Tiny black doorways linked the elevated sections, providing an alternative route for those who knew the cathedral well. I imagined the ghosts of Catholic priests prowled there, including the one the old woman told me had disappeared.

"Hurry up, Alexander. We don't want to linger here."

That was true. The cathedral was chilling after dark. I envied Geoffrey's expensive coat and warm shoes.

I realised that I was taller than him now, although he still looked better fed. It was hard to guess Geoffrey's age. He walked upright, at a good pace, but could be over forty years of age.

Turning a corner, I saw the noble woman's shrine ahead, lit by a line of slender candles.

"This lady is Katherine Swynford," Geoffrey said, stroking the inlaid folds of her dress. "She was a mistress of John of Gaunt and governess to his children. When he married her in his old age, he arranged for their children to be de-bastardised. Our Queen's grandfather claimed the throne through Katherine's line."

"Through a mistress? Is that allowed?"

"Tudor monarchy is built on fragile foundations, as is the Church since England broke from Rome."

I frowned, not understanding the constitutional intricacies.

"Our Church and monarchy depend on each other for legitimacy. The Church derives its authority from the Queen, its supreme head, whilst she received hers when anointed by the Church."

Geoffrey interlocked his fingers to illustrate his point.

"These are unprecedented times. Undermining one institution is risky enough, but we have an obstinate childless monarch who refuses to name a successor, and a growing band of fanatics who threaten the Church.

"Are you talking about Anabaptists?" I asked remembering the Dutchman on the *Mary-Anne*.

"No, re-baptisers are a threat on the continent, not here to my knowledge. I mean Puritans," he whispered, "Extreme Protestants, who print treacherous books, denouncing the bishops and their courts. It is bad enough when French and Spanish-trained Catholics spread foreign lies here, but Puritans are Englishmen who imperil their own island."

Geoffrey convinced me, as he always did, that Puritans were dangerous like the Spanish. Their name sounded haughty and uncompromising too. Not the sort of people I would wish to concern myself with.

He lifted a candle holder from the end of the row behind the tomb, and led me on.

The Russell Chapel was small and bare, except for a rough stone altar. Geoffrey held open the door for me before placing the candle there. Standing close, the light accentuated his plump cheeks, making him look younger. He stared at the flame for some time, smoothing his moustache with his thumb and forefinger, from the centre towards the sides. Women found this habit attractive, although I never understood why.

"I was forced to make changes while you were overseas, but see no reason to terminate our arrangement."

"Do you work for the Church now? Is that why we're meeting here?"

Geoffrey did not answer, but gave me coins and promised more. My patron remained frustratingly evasive, but at least I could afford to eat again.

"We've recognised your value. You've been offered a position here in Lincoln."

"I can't work for Sculthorpe. He doesn't listen."

"You would work with him, not for him. He'll pass on my instructions and pay you each week."

"Why all the secrecy? Where's the important guest the Secretary promised? Is this on account of the letter he sent to Crackleton, telling him that his wife died? Your letter was delivered by the same boy. Did you meet her here?"

"I've been in London. Please forget about letters. Tonight, you will meet the eminent Bishop you need to impress. If he is satisfied, we can discuss more details later."

"You must tell me everything in advance this time, and increase my pay, especially if I've got to work with Sculthorpe."

"I think you'll be pleased with the immediate remuneration, and the longer-term prospects. Wait here until I return with the Bishop."

11

Geoffrey left me alone in the tomb-like chapel, without food or drink. Outside, the coins in my pocket would buy female company and a seat by the White Hart fire. I wished Agnes would appear beside me again, with more apples and a blanket this time. I rubbed my finger along the altar, and held it to the light. It was covered in dust. No cleaners had visited the Chapel recently. Agnes was probably tucked up in bed with a well-paid husband. She looked too well fed to rely on cleaners' pay. They rarely had such attractive curves, nor her self-assurance either.

When the candle burnt out, I fell asleep on the cold stone floor. Voices woke me. Shadows leapt across the ceiling, as a light approached outside. I trembled as the door creaked open slowly, remembering the ghosts I had sensed in the nave. Sculthorpe peered in, with a lantern illuminating his wide nostrils. I quivered on the floor as he set it down.

"Baxby where are you? Get up boy! This is important. Don't waste our time!"

After I pulled myself up, Geoffrey presented me to the Minster's illustrious guest. Richard Bancroft, the Bishop of London, had travelled a long way north for this nocturnal visit. I had never met a bishop before and was shocked by the encounter. His face was as white as his wide surplice sleeves, with a high creased forehead beneath his pointed clerical cap.

Throughout Sculthorpe's speech in praise of the Bishop's insight and judgement, Bancroft kept his dark eyes fixed on me. I did not know where to look, a disconcerting experience. Geoffrey kept smiling, but without the customary display of perfect white teeth. He had never looked so nervous before.

Then the interview started.

Sculthorpe explained, "When the Bishop asks you a question, you must answer immediately, without hesitation. We mustn't waste His Excellency's time."

Patience was not a virtue these churchmen valued.

PAYING IN BLOOD

Bishop Bancroft lifted my chin, with his staff, before speaking. I smelt his strong scent for the first time.

"Young man, I understand that you showed good aptitude at Nieuwpoort. Also, you're ambitious and keen to serve your Queen."

His northern accent surprised me, having assumed London Bishops would be born there. Bancroft must have moved south at some point in his life. Fortunately, I managed to ignore the sickening smell of his perfume, as he made his astonishing offer.

"We will provide an apprenticeship here in Lincoln, with a view to securing a future position at court."

An apprenticeship! Court! Was this a cruel trick? Or had Sibsey been right after all? There was no time to consider the implications. As Bishop Bancroft brought his face close, pummelling his eyes into mine, his perfume irritated my nose. The jewelled pomander, on a chain round his neck, was filled with cloves.

"An apprenticeship?" I stuttered, trying not to sneeze.

Geoffrey muttered something about handkerchiefs, starting to search his pockets. The Bishop raised a hand to silence him, then continued undeterred.

"Tell me, is there something I should know? Anything that prohibits you from accepting this post?"

Bancroft banged his staff on the floor, perilously close to my toes. The sturdy oak rod would make a formidable weapon.

"Anything? Tell me now!"

Geoffrey found a handkerchief, just in time before the first sneeze exploded. I had no idea how to reply.

"I've been loyal to my country since ..."

"No religious affiliations? No grandmother who served porridge to Mary Queen of Scots before she lost her head?"

Then, without warning, Bancroft grabbed my arm and raised his voice, "No Puritan allegiances or alternative confessions?"

I stared back, trying to ignore the folds of flesh on his face. His perfume was overwhelming. My arm hurt.

"None," I whispered.

Bancroft let go, stepped back and waited until I had finished sneezing.

"This is not the time to take chances. Every day, England's enemies plot new ways to usurp her power. Soldiers fight bravely overseas, but who will stamp out the vermin within? Baxby, we need your help."

He turned his heel on a tombstone, adding dramatic effect. I nodded, not realising the full significance of his pronouncement at the time, but sensing its importance nevertheless.

"You can rely on me, Your Excellency."

Geoffrey looked relieved. Sculthorpe picked up the lantern to leave with the Bishop, their business done.

Afterwards, I rubbed my arm and tried to recompose myself. Realising that my hands were shaking, I hid them behind my back.

Geoffrey patted my shoulder, "Congratulations, Alexander. That was worse than I expected. You did well. You're unlikely to meet such a powerful man again. The Archbishop of Canterbury is often ill, and relies on Bancroft more than any other prelate. Come on, let's leave this place. I'll pay for a room at the White Hart and buy you a meal."

"Wait! An apprenticeship? Did Bishop Bancroft mean what he said before he hurt my arm? Can I train to be a barber-surgeon?"

Geoffrey laughed, "Not a surgeon, a physician. I told you not to worry."

"A proper physician! Are you certain?"

"The Church has agreed to pay your fees, and given your previous experience, you won't even need to serve the full seven years. Sculthorpe has made a special arrangement with a local practitioner, and budgeted accordingly. You will treat the Bishop of Lincoln as part of your role, a great honour."

"I don't understand."

"Just do what you're told."

"But why did the Bishop hurt my arm like that? It's still painful."

PAYING IN BLOOD

"Bancroft isn't high born. He comes from an ordinary village in Lancashire. Archbishop Whitgift relies on him to protect us all. I've heard that the Queen can be demanding too. How would either of us cope with such a role? I have no interest in religion, but we must take precautions when national security is at stake."

Remembering his previous misgivings, I doubted he would have worked for the Church before William Cecil died, but Geoffrey was astute. He knew how to secure the best outcome for himself and his business. As he said, these were serious times.

"Sleep well," he called after me, as I stumbled up the White Hart stairs, after eating a generous meal, and drinking more than I had for some time, "You will be busy tomorrow."

London 1613

12

Recalling Bancroft's tight grip and the subsequent bruise, Baxby breaks from his tale to sip some drink. Despite all that has happened since, he has never forgotten the interview in the Russell Chapel and the way it changed his life. An apprenticeship was an incredible opportunity. He also made new friends in Lincoln, who are dear to him still. Some have searched but cannot find him. They do not know if he is alive or dead.

Outside no-one else cares about Baxby's condition. London is consumed by royal wedding fever, at the start of the year. Soon, King James will give his daughter Princess Elizabeth's hand in marriage to her handsome German suitor. Even the oldest residents cannot remember such excitement. The late Queen was single for so long, and kept a tighter grip on the Privy Purse.

A peel of bells reminds Baxby's cell-mates of the imminent celebrations. They hope to be released in time to watch the fireworks and sea-pageant on the Thames.

Baxby does not expect to see any wedding events. His thirst quenched, he returns to his story.

PAYING IN BLOOD

Lincolnshire 1600

13

When Geoffrey handed me my apprentice robes, I still struggled to believe this was true. A medical apprenticeship surpassed all my previous dreams. Once qualified, I could practise anywhere, even at court. My earlier assumptions about Geoffrey had been wrong. He had rewarded my loyal service, as Sibsey predicted he would.

I tried on the robes with trepidation, wondering whether they would fit. The sleeves were a little short, but the cloak reassuringly long and warm. The cap kept my hair in place, and showed off my pencil beard to good effect.

If only the nay-saying Boston neighbours could see me now. That barber would not taunt me. My mother would be proud. Crackleton would say that he knew I would do well. I was dressed for a promising future.

However, it proved harder than I expected to uncover the truth about Catherine. Geoffrey was evasive when I raised the subject again, "There were two letters when I returned from Nieuwpoort, both sealed with the Bishop of Lincoln's mark. You wrote one, instructing me to meet you in Lincoln. Secretary Sculthorpe wrote the other, telling Crackleton that his wife Catherine died here, but it didn't give many details."

"I have never heard of a second letter."

"Don't you chat with Sculthorpe?"

"We had a long conversation about your apprenticeship this morning. There is no time for idleness. The Secretary is a very busy man. He manages the diocese finances for Bishop Chaderton. It's a responsible role."

"Is the Bishop busy too? Why don't they care about my poor friend's wife?"

"They are men of God. Of course they care. They just care

about other things too. The Church is giving you a wonderful opportunity. You should be more thankful."

"I am grateful, Geoffrey. Thank you for arranging this with Sculthorpe. It's just frustrating that no-one will discuss Catherine Crackleton."

To my annoyance, Geoffrey made me promise not to mention the subject with any clerics. I had hoped to hire a horse and visit Crackleton's village, once I had discovered how Catherine died. This was going to take longer than I had foreseen.

Surprisingly, my patron answered all my questions about my new role, without licking his lips. He appeared to be telling the truth this time, although I remained suspicious.

From tomorrow, I would be apprenticed to a Cambridge-educated physician called Matthew Mobley, who lived with his wife and family on Michaelgate. Matthew would supervise my training, and ensure I gained sufficient skills to justify my licence. He would expect me to work and study hard. Geoffrey said that my conduct at Nieuwpoort had helped convince him that I was suitable.

Even more astonishingly, the Minster had agreed to pay my fees, and buy my robes and equipment. Geoffrey explained that this was because I would treat Bishop Chaderton as part of my apprenticeship. Understandably, I was nervous about meeting another one, given my experience in the Russell Chapel.

"Why does the Church want me?" I asked.

"Chaderton has lost faith in so-called renowned physicians. He's seen too many over the years. He wants someone new. You'll visit him twice a week."

"Is he like Bishop Bancroft?"

"They couldn't be more different. Chaderton is much more sociable, although he doesn't tolerate fools. You'll enjoy your time with him, but you must pay attention. Don't mention Crackleton or letters. Sculthorpe's done well. The Bishop of Lincoln will get the treatment he needs, and you'll settle back into everyday life and learn a valuable profession. Having done so well overseas, I feel sure you'll be able to adapt."

Geoffrey had arranged for the Secretary to pay my allowance, which meant I would need to visit his 'lair' in the north-east transept each Saturday. Given the generosity of the rest of the agreement, I could not complain about that unfortunate detail.

There was an additional benefit too. The Minster would provide free accommodation in one of its properties. It owned numerous such houses, in the streets surrounding the cathedral. I would board with two unmarried sisters, near Greestone Stairs.

"I've heard the food is very good there," Geoffrey advised, pointing the way.

My new home was further down the hill, below Vicars Court. As I struggled down, with my bulky robes and bag, embarrassingly the cleaner Agnes overtook me. She must be more practised on the slope. I was taking care, because the broken cobbles were slippery.

"Mister Baxby," she smiled, "I said we would meet again."

Taking a key from her apron, she stopped a short distance in front of me.

"Welcome to our home."

I stood there speechless, like a fool, as she opened the door.

"Didn't they tell you that you would be staying with us? My sister Susannah lives here too. You must treat her kindly, as she is very shy. Pass me your robes so I can hang them up."

Susannah did not speak as we passed her in the kitchen. After following me up the stairs, Agnes opened the shutters, letting in a great gust of damp air.

"I'm afraid we only have glass in the windows downstairs. Secretary Sculthorpe ignores me when I ask him to buy more for the bedrooms."

Agnes stood close, showing me the view of Waddington Heath, beyond the flooded lower Witham valley.

"Are there ghosts here?" I asked, having been warned by White Hart guests that many local houses were haunted.

"You don't have to worry about this house. Susannah and I are the only ones here, but be careful on Greestone Stairs. St. Hugh's head fell off when they carried his relics up to the cathedral. You might feel it brush past your legs if you take that route."

Agnes left after helping me unpack. It was a comfortable room, with a spare blanket on the chest and candles on the shelf. Ideal apart from the lack of glass, I had never had such a pleasing room of my own.

When I came downstairs, Agnes had prepared a feast in the kitchen. She kept offering me more food and drink. Her younger sister helped, but said nothing throughout the meal. Both sisters were cleaners at Vicars Court. Susannah was taller and prettier than Agnes, but less interesting.

After eating, I mentioned Crackleton and his letter. Geoffrey had not prohibited me from talking to them about the subject.

"How amazing to save your friend's life, by sawing off his foot. I would have fainted, as soon as I saw the first drop of blood."

"I'm more interested in discussing his wife's last days in Lincoln. Do you know if Catherine had any friends? Did you meet her here?"

"If Secretary Sculthorpe wrote the letter, I recommend asking him. He is very clever and remembers everything."

"He refused to speak about Catherine."

"It might have been a busy day. How exciting to start your apprenticeship tomorrow! Matthew Mobley is well respected in this city."

Agnes remained evasive on the subject of Catherine, no more helpful than Sculthorpe. Susannah studied the floor throughout the conversation. Why would they not talk about Crackleton's wife? Someone must have seen her in the city before she died.

PAYING IN BLOOD

14

Geoffrey was angry when he led me down Michaelgate to the Mobleys' cottage, another steep street.

"Why did you ask the sisters about letters? I told you to forget about them."

"Agnes works as a cleaner, so might know something."

"You're not here to ask questions. You're here to work hard. Bishop Bancroft travelled from London to check you were suitable for this apprenticeship. Do you want me to report back that he made a mistake? Can you imagine how cross he'd be if he had to find someone else? Don't pester Matthew Mobley, his family, Bishop Chaderton or anyone else. You're an apprentice not an inquisitor. Do you understand?"

"Yes, Geoffrey."

"And take this handkerchief. You're always sniffing and sneezing. Physicians mustn't drivel on their patients."

The Mobleys lived in an old stone cottage, built into the hill, with the front door and a small shuttered window visible from the top of their steps. While Geoffrey knocked, I peered through a crack in the shutters to see the tiny treatment room for the first time. Rows of jars and potions lined the walls, a strange new world that I was about to enter.

When Matthew opened the door, he was smaller and more timid than I expected. The physicians' furs hung low on his shoulders. He kept his head bowed, never meeting Geoffrey's eyes. I sensed that he knew him, or at least, knew of him. His wife Eunice seemed blissfully unaware.

"Come in," she called out, from behind her husband, "Are you hungry? There's food in the pot and beer in the jug. Make yourself at home."

Eunice's exuberance seemed to scare Geoffrey. Larger and louder than her husband, she protested when he turned to leave.

"Please don't go, Sir. There's plenty of pottage for everyone."

"I've already eaten," he lied.

Moving closer, he whispered to me, "Remember what I've told

you, Baxby. Do what you're told."

Geoffrey ran up the steps, shouting good-bye. It would be several months before I saw him again. I refrained from mentioning Catherine Crackleton when the Mobleys welcomed me into their home.

The family lived in a large room on the far side of the cottage, overlooking Brayford Pool and the upper Witham valley. A small boy pointed out the long straight line of the Fosse Way, running through the fields below. The flood water was subsiding.

"What an impressive view!"

Eunice sighed, "We have always loved this home, but it's becoming too small for us all."

In addition to their two sons, Eunice was obviously expecting again.

"Matthew hasn't had an apprentice before," she continued as she dished the pottage, "Please don't hesitate to let my husband know if you have any problems."

"Thank you."

"Who was that man who brought you here? Why did he smile all the time, even when he was being rude?"

Unusually, she was not fooled by Geoffrey's charm.

Matthew spoke, "Eunice stop. We can't batter Mister Baxby with questions, and comment on his friends. We must take this apprenticeship seriously."

Although Eunice talked more, Matthew was clearly in charge. The boys behaved well throughout the meal, not looking up from their pottage until they had finished. Both shared their mother's curls. Matthew's hair was straighter, and already greying at the sides, perhaps on account of his burgeoning family responsibilities.

"This is excellent," I thanked Eunice, "You're a very good cook."

"Come and eat with us whenever you want. Let us know if there is a friend or special girl we should invite too."

"Baxby is staying with Agnes and Susannah at Greestones," Matthew informed his wife. "There won't be time for women. He has too much to learn."

Clearly disappointed, Eunice started clearing the bowls.

Matthew turned to me, "I'll teach you how to handle a leech when we've finished eating. Bishop Chaderton wants to see you at the end of the week, so we haven't long to prepare."

The Mobleys' elder son Luke climbed on a stool in the treatment room to reach an earthenware pot on the shelf.

His father encouraged him, "Now open the lid to show Mister Baxby the leeches."

Black flecks swirled in the water inside, too numerous to count. I had never been bled myself. They were smaller than I had envisaged.

"Don't put your finger in. It takes an hour to get them all off."

"Do they hurt?"

"Leeches are like old friends, who still nip you if given the chance."

Matthew noticed my grimace. Was he talking about Geoffrey or the creatures in the jar? He might have learnt about him whilst arranging my apprenticeship.

Luke pulled up his sleeve, for his father to drop the leech from the pincers. He winced as it attached, a brave boy.

"It's harder to remove one before it's full," Matthew explained.

He showed me how to slide my finger nail along Luke's skin, until the suction broke.

"Look after this. They're expensive," he pronounced, dropping the swollen beast in a second pot for me.

After sending Luke to play with his brother, Matthew explained the Bishop's treatment. He needed to be bled in a sensitive place, which would require care and discretion, but sounded simpler than sawing limbs at Nieuwpoort.

"Just drop the leech as I showed you. Chaderton won't complain. He's an easier patient than many."

"Why don't you treat the Bishop yourself?"

"You'll need to convince him that you're competent. You've made a good start today. We'll practise more tomorrow."

Matthew did not tell me why he did not treat the Bishop.

15

During the following week, Matthew took me with him on his visits, and let me watch several bleedings in the treatment room. He showed me which books he expected me to read first, plus a long list of illnesses I must learn to diagnose. Although providing a helpful stream of explanation throughout, he remained more reticent on other subjects.

When I asked him if he had treated Chaderton again, Matthew refused to answer as before, "Just concentrate on the leech when you visit the Palace. That's all you need to do."

My new master seemed to dislike honest enquiry as much as Geoffrey.

Agnes was interested in my apprenticeship, particularly the people I met each day. Matthew expected me to respect the patients' privacy, so I tried not to say too much.

"Have you been busy, Baxby? How is Mistress Mobley? I've heard she is expecting again. I don't know how the family will fit in their cottage once the new baby is born. How many bedrooms do they have?"

"They have two."

"Do they have glass in their windows?"

"Yes, all of them."

Agnes always chattered while cooking and during the meal. She proved a generous landlady throughout my stay, supplying enormous slabs of bacon for breakfast each morning, and plenty of beer each night. The Church provided the sisters with an allowance, which Agnes used to good effect.

Susannah listened intently, but never joined our conversations. Agnes told me she was not dumb, just chose not to talk in the presence of men. I wondered whether Susannah might be more willing if Agnes was not present. One of the cathedral guards told me that they were only half-sisters, sharing the same late mother, from whom they took their colouring. Susannah's hair

PAYING IN BLOOD

was a slightly lighter shade.

By Friday, Matthew was confident that I was ready to treat Bishop Chaderton. He left me at Exchequer Gate, after checking the leech in my pot. The guards waved me straight through, recognising me by then.

I had to take the longer route down the driveway, obstructed by brambles, as the passage opposite the Galilee Porch was reserved for the Bishop's private use. The interior of the Palace was in poor repair too. The servant who took me upstairs, pointed out holes in the treads to avoid, before carefully knocking on a big rotten door.

"Come in, Mister Baxby," Bishop Chaderton boomed from his chamber, "Don't be embarrassed young man. I've done this many times before. It doesn't take long."

In contrast to his Palace, the Bishop appeared in surprisingly good form, beckoning me across to the window where there was more light. Although his skin was as pale as Bancroft's, he was dissimilar in other aspects. By the time I had found the pincers and jar in my bag, he had moved the furniture into place and was ready for his treatment.

Having seen guts and gore on the battlefield, skin problems seemed relatively straight-forward. I did not comment, or show surprise, but was nervous dropping the leech.

"This may hurt," I warned, as I curled the creature out.

"It will," Bishop Chaderton spoke from experience, "We're called to suffer on earth. Don't chase idle pleasures. Seek the treasures of heaven."

Unaccustomed to the Bishop's favourite sayings at that time, I tried to concentrate as Matthew had advised. Chaderton kept his clerical cap on his egg-bald head throughout. The full leech was easy to remove afterwards.

"Thank you, Baxby. That was better. No fawning or fuss. I'll see you again next week."

Success! I had passed the test. Relieved, I tripped back across Minster Yard without noticing the gruesome sculptures. My apprenticeship was secure.

Matthew was delighted when I reported back. It was the first time I had seen him smile. He had been more worried about my visit to the Palace than I had realised.

"We'll keep this leech for Chaderton," he laughed, returning my pot to the shelf, "Some leeches live for years. We'll see how this one fares on bishop's blood."

When I told him about the holes in the stairs and broken furniture, Matthew did not seem surprised.

"You must have visited the Palace," I ventured.

"A long time ago."

"Why don't you treat the Bishop instead of me?"

"I'm not welcome there."

It was hard to imagine why this should be true, but this was not the time to press him further on the matter. Eunice was serving pottage in the back room. As the Mobleys' toasted my success, I wondered if Matthew knew more about Catherine too.

Agnes was impressed to hear that I had treated the Bishop. Having previously cleaned the Palace stairs, she knew how rotten they were.

"Once I opened a cupboard and a whole flock of moths flew out. Bishop Chaderton never complains though. He is a godly man, a true saint. We're so fortunate to have such clergymen."

Ever loyal to her employers!

Seeming less convinced, Susannah disappeared into the yard with the laundry before Agnes had finished her praise. Sensing an opportunity, I followed the younger sister outside, "Is there a problem, Susannah?

She pegged an apron on the line, ignoring me.

I persisted, "Why don't you like the churchmen? What have they done to you?"

She pointed back towards the door, making it clear that she wanted me to return inside.

"I won't hurt you, Susannah. You can talk to me."

She rapped on the kitchen window, prompting Agnes to run out.

"Come inside, Mister Baxby. Have more beer. It's hot out here. You mustn't stop Susannah working."

It would take more skill and patience to encourage Susannah to talk. Agnes was very protective.

16

After a few more days of September sunshine, I settled into my new routine under more familiar grey skies. It was easier to find my way around the city, once I had learnt the names of all the gates. Building them must have kept an army of stonemasons busy for years. Steep Hill was the hardest street to climb. Eventually I mastered the incline, no longer needing to pause for breath. I also established which inns served the best beer.

Matthew gradually introduced me to his patients. Trusting me with mundane tasks, I learnt how to bandage boils and lance them cleanly.

Few people in the quay-side cottages could afford physicians' fees. Most of Matthew's patients lived respectably high up the hill, and were particular about their treatment. I liked learning new skills and medical theory, but found some people problematic. Matthew was more patient than me. He was sensible and straight-forward in every respect, apart from discussing his previous involvement with Chaderton.

Some patients were reluctant to let me treat them. Matthew tried to convince a magistrate's wife, who refused to let me enter her Bailgate house.

"Mister Baxby is my apprentice. He is very capable and only acts on my instruction."

"Baxby isn't like you. Although I could overlook his youth, I can't ignore where he lives."

Matthew replied, "Greestones is a respectable area although I believe it is haunted."

"I'm talking about the sisters not the ghosts."

"Agnes and Susannah?"

"Don't mention their names here."

The magistrates' wife disapproved of them, even more than me. Matthew informed her that she would have to wait until later in the week. He tried to calm my protestations as we walked back through Castle Square.

"I can treat her warts as well as you can."

"She doesn't object to your skills, Baxby. It's the company you keep."

"Some people are born lower than others. It's not their fault, and the Minster chose my accommodation for me."

"Then you'll have to put up with adverse comments until you can afford to move. Try to be more patient. "

The magistrate's wife was out or order. Matthew could have made a stronger case.

My trips to the Palace provided a welcome contrast to such prejudice in the town. Chaderton liked to talk once the leech had attached. Although his historic home was crumbling around him, he retained his good humour and stoicism through. The Bishop taught me history whilst my leech consumed his blood, finding me a willing student despite my religious ignorance.

"I gained some fame through preaching at the Scottish Queen Mary's funeral," Chaderton smiled, "She suffered from ill-health. Her so-called reputable physicians were no better than mine."

The Bishop seemed to prefer my relative inexperience, trusting me to do what I was told.

"Who's on the Scottish throne now?" I asked.

"Her young son James became King when she abdicated, a very different character."

He patiently explained it all. Bishops would not be a problem if they were all like Chaderton.

After returning from the Palace, I confronted Matthew again. Had he ever treated Bishop Chaderton there? Worn down by my persistence, this time he admitted he had, before I arrived in Lincoln. He told me he had taken a rabbit into the Palace, intending to eat it that evening. The rabbit escaped and ran amok in the library, ruining several books. Sculthorpe caught it but banned Matthew from treating Chaderton again.

Obviously, Matthew's rabbit story was not true. He was too

intelligent to behave in such a way. Also, I knew that the Palace was too damp for books, which were kept in the cathedral library, near the Chapter House.

However, encouraged by Matthew's admission, I told him about Crackleton's letter. My master shook his head. He told me to let the matter rest. I should concentrate on my apprenticeship if I wanted to qualify.

What was Matthew afraid of? Why invent the rabbit story? Surely, the city's most noteworthy physician must know something about Catherine's death. He knew about all the more recent ones.

The next time I visited Sculthorpe, I resolved to ask him about her again. He was wearing a new cassock, with embroidery round the neck. His lair was more untidy than usual, with vestments piled on his chair. To me, he seemed to have always lurked there, chiselled by the first masons, like an ugly imp or gargoyle. A figure on the screen in the Crossing had a similar nose, perhaps a likeness of one of his ancestors.

In truth, his father had been Secretary before him, and his mother was a seamstress. There was a Mistress Sculthorpe some miles away, but he rarely travelled back to see her.

When I asked about Catherine, Sculthorpe lost his temper, demanding I answer his questions instead. Why was I interested in a peasant woman? Did I know her personally? He did not understand that I wanted to help a friend. His obfuscation only increased my suspicion. Something untoward must have happened during the summer.

Having had no success elsewhere, I mentioned Catherine's name to a couple of patients. Matthew was furious when he found out, "Baxby, I'm pleased with your progress, but you mustn't interrogate patients. They deserve their peace and privacy."

"When I promised to help Crackleton discover how his wife died, I didn't expect it to be this hard. No-one talks openly in

Lincoln."

"Respectable people don't pry into others' business. The poor souls down at Brayford Pool may stand around gossiping all day. You mustn't be so forward with reputable residents, higher up the hill."

I apologised, and promised not to repeat my mistake. However, Matthew was soon proved wrong, when the whole city became gripped by a frenzy of gossip about a despicable crime.

17

Someone woke me before dawn, throwing stones at the shutters. The lack of upstairs glass was still a source of irritation to Agnes. I turned over to sleep more.

"Baxby!" she called up from the kitchen, "One of Mister Mobley's neighbours needs to speak with you."

"At this ungodly hour?"

"It's urgent. Get up! Someone's ill."

The neighbour's ashen face suggested this was serious. It was gratifying that Matthew wanted my help with such a case.

"Be careful on Greestone Stairs. They're haunted," Agnes reminded us as we left.

The neighbour demanded we take that route, being keen to get back to bed. The scratching rats were disconcerting, but we reached the bottom of the flight unharmed.

"No ghosts this time," I laughed, but as I turned the corner, I was pushed back against the wall by someone moving fast. He winded me, and ran on towards Potter Gate, before either of us could see his face.

When the neighbour left me at the end of Flaxengate, I was unprepared for the crisis I faced. Most shops were still shut, but a small crowd had gathered outside the bakery, obstructing Matthew's route to the door. No-one else appeared to have noticed the ominous burning smell, drifting down the street. I had a more sensitive nose than most.

"Baxby, we must get into the shop. The Bucklers need our help."

Previously, Matthew had treated the baker's wife for minor ailments. He reached the door first, as I was delayed by a small boy tugging on my sleeve.

"I saw a man with a sword and a cape." he said, waving an arm to demonstrate his movements.

"In the bakery?"

PAYING IN BLOOD

"Outside in the street."

The child trembled, bringing his finger to his nose, "He pointed it here,"

"Wait here until I return. I've got to help Mister Mobley in the shop."

I could have asked the boy more, but was more concerned about the risk of fire.

The bakery was larger than I expected. Buckler's business was obviously profitable. He had recently joined the St. Anne's Guild, the most influential in the city. The ground floor was packed with over-heated relatives, guildsmen and neighbours.

Mistress Buckler was resting in a sturdy chair, too shocked to answer questions. Matthew gave her a potion to calm her nerves, whilst I tried to clear the building.

After watching the slow procession of burnt loaves and busybodies file out, I felt a warm sensation on my head, spreading down the crown. I touched the sticky spot, and lifted my fingers to show Matthew. My hair had brushed through blood, which was dripping through the ceiling boards above our heads.

Once the room was clear, we heard the frantic gasps above. With trepidation, I followed Matthew up the floury stairs, and watched while he pushed the first door open.

"Empty. Try the next."

The second door was split. When I tried to edge it forward, it crashed off its hinges to reveal the baker's plight. Mister Buckler lay on the bedroom floor, barely alive, with a serious blow to his head. Blood had soaked his clothes and ruined papers from an overturned chest. As I knelt to examine him, it was difficult to avoid the spreading pool.

"This is a rapier wound," I said, astounded.

Although common in London, neither of us had seen one in Lincolnshire before. Matthew tried to stem the flow as Buckler laboured for breath.

"Can you hear me?" he asked repeatedly, but the baker did not reply.

The nosiest neighbours, who had followed us upstairs, witnessed our desperate attempts to save Buckler's life. We bandaged his side without success. The baker was slipping away. There was little more we could do.

"Get out!" Matthew snapped at the on-lookers, "We need more space to work. Mister Buckler deserves more dignity than this."

I stared in disbelief. Matthew had never lost his temper before.

"Baxby, get them back downstairs!"

I shouted at the intruders, "Do what Mister Mobley says!"

When I returned to the room, something odd caught my eye. There was a pamphlet, nailed to the beam above Buckler's bed. We had not noticed it before. I stood on the bed to pull it down, as Matthew pronounced the patient dead.

"What's that, Baxby?"

"It looks like a religious tract."

From the first page, I could see that it was comical, mocking bishops in an amusing way. I could not stop myself from smiling, which was inappropriate given the brutal death.

"It's written by someone called Martin Marprelate," I said.

"Hide it away and concentrate. Burn it as soon as you get home."

My master needed my help to tidy Buckler's body, before taking his widow aside to break the tragic news. She wailed, seemingly incapable of comprehending any details. Matthew would not let me ask her any questions. None of the relatives and neighbours seemed to have seen anyone suspicious. I had to leave when someone started to clean, as the flour triggered a sneezing fit.

Outside, there was no sign of the boy who saw the threatening sword-bearer. When the constables sauntered down Flaxengate, they were not interested in him or the man who bumped into me at the bottom of Greestone Stairs. What idiots!

PAYING IN BLOOD

London 1613

18

The vicar, to Baxby's right, can keep quiet no longer, "I'm surprised God didn't strike you down the minute you touched that tract."

"I didn't realise how infamous they were at the time," the story-teller replies.

"Secretary Sculthorpe was right to question your intelligence."

"I was shocked by Butler's death. It was a bloody crime."

"Yes, horrific, but murders happen every week in London. A Martin Marprelate sighting is rare."

The printer opposite is interested in the pamphlet's origins, "Was it really a Martin? I thought the last ones were destroyed years ago, and the author hanged."

"Someone must have printed the one I found."

"I would never risk that, however amusing the contents. Is that why you're here? Were you arrested on account of the tract?"

Baxby shakes his head, having been imprisoned for greater crimes.

KAREN HADEN

Lincolnshire 1600-1601

19

After the funeral cart took Buckler's body away, Matthew and I trudged up Steep Hill. The climb took longer than usual, because people kept asking us about his death. Each time, Matthew confirmed that the baker had passed away, and referred them to the constables for more information. He told me to respond in a similar way. It was not our place to speculate.

However, the citizens of Lincoln were not easily satisfied. Matthew's earlier analysis was completely wrong. Even the smartest gentlefolk craved gory murder details.

My master looked exhausted by the time we reached Castle Square. Buckler's death affected him deeply. After finding a quiet table in the Hart, I tried to cheer him up by reading from the pamphlet.

"Martin Marprelate says bishops are proud *pope-lets*, *swinish rabble*, and *anti-Christs,* who meddle in other people's business without addressing their own."

Matthew kept sipping his beer.

"The Church destroyed a Puritan's printing press, leaving him and his six children destitute, but protected a papist's in Wales. Are Puritans more dangerous than Catholics? I thought they were Protestants."

Matthew made me hide the pamphlet in my bag, before whispering behind his hand, "There are different types of Protestants, Baxby. Puritans are those who want to purify the Church, by including more preaching, teaching and other practices mentioned in the bible.

"Is Martin Marprelate a Puritan?"

"That wasn't the writer's real name, but yes."

Remembering Crackleton's family, I wondered whether the printer and his children were still alive.

Matthew replied that he did not know, adding, "In my

experience, bishops rarely understand how ordinary people live. They don't go hungry or watch their child die on the bed in a one-roomed house."

We had such a case the week before. Matthew moved closer and clutched my forearm.

"Baxby, this isn't the first Martin to be found with tragic consequences. Be careful. Lincoln isn't safe."

Another one! Naturally, I had assumed this was a unique occurrence. Matthew reminded me to destroy the tract when he said good-bye. On no account should I show it to Agnes, Susannah or anyone else.

It had rained while we were drinking, so the air outside was cold and damp. Weary and confused by what I had seen and heard, I decided to take the shortest route back through Minster Yard.

The Exchequer Gate guards wanted to talk about the murder. One suspected a jealous rival had taken Buckler's life. Others blamed the Flemish immigrants who lived near the Pool. Rapiers were costly so that was unlikely, but it was an interesting discussion and late when I left them.

The Yard was deserted, with a late shaft of light illuminating the lurid friezes on the great west wall. I stepped in a puddle, distracted by the way the cunning serpents coiled their victims' limbs, dragging them down to hell. The line of haughty dignitaries, seemingly sitting in judgement above the central arch, made me feel guilty despite having done all I could to save Buckler's life.

A herring gull cast an eerie shadow as it flew overhead, momentarily reminding me of the one at Nieuwpoort beach. It folded its wings on St. Hugh's mitre, high on the turret above.

I trudged on, past the gaping black mouth of the Galilee Porch. It was almost All Hallows' Eve, when spirits break free from their graves. Countless bodies lay nearby. I wished I had taken the longer route.

As I passed the turning to the Bishop's Palace, the gull

swooped low overhead, and landed on the apex of the south east transept roof. Arching its throat, it released a piercing screech, which echoed round the stonework, magnifying the effect.

I stopped, startled by the bird, then my heart beat even faster when I heard a dull metallic thud, much closer, repeated several times. The bolts of the Judgement Porch door were being unlocked from inside.

Pressing back against the cold transept wall, I was scared but also intrigued. Who could be leaving at this hour? The gull had given me a warning sign. I stood there, rigid between two buttresses, like a statue myself.

When the heavy oak door opened, I heard a woman's voice, then recognised her curves as she stepped out. Agnes was leaving the cathedral, at a surprisingly late hour. The door shut behind her so I could not see who she had been talking too. I knew she visited Sculthorpe's lair each week, after finishing her work at Vicars Court, but she refused to tell me why.

Agnes pulled her shawl over her head to protect it from the weather. She picked up her skirt to avoid the wet, revealing her shapely calves, and set off towards Greestones with a purposeful stride. I do not know how far she went. Suddenly, I was overcome by a sinister episode which is difficult to describe even now.

When the gull on the roof top released another guttural cry, my mind was transported back across the Narrow Sea to Nieuwpoort. Flanked by monstrous sand dunes instead of cathedral walls, vivid battle scenes appeared before me. The lad and his Spanish adversary tumbled down the bank, whilst the old Boston militiaman laughed, "We might as well dig our own graves. We can't rely on Baxby."

I was in the sea again, buffeted by the breakers and showered in spray. The gull squawked overhead as Lupton's corpse washed past, rising and falling in the shallows, followed by a severed arm, tangled in seaweed. I watched, helpless in the swell, bewildered and angry.

PAYING IN BLOOD

I screamed, "Lupton! We need you in the tent."

Opening his eyes, the surgeon looked into mine.

"We can't save them all," he smiled, before slipping back into death.

What was wrong with me? Was I going mad? Was I at Nieuwpoort or standing in Minster Yard? When I tried to wade ashore, the ebb pulled me out. Something touched my arm. I tried to push it away, but could not break free.

"Mister Baxby, are you alright?"

I saw the Judgement Porch again. The sea started to drain away.

"Baxby! It's Agnes."

She was pulling my arm, bringing me back from my living nightmare.

"You look like you've seen a ghost. You're deathly cold."

Embarrassed by my behaviour, and still exhausted from the waves, I muttered something about herring gulls.

Agnes chastised me, "I don't know what you're talking about. You need to get home and warm through."

Was I feverish? Had I caught a chill? My medical knowledge was too limited to diagnose my condition. Thankfully, she was there to save me. No-one else must know what had happened.

After finding a blanket, Agnes made me remove my wet clothes. She stoked the fire and filled a bowl with thick meat stew. The Church allowance enabled her to afford better ingredients than Eunice.

"This is excellent," I said, finishing it quickly.

"There's plenty more. Tuck in."

The food revived my mind as well as my body. Agnes sat on the bench beside me to pour more beer.

"What were you doing in the cathedral?"

"No, tell me about your day. Were you really at the bakery when Mister Buckler died?"

Agnes loved to gossip about Bail and City folk, having low opinions of both. She thought the St Anne's Guild 'a disgrace', and the Sheriff 'not fit for office'. Now, she wanted to know everything about Buckler's death, although, of course, I omitted to tell her about the tract.

"Why does everyone want to talk about Buckler's death, but not Catherine's?" I asked, "Someone must know how she died. And why Sculthorpe paid for her burial?"

"There's no point asking me. I don't know. Do you want more beer before you go to bed?"

In contrast to her chatter about Bail and City residents, Agnes remained silently loyal to her Minster landlords. Her repeated refusals to answer questions about Catherine, aroused my suspicions further. I did not accept Agnes' non-answers any more than I believed Matthew's rabbit story. Little happened in Lincoln without her knowledge.

Reluctant to be alone, I let my landlady help me upstairs that night. I knew I was attracted to her, but was unsure of her feelings towards me. Her breast brushed against me, when she bent forward to pull back the blanket, but she carried on regardless.

"Who's Lupton?" Agnes asked, as she snuffed out the candle, "You mentioned his name in the Yard."

"Lupton was the surgeon at the Battle of Nieuwpoort, a good man. Good night, Agnes. Thank you for your help."

The beer and her soothing presence must have helped me settle. I slept better than I expected that night.

PAYING IN BLOOD

20

The days after Buckler's murder were confusing. Matthew seemed distracted. Bishop Chaderton was away visiting deanery courts. Buckler was Agnes' favourite topic of conversation until she visited the cathedral, then she fell strangely quiet on the subject, as if the baker had forged a mysterious link with the Minster clerics beyond the grave. She talked about everyone else. Perhaps Buckler had joined the ghosts looking down from the galleries. Agnes told me she also sensed their gaze, when she walked through the nave.

I decided not to destroy the pamphlet immediately, reasoning that if someone had seen me with it, it would be safer to hand it over intact. I almost wished Geoffrey was there, as he always knew what to do or at least what to say. However, I could not blame him for my current predicament, and knew I should not risk my apprenticeship on account of an illegal tract.

After much deliberation, I decided to ask Bishop Chaderton about Martin Marprelate, without revealing my true purpose. Unfortunately, his return was delayed by further floods. I kept the pamphlet in my bag, nervously biding my time, until summoned to the Palace again.

His servants were mopping up after another deluge. There were insufficient buckets to catch all the leaks. Rain came in through the roof, and damp up through the floor.

Unconcerned by the puddles, the Bishop wanted to talk about his recent court cases at length. Clearly vexed by what he had witnessed on his travels, I had to wait for an opportune moment to find out more about the tract.

The Bishop groaned, "An apparitor accused a vicar of baptising a cat. What nonsense!"

"What are apparitors? I've never met one."

"You're fortunate. The Church employs them to investigate cases that the parish wardens miss, but they seem to pride themselves on spotting the most ridiculous. They've no sense of proportion or common sense. Keep away from all Church prosecutors, young man. It's easy to fall foul of ecclesiastical law."

"There's so much to learn."

"Pursuivants are even harder to please. They prosecute the most serious cases and report to the High Commission Court."

This was my chance.

"This is more complicated than I realised, Your Grace. How can I learn more? Have you heard of a man called Martin Marprelate? Does he write on the subject?"

The Bishop frowned, no longer so concerned about his courts, "Where did you hear that? I fear you have been misled. The name was used some years ago, but Bishop Bancroft hanged the likely culprits, and burnt the tracts which were highly critical of the Church. It would be dangerous just to see one."

What would happen if he spotted the one in my bag? Bishop Chaderton had convinced me that Martin Marprelates were no laughing matter.

Sculthorpe was talking with the Dean at the top of the drive, blocking my way.

"There's something I want to ask you, Baxby. Can you come to my office now?"

As I waiting for them to finish their conversation, I tried to steady my breath and devise a strategy. Could he have found out about the pamphlet? What was the least bad option for me?

If Sculthorpe knew about the pamphlet, denying it was dangerous.

Saying I had burnt it was risky too, as evidence from a murder scene should be handled appropriately.

What if he found the pamphlet in my bag? He could trick me into confessing heretical beliefs.

Following Sculthorpe across Angel Choir, I was terrified, concerned that even my walk might give me away. Neither of us talked until we reached his office. He squeezed round the desk to his chair, a route he found harder now his stomach had grown.

"Sit on that stool. Let me move these candles out of the way."

Strangely, the Secretary seemed more pleased to see me than usual. Perhaps he did not know about the pamphlet after all.

"Now Baxby, what can you tell me about Buckler's death? I understand that you were at the bakery when he died."

Sculthorpe wanted information, the reason for his abnormal pleasantness. Nevertheless, I knew I must not drop my guard.

"The baker was killed by a rapier wound to his side, and also suffered a blow to the head."

He scrutinised my face, reminding me of Bishop Bancroft's penetrating gaze.

"Matthew Mobley could not save the baker. The manner of his dying troubled us both."

"Did you find anything else there?" Sculthorpe probed, "Any clues? Mistress Buckler thought the murderer might have left something behind."

I made my decision quickly. His eyes were watching me still. Reaching into my bag, I found the pamphlet and pronounced, "This was attached to the beam above Buckler's bed. I kept it safe for you to see. Do you know what it is?"

His eyes widened, "Why didn't you show me this before?"

Managing to hide my fear, I replied, "I thought it was best to be discrete, so waited for an appropriate time. It's good that we can talk privately today."

Sculthorpe snatched the tract from my hand, turning redder with each page he read.

"Beelzebub! Another one! How can we afford another investigation? The Palace is falling apart. Worms are destroying the wood. The Treasurer refuses to release more funds, except in an emergency."

I ventured, "Isn't this an emergency? A man has died."

"What do you know about running a cathedral, or seditious tracts? You should have brought this to me earlier. You've caused unnecessary delay."

He banged open the door. I had never seen him so enraged.

"How can I balance the books? We should charge pilgrims to see St. Hugh's relics again. The Minster wasn't poor in those days."

Sculthorpe strode off, back towards the Angel Choir. It was a relief to escape, and know that the Martin Marprelate was no longer in my possession. I only told Sculthorpe and Matthew about the tract. No-one else knew.

PAYING IN BLOOD

21

When I returned from Sculthorpe's lair, I found Agnes in my room with a duster. Although there was little dirt, she cleaned it every day.

"Mister Baxby! I've been so worried about you. Treating the Bishop has never taken this long before. You weren't well in Minster Yard."

"I'd just witnessed Mister Buckler's death. I'm feeling better now."

Agnes persisted, "Is Susannah a problem? I waited for you up here because I thought you might prefer to talk without her."

She sat down next to me on the bed, spreading her skirt, so that her ankles showed below the hem. It was tempting to touch her then, but I talked instead, mainly about my plans to move to London. Having never been to the capital, I knew she was suspicious of those who did. However, I was taken aback by the strength of her reaction. Clearly, she was upset.

"Why do you want to go away? You have so much here."

"I can earn more and …"

I had never seen Agnes look that way before. She had always seemed so independent and strong, now, I saw a softer side.

"Don't go yet," she sighed, looking up into my eyes.

When I turned to stroke a lock of chestnut hair, she took my hand in hers and held it tight. I felt her heart beating beneath. My landlady was attracted to me, as I was to her. How did I miss that before? She released my hand when we kissed.

We slept together for the first time that night. Living in the same house meant there was nothing to prevent us. It happened easily, perhaps inevitably.

Susannah showed no surprise at our changed relationship. She still did not speak to me or other men. Sometimes, I heard her whisper downstairs when women came to visit.

Gradually, Agnes slept with me more nights. Other lodgers may have enjoyed a similar arrangement before me, but I did not dwell on that. It was reassuring to return to the same warm woman each night. I had slept with women before, but never regularly.

Agnes continued to compensate for her sister's rectitude with endless conversation, on every topic, except the Minster clerics and Buckler's death. Her willingness to share my bed was not accompanied by a similar willingness to divulge more information.

As the days shortened, another aspect of my life changed too. Before Buckler's death, Matthew's contemporaries would occasionally buy me a drink, as a generous act when thanking us for sitting with a sick father or restoring a dying aunt. More usually, I had drunk with those of similar rank. After the Flaxengate murder, I gained fame and notoriety by being present at the scene. Lincoln's most distinguished citizens brought beer to my table. Aldermen, magistrates and even the Sheriff sought me out, all wanting to analyse motives and potential murder suspects.

Some thought that Buckler's rivals on the St. Anne's council had sufficient reason to kill him. I learnt how the different factions vied for power. The presiding grace-man was always the previous year's mayor. A simmering grudge could easily boil over, given the intense competition.

People seemed pre-occupied with the baker's last hours, but not Catherine Crackleton's. Why the inconsistency? Unfortunately, Buckler's murder seemed to make it even harder to discover the truth about her. Everyone wanted to ask me questions rather than answer mine. There might be a connection between the two untimely deaths. No-one else in Lincoln seemed interested in comparisons.

Speculation about Buckler's murder continued as winter approached. After eliminating current and former councillors, the conversation widened to consider prospective candidates who might have a motive to kill him.

PAYING IN BLOOD

One evening in the Hart, a name attracted my attention. Busy with my apprenticeship and relationship with Agnes, I had almost forgotten the annoying deputy who hurt Crackleton in the Sailors' Inn.

"What about Julian Felde?" someone asked, "Could he be Buckler's killer?"

"Which one is he?" came a reply.

"The Muster Lieutenant's ambitious deputy, with the bright cape and strong scent."

"I bury my nose in my ruff whenever he passes. Where does Felde buy that?"

"In London, which he visits frequently. Although he was born here, his father took him to live there as a child."

Where was Felde at the time of Buckler's death? None of them knew. My fellow drinkers summoned a guildsman from another table, who was unable to recall Felde's whereabouts either.

"You should talk with to him about enclosing your fields," the newcomer advised, "Felde owns land further north. He is an expert on the subject."

Henceforth, the discussion deteriorated into a dreary debate about the relative merits of various drainage and farming methods. Someone mentioned the Fosse Dyke ditch which linked the Witham to the Trent, a perennial bore. Many locals assumed they would be prosperous again if someone else paid to clear it out.

More interested in Felde's movements, I asked, "Where does Felde stay when he is in Lincoln?"

They claimed not to know the address. As with my previous attempts to find out about Catherine, I was forced to give up.

That night, I opened the shutters when Agnes was asleep, staring out into the clear sky. The black edge of Waddington Heath framed the hemisphere of stars. Fainter ones twinkled between familiar constellations, far too many to count. The darkness helped me think.

Although grateful for my apprenticeship and Matthew's

support, Lincoln irritated me. Despite all the chatter in the inns and market, much went unsaid. People swapped shocking murder stories, speculated where the killer might strike next, but no-one had been arrested. The magistrates and constables were lax, too busy fussing about guild politics instead of tackling crime. Why would they not answer simple questions? What were they scared of?

Staring out, I concluded that some locals told lies deliberately. Accustomed to secrecy, others hid truth from themselves, like patients who refused to confront an obvious illness, or amputees who claimed they still sensed their missing limb.

Leaning further, I could see the upper River Witham, reflecting the moonlight as it snaked round the straight Fosse Way. I missed my old comrades. Soldiers spoke plainly, and answered questions when asked. Why meander up the Witham when you could ride on the straight road? Crackleton would not have deviated unnecessarily.

The shutter banged against the wall, waking Agnes.

"What are you doing, Baxby? Close the shutters and come back to bed."

"I can't sleep."

"Just close the shutters then. It's hard to keep this house warm. Secretary Sculthorpe won't pay for upstairs glass, however much I complain."

"Why do you visit him when you finish work at Vicars Court? What do you talk about?"

"It's the middle of the night."

"I was thinking about my friend Crackleton."

"Not now, Baxby."

PAYING IN BLOOD

22

Soon afterwards, Matthew took me with him to my first delivery, a harrowing experience. The father, who worked for the Sheriff, disappeared, unable to bear his wife's screams. Why was it taking so long? Matthew stayed all night whilst the labour progressed, but kindly let me go home to get some sleep.

I witnessed the birth when I returned in the morning. There was much more blood than I expected. Twisting the baby's head out, Matthew found the cord was wrapped around its neck. He cut it and made the infant cry, then left me to wait for the afterbirth. I had never even heard of one before that day.

"A beautiful boy," Matthew pronounced.

The mother was delighted with her tiny bundle, as was the father when he re-appeared. They kept thanking us both, overwhelmed with joy. Matthew told me that had been a relatively good first labour, although it seemed grim to me.

"Some babies take several days to be born. Many don't survive."

"Do you deliver many?" I asked.

"A few each year, to richer parents who don't trust the local midwives. They're paid per baptism, so can seem pre-occupied with tying the knot to the Church."

"What about your own children?"

"Yes, I delivered both."

The experience made me view my mother differently. It was incredible to think that she had given birth to me, in the way I had witnessed. I knew she was very young at the time, but not whether a midwife helped her, or who arranged my baptism.

Agnes had told me that she could not have children, which puzzled me. Matthew's medical books stated what I already knew, namely that women conceive when fully aroused. They did not mention conditions that would stop this natural process. Agnes must be confused.

I came home late one night, after another difficult visit, where a young woman had bled to death. Matthew told me not to mention the details to anyone. Agnes was sleeping soundly, curled like a small child herself. I lay beside her, listening to the rain on the roof.

When I eventually fell asleep, I drifted into a disturbing dream, floating through waterlogged fens in a flat-bottomed boat, with no stars for guidance. A thin moon shone over-head, leaving a wispy reflection on the sea. An occasional tree punctuated the surface, between clumps of sedge and reeds. Otherwise, the horizon stretched in all directions, like an infinite sea.

Without making ripples, my boat slid on silently, until the hull hit an object in the water, then another and a third. Peering over the side, I saw that the sea was writhing with human body parts. Gruesome hands tried to grasp my ankles. Limbs and torsos floated by.

The dream was worse than my experience in Minster Yard. Which way should I go? The pole star appeared, but where was I?

Sailors tell tales of beautiful sirens who lure ships to the rocks, but there was nothing enticing about my dream. I was drawn towards the edge of the boat. Balancing there, the water drew me down. Time slowed as I fell into the cold darkness, unable to swim.

I woke in a cold sweat, surprised to find myself in bed not underwater. Agnes was pulling my sleeve.

"There were bodies in the water."

"It was just a dream. You're safe in bed with me."

Thankful I was not alone, I nestled against her, hiding my fear,

When I apologised for my behaviour at breakfast, Agnes had already been out to buy bread. She wanted to help, "You could talk to someone about your experiences. I'm happy to listen whenever you want. It must have been awful to see so much blood at that battle, and chop off your friend's leg."

"I sawed it off with a blade."

"If you prefer to talk to a man, I understand. Why not ask Mister Mobley? He's seen more than most in the city. Or you could write to that nice innkeeper in Boston?"

Agnes did not suggest Geoffrey. I had not mentioned his name to her.

"I've recovered now. This is lovely bread. Please don't fuss over me. I'm not a child."

Worryingly, the dream did not vanish from my mind in the usual way. Troubling images re-appeared during the following days. Body parts surprised me, when I was meant to be assisting Matthew or treating the Bishop. The intrusive thoughts were not debilitating, like my seizure in Minster Yard, but disturbing nevertheless.

I did not tell Matthew, or anyone else, about my dream. However, I could not forget the fear I felt on the edge of the boat, and the subsequent terror when I hit the water.

23

I was grateful when Agnes ceased nagging me and hatched a more agreeable plan, "Why don't we visit Crackleton's village? The owner will let us ride in the bread charity cart."

"I doubt Crackleton's still lives there. He may even have died."

"The driver makes the journey regularly. He is willing to help. And if we find that Crackleton has passed away, you can stop worrying, because you won't be able to help him anymore."

Although her logic made some sense, I doubted that Crackleton's death would have that result. My vow would remain. Buckler's murder had re-enforced my desire to discover the truth about Catherine.

Matthew only gave me permission to travel the evening before, then the driver had trouble with one of his wheels. Agnes never stopped talking while it was being repaired. I suggested we abort the visit, but she insisted we go. The weather was deteriorating, so this would be the last opportunity before the spring.

The bread charity horse had been donated by a yeoman, who found it too weak to pull his plough, so progress was slow. Although only November, the overcast sky grew lighter, threatening snow. Agnes remained enthusiastic, spotting walls that needed mending, and pig-pens that should be cleaned, but most of the cottages were tidy, and the strip-fields well dug.

Drawing nearer to our destination, the driver sighed, "It all used to look like this."

"What do you mean? How has it changed?"

"The land on the south side of the village has been enclosed. You'll see soon."

"My friend Crackleton is a strip-farmer there."

"Let's hope he lives on the north side then."

Even Agnes went quiet as we neared the village and saw the dereliction. An isolated farm first, then rows of wasted cottages, with sagging thatch. Weeds choked doorways and broken shutters. No people, no animals, no movement except our cart.

"How has this happened?" I exclaimed.

"The new owner imported a tenant farmer from Northamptonshire, an outsider who doesn't understand our soil and weather. God should fire down lightning bolts to strike them both. No wonder there are food shortages when land is neglected like this."

No longer divided into strips, like the ones we had seen before, the fields appeared larger and uniformly drab. How could Crackleton or his children survive such desolation? How could any family?

The church stood in the centre of the village, surrounded by bare-branched trees.

"You can stay with the cart if you wish, and help me load sacks," the driver offered, "I wouldn't blame you for changing your mind."

"No, I need to see this place, even if Crackleton isn't here."

"There was blossom on these trees when Crackleton married Catherine," I told Agnes.

"I can't imagine another wedding here. There's no one left to marry."

The entrance to the church was locked, so we huddled in the porch to eat the bread and cheese she had brought. When I finished, I stood up to check the graves. Sculthorpe's letter said they buried Catherine in the churchyard. Crackleton might be here too, possibly the children. I refused Agnes offer to help, needing to search alone in peace.

I found a line of forlorn wooden crosses, by the wall on the north side. Several locals had died recently, which was not surprising in the circumstances. Their names were scratched in the uprights, with Catherine's adorning the last. As I stared at the sad little letters, snowflakes started to settle on the arms of the cross.

The letter had said that Catherine was buried 'in full accordance with the Book of Common Prayer'. What did that mean? Did a fat, old cleric read whilst another shovelled dirt?

Nothing a churchman said or did, would bring her back.

I searched on, relieved not to find the others.

Agnes came round the corner, shouting, "The grave-digger is at the gate. He wants to speak with you."

The neighbour, who had known Crackleton since they were children, remembered seeing him when he returned from Nieuwpoort.

"Poor John came back to find his cottage empty, and his children gone."

"Did the Poor Law Commissioners take them away?"

"I sincerely hope not. He left to search for them."

"Was he managing to walk with his crutches?"

"He was doing well. It was sad to see him with just one leg. John shouldn't have left Catherine with the two little ones, like that, although we didn't know what Felde was planning to do with the land back then."

"Felde! Julian Felde? Was he Crackleton's landlord?"

The grave-digger nodded, "Fortunately, my parents rented a house further north."

The cart was coming towards us on the track. We did not have much longer to talk.

"Is Felde here now?"

"No, he rarely visits. I think he lives in Lincoln or possibly London."

"Thank you. If Crackleton returns, please tell him that Baxby came to find him. Say I asked after him."

"I will, although I doubt he will return. What's here for him now?"

Nothing, but his wife's grave and memories.

PAYING IN BLOOD

24

The weather had not improved by the following Sunday. I was surprised when Matthew told me we needed to visit Brayford Pool. The City Preacher had requested we help a woman who had fainted there.

"You'll like Smyth," Matthew assured me, as we walked down the hill, "He's employed by the City, not the Minster."

I had never heard of a cleric who did not work for the Church.

Matthew explained that his appointment was controversial, "I think the others may be envious. Smyth can command an audience of a hundred in the open air. People prefer his sermons to those they hear in church."

When Smyth shook my hand for the first time by the Pool, I thought he looked a little odd, with his wavy hair hanging in untidy clumps, and a creased preaching gown which seemed too big for his frame.

"I'm pleased to meet you Mister Baxby," he smiled, "There's so much sickness in this city. We're pleased you're helping Matthew."

"Baxby came at the right time," Matthew agreed.

"Mistress Sudwell is waiting at our cottage, with her little boy. The poor woman fainted during my open air service earlier. I hope I didn't cause her unnecessary stress."

"It's probably on account of the cold", Matthew assured him, "Did many come to hear you today?"

"More than thirty adults, but I'd preach if only one or two came. Every soul matters to God."

Although he looked inconsequential, the Preacher's calm, deep voice commanded attention. It was not surprising that some would want to listen to him. However, there was nothing to suggest the day's encounters would prove significant.

Mistress Sudwell was sitting on a bench in the Smyths' cramped room, with her young son on her lap. Too well-dressed to live nearby, she must have brought him down the hill to attend the outdoor service. Both had striking blond hair.

"What seems to be the matter?" Matthew asked.

"It's very kind of you to visit at the Preacher's behest, but I'm perfectly well as you can see," Jane Sudwell replied.

Given the strength of her protests, I was happy for Matthew to take charge, and warm myself by the stove. Smyth's wife Mary beckoned Jane's little boy to the table, to look at the pictures in a book. There were a surprising number on the shelves, including some in other languages, suggesting Smyth was well-educated.

On finishing the examination, Matthew pronounced, "You're perfectly well, Mistress Sudwell. The cold may have made you feel ill. Would it be possible for you to attend indoor services during the winter months? Lincoln has plenty of churches to choose from."

Looking across at the Smyths, Jane smiled, but kept her opinions to herself.

"Thank you for your help, Mister Mobley. How much do I owe?"

"There won't be a fee today. I was helping friends."

"Then I shall make a charitable donation to the bread charity. There are so many hungry children in this city."

"They will welcome your gift."

Jane refused our offer to accompany her up the hill. Many would have welcomed the opportunity to gossip about Buckler's murder, but not her. Walking back, Matthew told me she managed her late husband's glove business and ran it well, employing two journeymen.

The following week, Matthew invited Smyth to eat at his home. Eunice lifted an enormous pot of pottage on to the stove, but let me carry the bowls across. Her swollen belly was tight against her dress, evidence that the baby was due soon.

The Mobley boys closed their eyes when Smyth blessed the food, then listened attentively to everything he said. His voice had that effect.

When the meal was over Eunice busied herself cleaning pots.

PAYING IN BLOOD

Matthew took the boys to the treatment room, leaving me alone with Smyth.

"You look tired, Mister Baxby."

"I haven't slept well recently," I confessed.

Speaking more openly than usual, I told him about my trip to Crackleton's village, albeit omitting Agnes' role.

"I promised Catherine's husband that I would help him discover how she died, but it's proved harder than I expected."

"I saw her at the bread charity," the Preacher stated, an admission which nearly caused me to fall off the bench.

After so many months asking fruitless questions, I had almost given up hope. Now Smyth had told me that he saw Catherine, voluntarily.

"No-one else has admitted seeing her," I explained my shock.

"These are difficult days for everyone. People are hungry and scared. It's often safer to say less rather than more."

"What do you remember about Catherine?"

"I think she came to Lincoln to settle a dispute with her landlord."

"His name was Julian Felde. Did you see them together?"

"No, I only saw Catherine once, at the bread charity. The overseer pointed her out. I remember she had dark hair beneath her bonnet, and looked a little agitated."

At last, I had found someone who was open and honest. How strange that he should be a clergyman of sorts!

"Thank you so much," I shook Smyth's hand several times before he left.

"People are rarely so easily pleased. Come and listen to an open air sermon by the Pool one Sunday. You may find that helpful too."

I was not interested in sermons, but the City Preacher's compelling style impressed me. It was not surprising that Sculthorpe did not like him.

As I walked back to Greestones that evening, I did not feel the cold or fear the ghosts. Now, I knew that Catherine had visited

Lincoln to challenge her landlord Felde. Although I still suspected Sculthorpe's involvement, he was not the reason she travelled to the city. I would search for Crackleton in the spring and tell him.

Also, Smyth's revelation changed my perception of Catherine. She was no longer a weak, simple wife in my mind, but more like my mother, battling her cause. It took great courage for a woman to travel to Lincoln to confront an unjust landlord.

25

Back at Greestones, I discovered that Agnes had been sick during the day. She assured me there was nothing to worry about. Susannah was sitting at the table, silent as usual.

"Are you certain that you're not pregnant, Agnes? Sickness is one of the first signs."

"I've told you before, I can't have children. I just drank too much yesterday."

"But women get pregnant when aroused. You can't refute centuries of accepted medical truth."

Agnes snapped back, "That's just men's truth. Men should listen to women more."

She argued about conception, as if the science was my fault, citing Susannah and herself as examples to the contrary.

"I enjoy copulation but am childless. Susannah loathes it but is expecting."

"If your theory was true, men would stop trying to please their wives," I laughed, trying to hide my shock at the news.

Eunice was not the only one, Susannah was pregnant too.

"They would stop judging women who are raped," Susannah spoke to me directly, for the first time.

Astonished by the anger in her voice, I did not know what to believe or say. I tried to catch her hand, "Susannah what happened?"

"Don't touch me, Mister Baxby!"

Agnes snatched my handkerchief to dry her own tears.

"I'm truly sorry Susannah, but you can't make accusations without explaining more."

"Susannah can say what she likes," Agnes contended, "It's not for you to decide."

She followed Susannah upstairs, banging the door on the way. I slept alone that night.

Over the next few days, I studied Susannah's belly size. The magistrate's wife would feel vindicated by her condition.

"Was she really raped?" I asked Agnes, when we were alone.

"It's none of your business, Baxby. Keep away from her."

"Have you found a midwife? Do you need money?"

"Susannah shouldn't have said what she did."

"Who's the father, Agnes? You can trust me."

"I know people talk about the two of us behind our backs, but I'll never betray my sister. I'll judge who I can trust."

I offered to move out, but Agnes assured me my presence was not problematic. Matthew had not taught me much about female ailments by that time, but I suspected that Agnes was afflicted by one. I could not predict when she would burst into a rage, or sob uncontrollably.

Coming in late from the White Hart, I was surprised to hear both sisters conversing with a better-spoken female. After flattening my hair to make myself more presentable, I pressed my ear against the kitchen door.

"They're good people who will look after you well. After Plough Monday, you can use the bread charity cart.

"Thank you, Lady Isobel."

The mystery lady nearly bumped into me on the way out.

"My apologies," I stammered, "I didn't expect to disturb a visitor at this hour."

"This is the lodger you let ride in your cart," Agnes scowled.

I had naturally assumed that the bread charity owner was a man, not a handsome woman like this. Isobel was older than Agnes but better kept. Her felt cap was slightly askew, which was unusual for a lady of high standing. Perhaps she had been out all day, away from her home.

"I'm pleased to meet you, Lady Isobel," I said, bowing low.

She smiled, "I'm not really a Lady, Agnes and Susannah just call me that."

Her perfume did not cause me to sneeze like some gentlewomen's. It seemed to melt my reasoning instead. I struggled to find a suitable topic to engage her in conversation,

PAYING IN BLOOD

"Thank you for letting me ride in your cart."

"Agnes told me that you were concerned about a friend who only has one leg."

"Yes, John Crackleton."

"Crackleton? The name sounds familiar."

"His wife Catherine could have been one of your bread charity customers. Do you remember seeing her?"

"Isobel needs to get home," Agnes interjected, "She hasn't time to answer questions."

"It's true, Mister Baxby. I have start work early tomorrow."

"I shouldn't have assumed ..."

"Why don't you visit the bread charity? I can check our records there."

"Thank you, I'll come as soon as I am allowed time off work. I'm Matthew Mobley's apprentice."

"I know."

My inferior status was obvious, I wore the robes.

I held the door, and watched Isobel walk to the top of Greestone Stairs, obviously not scared of ghosts.

"Don't pester her," Agnes warned, "She's too good for you."

Agnes was right but I ignored her advice.

26

I avoided the Minster in Advent whenever I could. The pre-Christmas fasting and preparations adversely affected the clerics. Sculthorpe made Agnes cry by refusing to buy a replacement mop when hers broke. Even the sheep in the stained-glass nativity scenes would keep away if they could.

Matthew and Eunice showed more tenderness towards their Mobley flock. Little Constance delayed her arrival until after the Christmas blizzards, wise from the start. Matthew delivered his daughter safely, but Eunice was poorly afterwards and had to spend more time in bed than with previous labours.

The Smyths walked up the hill to help the family. Mary cooked, whilst her husband entertained the boys by telling bible stories. Excited to have a new sister, they helped by rocking the baby's cot. However, Matthew had to discipline them, when they wrapped bandages round Constance's head, pretending she was a patient. The pair made a terrible mess in the treatment room that day.

Matthew was exhausted, and grateful when I volunteered for extra work. In truth, I was glad of an excuse to keep away from Michaelgate and Greestones. One house overflowed with visitors and pungent baby linen. The other drenched me in a snowstorm of criticism, from Agnes who kept complaining about men.

Steep Hill was treacherous in the cold. Careless citizens kept me busy with snow and ice-related injuries. At least the wealthy patients could afford to heat their homes. I lingered by the largest fireplaces whenever I could.

Without Matthew monitoring my movements, I had more freedom to explore the city. I found the bread charity by following a baker's donkey. A line of hungry mouths queued at the door. Isobel beckoned me straight in, looking regal in fur, her sickly customers grateful for every gracious smile.

"Lady Isobel, how good to see you again."

PAYING IN BLOOD

"Good afternoon, Mister Baxby. You've called at a busy time. This is a terrible time of year."

"Shall I come back later?"

"No, please stay.

Many recipients were beyond medical help. We lost record numbers of children that winter.

"This is an admirable place," I commented, "Your reputation is well deserved."

"To its eternal shame, the Church stopped providing alms when the monasteries closed. We just feed as many as we can."

She seemed to soften as she looked around the distribution room, drawing strength from the shrivelled souls waiting there.

"From conversations with older folk, I believe the monks also brewed better beer."

"Yes, I've heard that too."

Her hat bobbed on her head when she laughed.

"Are you thirsty now, Mister Baxby? I should have offered you a drink."

As Isobel led me through to the back room, I felt more nervous. Might she see me as another project, a young man in need of kindness-balm? I was just an apprentice after all. Clearly, she was a capable woman.

Isobel beckoned me to the table beneath the window and poured some beer. An old man was unloading the donkey I had followed, outside in the yard. I should have asked her about the charity records, which she had offered to check, but I was eager to learn more about Isobel first.

She told me she had sold her alderman husband's properties in the country when he died, and moved to the city, where it was easier for a woman to live independently. Her gold necklace confirmed her continued wealth. It quivered on her throat when she talked, framed by the edges of her ruff.

The bread charity owner was beautiful in a way that Agnes and Susannah would never be, the sort of woman I would never touch. I did not pride myself on possibilities above my station, but wanted to give a favourable impression nevertheless.

"Do you miss your former life?" I enquired.

"I like to keep busy and serve a purpose. This suits me well."

"Some gentlewomen won't mix with those of lower birth," I said, picturing the magistrate's wife on her doorstep.

"We're all the same underneath," she smiled.

Isobel did not seem the same as everyone else. Her statement was generous, one few would make.

Before we could finish the beer, our conversation was interrupted by a commotion outside in the distribution room. Isobel jumped up more quickly than me. I followed in time to witness Secretary Sculthorpe burst through the door, knocking a small child to the floor. I had never seen him outside the Minster district before. He looked even larger, next to the bread charity customers. What was he doing here? Isobel's staff clung to each other in fear. Although not as angry as when I gave him the Martin Marprelate tract, he was alarming nevertheless.

"What are you doing in this flea-pit, Baxby? I've been searching the devil's-own alley-ways since noon."

To my astonishment, Agnes was standing outside in the street, fretting in the cold. Why was she there? What was her involvement in this drama?

Isobel regained composure first, "Reverend Sculthorpe, how lovely to see you. It's crowded in here. You may spoil your clothes. Let us talk outside."

She passed the fallen child to its relieved mother. Isobel did not have children of her own.

"I've come for Baxby," Sculthorpe boomed, "I can't waste time talking to you."

Agnes ran off when we stepped out into the street, ignoring my pleas. How did Sculthorpe know where to find me? Did she lead him there? I did not remember telling her where I was going, but she could have followed me. I should have been more careful, not trusted her so much.

Before leaving, I whispered to Isobel, "I enjoyed the drink. Apologies for this disturbance. Please don't worry about me."

PAYING IN BLOOD

As I walked off with Sculthorpe, I heard her sigh, "I thought I would disappear like that Crackleton girl. I thought he'd come for me."

In my eagerness to impress, I had missed an important opportunity. Isobel had seen Catherine at the bread charity. She knew more than I had realised. Turning the corner of the street, I looked back and saw her for the last time. The picture of Isobel's fur-trimmed figure in the doorway remained in my memory.

27

Understandably, I assumed this summons was linked to my disclosure of the Martin Marprelate tract. Sculthorpe unlocked the gate to the private passageway, opposite the Galilee Porch, the only time I used that route. Anticipating a confrontation with the Bishop, I tried to prepare my defence.

However, Sculthorpe turned away from the Palace at the end of the path. He briefed me as we walked towards the stables, where two horsemen were waiting, with a third saddled horse.

"These escorts will take you to London. Just do what you're told."

"What are you talking about? Geoffrey said I must complete my apprenticeship here."

"This is more urgent."

The Secretary handed me a black cloak and doublet, matching those of my two new travelling companions. I fastened the buttons, and secured my bag. He gave me three weeks' pay in advance, not enough to allay my fears. Had Bishop Bancroft heard about the tract? Was this his doing? My apprenticeship seemed to be over as abruptly as it had begun.

"Is this a trick? I know what you're like," I shouted, as we kicked off.

"Don't blame me. This is Geoffrey's idea. He needs you without delay."

I wished Sculthorpe dead as he stood there laughing, with my apprentice robes over his arm. He would return to his lair, draw a line through a ledger to confirm the task complete. He had used Agnes for his own purposes, now he was scuppering my plans.

Forced to leave Lincoln in such a hurry, I realised how much the apprenticeship meant to me. Would I be able to return? If not, I would miss Chaderton, the sisters and the Mobleys, even some of the more endearing patients. However, it was not just my physical appearance that had changed since the Battle of Nieuwpoort. Having known a measure of financial security, I did not want to return to my old precarious past.

PAYING IN BLOOD

The wind drove intermittent snow showers across the Fosse Way, hiding the Lincolnshire dirt and ditches beneath a deceptive white blanket. Snow slowed the horses and numbed our extremities.

When I dismounted to relieve myself, I discovered three frozen paupers crouched behind a wall. Two dead children clung to their lifeless mother. It was too distressing to linger, but also hard to remount.

We saw no other travellers before Newark. The weather improved after we turned south, on to the Great North Road. What fell as snow in Lincolnshire, fell as rain further south.

I recognised the road beyond Stamford, having taken that route before. The first time, I was ignorant of the distance, just a wide-eyed boy visiting Sibsey's cousin in London. Without his money, I would not have survived, possibly dead behind a wall like the frozen children, or arrested as a vagrant.

Although the purpose of the ride remained mysterious, its urgency was clear. The mission had been planned meticulously, with pre-booked rooms and horses along the route. I ate the more expensive dish whenever there was a choice, and drank well to ward off the cold.

The escorts did not let me out of their sight, so I felt like their prisoner, although they assured me this was not the case. They were silent at first, then grew more agitated and vocal after we experienced delays.

The horses were not ready when we tried to leave an inn.

"You're late," the ostler complained.

"We paid in advance. The horses should be here," the shorter escort answered back.

"They were here four hours ago."

"I'll speak with the landlord. Insist you lose your job."

The landlord saddled three horses himself. After setting off late, the next inn had stopped serving food by the time we arrived. Another reprimand sent that innkeeper scuttling to the kitchen to cook our meals. Both escorts drank more than usual, and conversed that evening.

"This place was poor last time. We mustn't book it again."

"Bancroft complained about the vermin and the beef. I hope we don't have to bring him up here again if another Martin appears."

I nearly spilt my drink. This pair had escorted Bishop Bancroft on a previous journey, and knew about a tract.

"Did you accompany Bishop Bancroft to Lincoln?" I asked, managing to hide my excitement.

"Both times the pamphlets appeared. We know this route well."

Heavens above! Bishop Bancroft had visited Lincoln on two occasions when Martin Marprelates were found. How could I find out more?

"I've heard Archbishop Whitgift regards the Bishop well."

"Yes, but Bancroft was in a foul mood when he travelled with us, especially the second time."

Matthew had mentioned an earlier pamphlet. I had not given it much thought since, having been concerned with the one I found on Buckler's beam. Mine must have been associated with Bishop Bancroft's second visit. I needed to know more.

"Was the first pamphlet linked to a murder?" I asked.

"We don't know much about that death. Bancroft seemed more anxious the second time. We think he knew the baker, or at least knew of him. He was more concerned about his death than the woman's before."

Two deaths, one female and one male, both associated with Martin Marprelate tracts!

"Was the woman murdered too? Do you know her name?"

"Bancroft didn't talk about her. He was more worried about the baker."

Although a disappointing response, I had discovered more during this short conversation with the escorts, than six months of enquiry in Lincoln. It was hard to stop myself shaking their hands. They were grateful for the drinks I bought them, without knowing the reason why.

PAYING IN BLOOD

London 1613

28

Baxby pauses to stretch, having been advised by friends who were previously imprisoned themselves. Weeks in a leg-iron have taken their toll. His muscles are no longer strong enough to control a horse.

Outside revellers toast the royal couple's health. London is in carnival mood, very different from the day, twelve years ago, when Baxby and his escorts arrived from Lincoln. Back then humanity hid behind bolted doors, with all sounds smothered except for the clank of armour as a patrol passed by.

From the beginning, it was difficult to establish the true course of events. Vicars loyally recited Bishop Bancroft's authorised account in every parish church. Conflicting rumours spread through the inns and markets. Although too frightened to speak openly, many remained suspicious, including Baxby's cell-mates who remember February 1601.

Both men are pleased when Baxby decides to rest and resume his story in the morning.

KAREN HADEN

Tuesday

London 1601

29

London had swollen since my previous visit. Filthy hovels bunched behind the frontages, long before we reached the city wall. The suburbs were strangely quiet though. My escorts pulled me aside to explain the reason, before we reached the gate. I was astounded when they told me Bishop Bancroft's authorised account of recent events in the capital. I heard other versions of the story later.

Earlier in the month, Robert Devereux, the revered Earl of Essex and commander at Cadiz, had led a rebellion to overthrow Queen Elizabeth. After he deserted his post in Ireland, she confined him to York House on the Strand, which his allies used as a base to rally the uprising. Fortunately, Bishop Bancroft saved the day, by mustering loyal troops to thwart the traitors' plans.

"Imagine what would have happened without Bancroft's intervention," one escort added, "Whitgift could be crowning King Robert now. How close we came."

Hearing this, it seemed less likely that our journey was on account of the Martin Marprelate tract I found in Lincoln. London had more serious problems, with implications for the whole country.

The escorts brought me into the city through Bishopsgate at dusk. Soldiers marched on the drill ground beside the wall, but the city streets were empty and most shutters closed. One locked-in lass peered out, otherwise we saw no other signs of life, nor heard the usual sound of ships loading and unloading at the Legal Quays. We turned into Eastcheap, heading towards the Tower.

In those days, the pig-houses backed on to the moat and

dumped their entrails there. We smelt it, long before we saw the dark damp walls of our destination ahead. As we drew nearer, I saw the cannons on the battlements above, trained on the city not the river.

The air grew colder as we neared the Tower, even the horses seeming to hesitate. I wondered whether high-born traitors shivered on arrival too. Were they surprised to lose the rosy glow of Tudor approval, expecting royal favour to last?

"You don't need to worry, Baxby," the escorts laughed, "Her Majesty only detains distinguished guests in here."

Nevertheless, I was nervous. We dismounted at the gatehouse, listened to the eerie rhythm of the river lapping below. There were no lights across at Southwark. Barrels broke free on a deck upstream, the clamour stopping as suddenly as it began.

Eventually, a gatekeeper appeared, disappeared and reappeared with Geoffrey and a torch. Despite my previous anger towards him, it was reassuring to see someone I knew. After he paid them, the escorts rode off into the night with my horse.

"Who were those men?" I asked.

"Pursuivants," he replied.

"Pursuivants? Don't they work for the High Commission Court?"

"Yes, they perform many useful duties, one of the benefits of working for the Church."

My escorts were two of Bancroft's enforcers that Bishop Chaderton had warned me to avoid. I would have been more anxious, if I had realised at the time.

"Do you intend to stay past ten?" the gatekeeper asked.

Geoffrey nodded, without smiling.

"If you're not out before we lock the gates, you won't get out until morning. You've been warned."

I was going to spend the night inside.

Many Londoners live within the Tower's shadow, but few pass inside its walls. The royal prison's infamous reputation was well deserved. As the portcullis closed behind us, Geoffrey's torch illuminated the broken drawbridge planks. How could I cross the foul moat on them? One of the Tower lions roared below, causing me to cry out. My shoes felt like they were nailed to the ground.

"Why have you brought me here, Geoffrey? My apprenticeship was progressing well. What have I done wrong?"

"Don't talk until we reach the chaplain's house. I don't trust these walls."

Geoffrey pulled me across the moat, then held the torch aloft as we negotiated the crumbling paving stones, between the curtain walls. I had expected the Queen to keep her prison in a better state of repair.

Nearing the foot of the Bloody Tower, we heard a deep rumbling sound, which caused me to panic again.

"What was that? Are the racks in use tonight?"

"They're opening Traitors' Gate. Hurry up, or we'll have to wait while they unload more conspirators."

"Essex's supporters?"

"Yes, he's here in one of the towers."

The people's favourite earl was being held close by. I had listened to the escorts' account, and seen the empty streets, but only fully appreciated the Earl of Essex's predicament when Geoffrey opened the inner gate. The timber-framed houses on Tower Green resembled those in Lincoln's Bail, but this regimented row encircled England's foremost execution site. The block was ready in the centre. Essex could lose his head. Loved by soldiers and commoners alike, even recognised in faraway Boston by Sibsey and his guests, how could our hero fall so far from grace?

Geoffrey knocked on one of the doors, "Let's get inside. I don't like to linger here longer than necessary."

Despite our other differences, we agreed on that. I hoped my stay in the Tower would be short-lived.

The house was small but comfortable. I never saw the chaplain there. His servant attended to our needs, re-stocking the fire before he left for the night.

"Now we can talk," Geoffrey said, "You'll have lots of questions no doubt. I'll ask one first. Do you know why the Earl of Essex is being held here?"

"He led a rebellion."

"It's too early to know what really happened, or which words are the most appropriate, but we'll call it a rebellion for now."

As we ate, Geoffrey gave me a different account of the key events, this time mentioning Shakespeare's play.

"Essex band of young earls and theatrical friends staged *Richard II*. Immediately spotting the danger, Robert Cecil called him to Whitehall to explain himself.

I scoffed, not understanding the significance.

"Baxby this is serious. In the play, feeble King Richard abdicates in favour of his manlier cousin Henry, which is why Queen Elizabeth banned it. I don't know if Essex's allies were planning to put him on the throne, or the Scottish King James, but Cecil moved swiftly, knowing this was a provocative act."

"People in Lincoln are preoccupied with the baker Buckler's murder. A rival on the St. Anne's Guild council may have killed him."

"No-one is interested in such murders here. This is politics at the highest level."

"Do you think Essex really believed the Queen would abdicate?"

"Our opinions don't matter. Cecil has played his hand well. Bancroft can spread his account in every parish church, but that may not be enough."

Geoffrey showed me the tiny room where I would sleep at the front of the house, with a small window overlooking Tower Green. There was a set of physician's furs on the bed, plus three ointment jars on a small table.

I asked, "What do you want me to do?"

"We need you to treat Essex's servant Crespin."

"Does he know I'm not qualified?"

"He has more pressing matters on his mind, such as the likelihood of losing his head. Sir Francis recommended you. Well done."

"Do you know what's wrong with Crespin?"

"I'm not a medical man. Just help the suffering servant, see what you can learn. I've borrowed these physician robes for you to wear."

It was good to receive such recognition. I had not been summoned to London on account of any wrong-doing on my part. On the contrary, Geoffrey had found an opportunity where I could be of use.

PAYING IN BLOOD

30

The cloud had lifted by the morning. The White Tower cast a continuous shadow over the chaplain's house. I could see the keep's crumbling stonework from the window above my bed. The room was neat and comfortably furnished, but far too cramped. I bumped my head on a beam when I got up.

Geoffrey had already finished breakfast by the time I descended the narrow stairs. The chaplain's servant was waiting to serve mine. I had grown accustomed to good food on the journey south, but the servant's cooking did not disappoint. As I savoured the bacon, Geoffrey said he needed to leave.

"Wait in the house until I return. Keep the door locked at all times. I have to attend to important business. If a Tower official asks what you are doing here, just tell them to speak with me. We've agreed this with the Lord Lieutenant of the Tower who has jurisdiction here."

"What about treating Crespin?"

"That will wait until my return. The chaplain's servant will look after you."

Geoffrey bundled papers into a bag and left.

My legs twitched under the table, aching after the ride. I wanted to visit my new patient, and return to Lincoln as soon as possible. Geoffrey had promised that I could continue my apprenticeship, but I still did not trust him. Why disappear now?

After I had finished eating breakfast, I returned to my room to try the borrowed robes. They were heavy, but the fur trim lightened my soul. They were real physician's robes, like Matthew's. Hopefully, one day I would wear my own. All those hours with minor ailments and grumbling patients, would eventually prove worthwhile.

While waiting, I cleaned my instruments, polished my shoes and shaved my pencil beard back into shape. The servant lit the fire early, before serving a delicious dinner of pheasant and wild boar, with two wines.

I napped afterwards, then watched the hands of the chaplain's clock and played patience with his cards. There was a portrait of Bishop Bancroft on the wall, with an enormous Bishops' Bible on the shelf beneath. I turned the pages until I got bored. This one had the same frontispiece as the one in Lincoln cathedral, with a picture of the Queen when she was younger, surrounded by cherubs and fruit. There were no other books in the house.

The chaplain's servant was courteous but would not chat, nor let me step outside. Why had Geoffrey not returned yet? How typical of him to cause this annoying delay.

In Lincoln, I had been surrounded with attentive enquirers since Buckler's death, now I had to sit in silence, sealed off from the world outside. Thank God I was never held in the Tower myself. Confined in the chaplain's house that day, I sensed its desolation.

Geoffrey had not returned when the servant left at seven, telling me to bolt the door after him. As the clock-hands climbed to ten o'clock, I accepted what I dreaded most, I was alone for the night in that place. When the last log went out, I went upstairs.

Lying in bed, unable to sleep, my mind wandered back to Lincoln. Had the snow melted yet? Were Eunice and Constance well? When was Susannah's baby due? I should have asked Agnes before I left. When would I be able to visit the bread charity again?

Picturing Agnes shivering outside, I remembered my sinister experience in Minster Yard. Could such a thing happen twice? It was cold and damp, as on that night, but there were no noisy sea-birds in the Tower.

An iron gate slammed shut outside, followed by a frightful howl, which did not sound as if it originated from a human or animal. I pulled the blanket closer but could not sleep. The Tower had cast its spell.

Shivering, I drifted into another flat-bottomed boat dream, lost on the endless sea again. Hands curled up from the seething waters, but this time I was not alone. A small woman crouched beside me in the bow of the boat, her damp, dark hair drooping over her shoulders. Somehow, I knew that she was Catherine

PAYING IN BLOOD

Crackleton.

"Baxby!" she smiled as our eyes met.

Her face was lined and kind. I was pleased that she was there with me, but she did not stay motionless for long. Catherine moved to the side, tiny and light on her feet, without rocking the boat.

I called, "Catherine, no!"

Momentarily, she turned and sighed, "Baxby, this is where we belong."

I shouted again but could not catch her. Catherine stepped over the side, a perfect circle of ripples marking the spot where she disappeared. Nothing else, ghastly silence. Then I felt the water drawing me closer too, as if coiled by the evil snakes on the cathedral's great west wall.

"No!" I screamed, "Not me!"

No-one heard me. I plunged into the icy depths, following Catherine. The water was too dark to see her. I was alone in the inky depths as before.

It was difficult to breathe when I woke. Sitting upright in bed, I heard the terrible noise outside again. I eased the shutter open, desperate for air, and peered out into the night.

The White Tower had disappeared into the blackness, but I could see the source of the noise below on the Green. Two guards were trying to push a shackled prisoner into the Bloody Tower, whilst another held a flaming torch, enabling me to see the captive's harrowed face. He screamed that he had seen a headless ghost inside. The man was out of his mind, delirious with fright. The guards threw him in regardless, before running away themselves.

Slamming the shutter, I crept downstairs to fetch the Bishops' Bible from its shelf. Of course, I knew a book could not protect me from Tower ghosts, but hugged it close nevertheless.

The bible was comforting although inconveniently large. When Geoffrey returned in the morning, it had fallen on the floor. I did not tell him about my dream, but refused to stay in the Tower on my own again.

31

Even in prison, peers of the realm do not share the privations of common folk. Devereux's tower was extravagantly furnished, the windows draped in his colours. There was a large throne-like chair in the centre of the room, which the Earl was circling round when I arrived, periodically pivoting to change direction. Servants buzzed around with plates of sweetmeats, urging their master to rest. A cleric was praying by the window, gripping a small statue.

The Earl looked magnificent as he paced the room, wearing spotless white hose on his long legs, beneath a silver tunic. More astonishingly, he bore a disconcerting red-headed resemblance to portraits of the Queen.

Although disgraced, it was an honour to be in his presence. The soldiers at Nieuwpoort would be jealous if they knew, but Geoffrey had sworn me to secrecy. My knees weakened as I waited for him to notice me. I pocketed a sweetmeat, when offered one, already hungry.

When the Earl stopped, I bowed as Geoffrey had instructed me to do. Recognising my robes, he smiled, "You must be Baxby. Thank you for responding to my request. We're very fond of Crespin. This means a lot in the circumstances."

Essex was authoritative and polite. The servant looked small beside his master, although of average height. He kept brushing his wavy fringe away from his face, not a sensible style.

Crespin admired my appearance, "What enormous eyes and adorable beard! I thought you'd be older."

"I've qualified recently," I lied.

"I'm glad they've sent you, not an ancient ogre with bad breath. Would you like another sweetmeat?"

Essex sighed, "Dear Crespin, I don't know how I'd cope without your smile and charming ways, but show Baxby to the side chamber. Don't keep this kind physician waiting any longer."

PAYING IN BLOOD

The Earl recommenced his pacing as we left.

Crespin munched more sweetmeats. This appointment was going to take longer than typical ones in Lincoln.

"Have you seen other physicians about your condition?"

"Yes, but please don't tell the Earl. He has more serious things to worry about."

When he had finished eating, Crespin produced a sample behind a screen, then held the bottle up by the window to examine its contents, instead of passing it back to me.

"Is this satisfactory, Mister Baxby?"

"Yes ample."

"No, is the colour alright? My father's was red before he died."

"He may have passed some blood, which is quite common."

"The Earl says the Queen's piss is purple. Have you ever seen that colour before?"

Shocked, I held Crespin's sample up to the light myself, trying to decide how to respond. Was he serious? Surely, it must be treasonable to talk about the Queen in such a way. Informers could be listening, even in the Tower.

"I've never heard of purple piss," I managed, "Is it caused by royal blood?"

"As a qualified physician, I hoped you'd be able to tell me."

"I'm happy to help, if you're able to find out more."

"Thank you. I'll ask the Earl once he's pardoned. He can't have long to wait now."

Crespin had the French disease, just the lesions not the rash. I prescribed the ointment, and said I would return the next day, but he would not let me leave so quickly. He wanted to tell me his account of the rebellion. The servant loved his master and could not bear to see him toppled. Tears ran down his cheeks, as he blamed Robert Cecil, casting him as an evil courtier and Essex as a gallant knight.

Also, Crespin was the one who told me about the earlier royal bedroom incident, saying that Cecil had confined the Earl to York House because he entered the Queen's privy chamber unannounced on his return from Ireland.

"The Queen loves Essex more than any other courtier. That's why she appointed him Master of the Horse. They had spent many happy hours playing cards together in her chamber, so naturally he visited her there."

I did not know what to believe, having now heard three different accounts.

"The Earl said the Queen looked frail without her make-up. Cecil had been bullying her about the succession all day. How could he be so cruel? He can't dupe her forever. Elizabeth will pardon Essex soon."

Crespin remained hopeful, as did many at that time, unable to believe the Queen would desert her favourite Earl.

I felt better after the appointment. In one-way Crespin was annoying, but in another a useful distraction. I understood why Essex wanted his company during his confinement.

In accordance with Geoffrey's instruction, I treated Crespin on three occasions during my stay in the Tower, and was pleased with the way the lesions shrank. Essex had received his sentence before my last visit. No longer pacing the room, he was like a cornered lion, mortally wounded by weaker cowardly men. Crespin still hoped for a pardon, but Essex knew the Queen better.

As the once-heralded commander sat with his head bowed, I summoned the courage to address him directly, "I'm sorry to interrupt your thoughts, my Lord. I wanted to let you know that I served under your command at Cadiz."

"Did you land? Did you drink the sweet wine? What a party! Those were good days. The Queen gave me the sweet wine monopoly as a reward, then took it away a year ago."

"Common people love you, Sir."

"Thank you for reminding me of better days. It's good to know that Crespin's health is improving too. Farewell, Mister Baxby."

We never spoke again. There was no royal pardon.

Geoffrey and I watched the execution from the chaplain's window. Initially, the proceedings appeared more dignified than a public hanging. The on-lookers, in jewels and fur, did not jeer when the condemned arrived. Essex removed his ruff and held his head high during the prayer, before placed it on the block. Bringing the axe down with considerable force, the giant executioner missed his victim's out-stretched neck and caught his collar bone instead.

Crespin screamed and looked away, holding his hand to his mouth. I doubted he would survive long without his master. It took three blows in total, scandalous incompetence! A surgeon would have sawed it off more quickly. Seeing I was shaking, Geoffrey put a hand on my arm.

"Don't worry, Baxby. You've done well in difficult circumstances. You will get your reward."

"What's the problem?" the chaplain's servant asked, "Haven't you seen blood before?"

I had seen too much.

32

When I emerged from the Tower, in the first hints of spring sunshine, London was already returning to business as usual. Crowds packed the Quays, from the gatehouse to the Bridge, with long queues for the ferry-boats. Ignoring the soldiers who still patrolled the streets, people were back in the shops again, buying and selling again.

Geoffrey gave me another three weeks' pay, and booked a room at the Cross Keys. He told me to rest in the capital for a week, before returning to Lincoln. The Tower assignment was not the end of my apprenticeship, merely an interlude. In fact, he was so delighted with my progress that he thought two more apprentice years would suffice, providing Matthew agreed. This was excellent news at the start of my week off.

I spent my days exploring the city. London was fun with money in my pocket. After visiting a barber, I bought a rapier and dagger, and ordered a new set of clothes. The grey cloak and capotain hat became treasured possessions. Fewer men wore the style back then. I had admired two merchants wearing similar hats on Cornhill.

Searching for presents, I found a comb for Eunice at one of the stalls on St. Paul's Walk. Guards kept order along the full length of the cathedral, but I did not see Bishop Bancroft or smell his cloves.

Back outside in St. Paul's Yard, I reflected on my good fortune, having reached a level of financial security I had never known before. However, my days in the Tower had lessened my enthusiasm for court. It might be better to work in Lincoln, occasionally visiting London for shopping or visiting a theatre.

As I sat, staring out towards the River, I heard a familiar deep voice, "Mister Baxby! How good to see you here. I didn't know you were in London."

"Preacher Smyth! What a lovely surprise! What are you doing

here?"

"I have a speaking engagement tomorrow. Would you be interested in coming?"

"I don't know …"

"Let's meet for a drink afterwards instead. I'm on my way to meet a friend, so can't stop now."

"I look forward to seeing you then."

In a Paternoster bookshop later, I found a wood-cut animal picture book for the Mobley children, then spotted a pamphlet about *Richard II* in a box at the back. Here was a way to find out why Shakespeare's play had been banned. The shopkeeper slipped the pamphlet inside the children's book when I paid, advising me to keep it hidden on the street.

My exit was blocked by a tall lawyer, with a neat, pointed beard, ducking to clear the lintel as he entered the shop. I clutched the picture book under my arm, hoping the pamphlet did not show. A lawyer might call a constable or arrest me for possessing illegal material. There was no other way out the shop.

As the lawyer apologised for obstructing my path, I noticed Smyth behind him, smiling. This was the friend he had mentioned earlier. Considerably younger, I had not made the connection. However, this did not mean he would ignore my purchase. I waited nervously as Smyth introduced us.

"I'm pleased to meet you," Thomas Helwys said, shaking my hand firmly.

"Baxby's apprenticed to Matthew Mobley," the Preacher explained.

"Sometimes my wife Joan visits Eunice when I'm in court. Have you met her at their cottage? You wouldn't forget Joan if you had. What brings you here, Mister Baxby?"

"I came to visit a sick friend."

Geoffrey had forbidden me from mentioning my time in the Tower, an unnecessary lecture.

"Matthew has been kind to me, and Eunice is a generous cook," I added.

"And what well-behaved boys. Our children are more unruly."

"The Mobleys have recently had a baby girl called Constance too."

"The family is growing fast. Let me take a look at that picture book."

Helwys had spotted the children's present, without me realising. It was impossible to refuse or snatch it back. He was persuasive, like Smyth. Lawyers and preachers share that trait.

I stood there trembling, as he flicked through the pictures of lions and elephants. There it was with the monkeys, a pamphlet about the banned play.

"It's for Matthew's boys," I stuttered.

"They'll love it. Keep it hidden. It should be a surprise."

Astonishingly, Helwys did not admonish me. After straightening the pamphlet on the page, he reclosed the book ensuring it could not be seen. Why would a lawyer behave like that? The play was banned, so clearly I was breaking the law.

After finishing our conversation, the two friends appeared familiar with the shop. Helwys ducked in all the right places as he moved around. Smyth talked with the shopkeeper at length. Had they bought illegal books there themselves? If so, the Preacher was more intriguing than I had originally thought, and his friend was not a typical lawyer.

Thomas Helwys was atypical in the way he treated a lowly apprentice too. When I met with Smyth, he told me that Thomas had invited us to join him at his lodgings, near Gray's Inn where he trained.

Smyth showed me the way, through lanes and courtyards filled with lawyers. I had never seen so many in one place before. They strode purposefully, with serious faces, too busy to exchange more than a cursory nod to each other.

Thomas welcomed us warmly, quickly making me feel at home. We compared the merits of our neighbouring counties, drinking his delicious wine. Thomas and his family lived at Broxtowe Hall in Nottinghamshire, where he was born.

When I grew sleepy, the friends discussed Puritan beliefs.

PAYING IN BLOOD

Thomas needed to know more about them, to help him understand a case. He absorbed the information quickly, despite the late hour. From the start, I admired his considerable intelligence and straightforward approach.

In keeping with others I met during my week in the capital, they did not discuss Essex or the rebellion, a disquieting omission. After their deaths, no-one discussed him, or his co-conspirators who were hanged at Tower Hill. It was as if our hero had never been born.

London 1613

33

Baxby's story has unsettled his audience, stirring memories. The printer looks around before speaking, as if those who made marks in the walls are listening still.

"I was an apprentice when the troops marched through. The Fleet Street journeymen wished they'd joined the Earl, but never mentioned him again after his arrest."

"I don't think Queen Elizabeth ever recovered. The episode shortened her life."

"I wonder whether the Earl saw anything other than pockmarks, when he entered her chamber,"

"I'm not convinced his death was justified," Baxby admits, "He may have been a tragic victim of circumstance."

The vicar reacts, "How can you question the Queen's judgement? You sound like a traitor yourself."

Like others, he would like to know what lay beneath Elizabeth's make-up and wig, but suggesting she could make such an error, threatens a myth he holds too dear. Having removed the pope from his pedestal, some seem to need an infallible monarch instead. The Queen was less attractive than her portraits, but few dare to state such an obvious truth even now.

Baxby states, "I haven't mentioned my association with Essex again until now."

The others agree that this was a wise precaution.

PAYING IN BLOOD

Nottinghamshire & Lincolnshire 1601

34

Smyth started to cough before we left London, grew worse as we travelled north. By Grantham, he could not ride his horse.

Thomas sought my medical opinion, "What do you suggest?"

"Preacher Smyth needs to rest. Can he stay at your home? Is it nearby?"

"I'll hire a cart."

When I signalled my intention to ride on with the other travellers in the group, Thomas insisted I accompany them to Broxtowe Hall, again the persuasive lawyer. Although he would not let me pay a share of the cost, it was gratifying to be able to offer.

It was dark by the time we reached the gate. The moon cast twisted tree-patterns on the track. An archway framed the approach to the house, with little candles twinkling in the windows.

"I've never been here before," the driver said, "It's beautiful."

The heavy oak door opened, to reveal a tall, slim woman. Thomas' wife Joan was immaculately dressed in a neat ruff and gown, with pearls on her necklace.

"We've guests," Thomas announced, "Preacher Smyth isn't well. This is Mister Baxby, Matthew Mobley's apprentice from Lincoln."

"It's a pleasure to meet you. Our home is yours."

Joan's teeth were as perfect as Geoffrey's, but her smile more genuine. She kissed her husband before helping me carry the luggage and settling Smyth in an enormous bedroom.

Thomas was right to say one could not forget his wife, not just on account of her height and strength. Back downstairs, she insisted on laying an extra set of silverware on the table for me, despite the servants' protests. He was fortunate to be married to such a woman, a gracious hostess and mistress of her house,

Later, it was strange to eat in such elegant surroundings, made to feel welcome by successful gentlefolk.

"You have a lovely home," I commented, "London seems a long way away."

Joan replied, "I'm relieved every time Thomas returns. It's safer here."

"Have you read your pamphlet yet?" he asked.

I was reluctant to answer, worried about informers and revealing how little I knew.

"You can trust our servants," Joan assured me, "There are no informers at Broxtowe Hall."

The couple were polite to all their staff, treating them with respect, so I was not surprised they were loyal.

"The writer's convinced that the Queen executed Essex on account of the play," I said, "I'm not so certain."

"We saw *Richard II* at the Globe some time ago. I was shocked when it was banned," Joan replied.

"What do we really know?" Thomas challenged, "Lawyers usually try to ask that question."

After some consideration I replied, "The Queen's relationship with Essex changed after he returned from Ireland. He could have seen something untoward in her bedchamber, or there could be other reasons.

"Yes, Cecil and Bancroft will have their own reasons for telling the stories they do. There are many ways to obscure the truth."

"Did you meet a young woman called Catherine Crackleton, when you were in Lincoln?" I asked, where it was similarly hard to establish facts.

Neither Thomas nor Joan remembered her.

"I promised to help her husband discover how she died when we were overseas, but it's proving difficult. People don't talk openly there, as you and your servants do. The Minster clerics must know what happened, but won't answer my questions."

"People are afraid of the Church in Lincoln, fearful of what lies beyond Exchequer Gate."

The couple understood my frustration, and were interested in my opinions which was astounding given how much they knew.

Broxtowe Hall provided a welcome sanctuary. I slept well, untroubled by my boat dream. The Helwys children were the only problem during my stay. The eldest chased his siblings round the room, with pincers he took from my bag. Smyth showed more patience despite being ill. Thomas and Joan did not discipline them firmly enough.

When Smyth's breathing improved, it was hard to say good-bye. On my last afternoon, I confided in Joan as she accompanied me on a walk through the woods, "I love Broxtowe Hall."

"It's been in Thomas' family for generations and is very dear to our hearts. These woods will be covered with bluebells, later in the spring. You must visit us again."

"Thank you for everything."

"Don't be silly, it's been our pleasure. Thank you for looking after Preacher Smyth. It's reassuring to know he has good friends in Lincoln."

On our way back, we admired the view of the house through the arch.

"Don't give up Baxby. Keep seeking the truth but be careful."

I promised I would do both.

35

Riding back from Broxtowe, I reflected on my time away, my perception of Lincoln having changed. Now I wanted to remain in the city when I qualified. London was too dangerous. Also, having valued my week with Thomas and Joan, I wanted to emulate their style one day, albeit on a smaller scale.

The sight of the cathedral caused me to stop and stare. How majestically she rose above the valley floor, with neat streets leading up to the tower and spires. St. Paul's was tangled in disorderly London alleyways. Lincoln's superiority was clear for all to see.

In order to fulfil my new plan, I realised I needed to improve my standing in the city. Influential townsmen and women should admire me, in the way I admired Thomas and Matthew. As the magistrate's wife had made clear, when she refused me entry to her house, this would not be possible if I continued to live at Greestones. I must speak to Sculthorpe without delay. Although I would miss Agnes' cooking and company, living with the half-sisters was not an acceptable arrangement anymore.

The Secretary was arguing with the Dean in the cloisters, so I slipped inside his lair. Taking a book from a pile, I was astounded by the cost of altar cloths. Fortunately, I managed to replace it, before Sculthorpe's stomach filled the door frame.

"Baxby! I didn't recognise you in those clothes. What a pleasant surprise."

He did not look pleased to have been caught unawares.

"Where are my robes?" I asked, tapping my fingers on his desk.

"I'll find them straightaway. Can you see the Bishop tomorrow morning? He'll be pleased that you're back."

I did not respond immediately. When he had finished rummaging through his vestment cupboards, red-faced and out of breath, I let him reclaim his chair. Then emboldened by his fluster, I stated my demand, "I need new accommodation Reverend Sculthorpe."

"Is Agnes not to your liking? Or is it the lack of glass? I must install more."

"I need a new residence, which I'm happy to fund it myself."

Sculthorpe neatened the ledger I had moved, before replying, "I see no problem with that. Tell me about London first. How was your time away?"

"It was excellent, but I'm glad to be back, and looking forward to a meal at the Hart."

As I moved towards the door, he manoeuvred his way round the desk to bar my exit.

"Was your mission successful?" the Secretary pressed, "How was Geoffrey? Take the stool."

His hunger for information provided an opportunity for me.

"Geoffrey briefed me. I know about Catherine Crackleton."

"Why did he tell you that?" he roared, "What's the matter with the babbler?"

It worked. Sculthorpe believed I knew more than I did.

"She died of natural causes," he insisted. "That's what we agreed with the Sheriff."

"In the castle," I added calmly.

The Sheriff was governor of the Bail, so it was the most credible guess.

"Well, at least Geoffrey got that right," Sculthorpe confirmed, before throwing my apprentice robes at me and striding off to see the Bishop.

What an excellent meeting. Not only did I have permission to leave Greestones, now I knew that Catherine had come to Lincoln to see her landlord, and subsequently died in Lincoln Castle. Guile had proved an effective method, hopefully one I could use again, to uncover what happened between those two events, and keep my promise to Crackleton. Leaving the Minster, with a smile on my face, I headed off to see the Mobleys.

Before I reached the top of Michaelgate, I saw a familiar man cross Castle Square to the market stalls. Julian Felde was a few yards in front of me, behind a pile of blankets. I had never seen him in Lincoln before.

Although I had not forgotten Crackleton during my time away, mercifully I had forgotten Felde. Now my anger re-surfaced, remembering how he had ruined the land and driven his tenants to destitution. Catherine would be alive if it were not for him. Could I challenge him in the square, without drawing too much attention?

Pretending I needed to buy something, I headed into the market. Ladies' bonnets were an unlikely purchase, similarly cooking pots. Damn! The rat was no longer behind the blankets. Where had he gone?

Felde was laughing with the Mayor, beyond the furthermost stall, in the adjoining row. They seemed to have common friends or relatives in Stamford, whose antics caused them amusement. I assumed Felde was endearing himself to the more powerful man. The Mayor did not know what that weasel was really like.

While I waited for the pair to finish their conversation, Agnes grabbed my arm.

"Mister Baxby, how lovely to see you! I didn't know you were back."

"Apologies, Agnes. There hasn't been time to tell you. I've only just arrived."

"When are you moving back to Greestones?"

"I'm going to find somewhere else to live."

I stepped away, but Agnes was not easily deterred. Much to my embarrassment, she tried to speak in my ear. We should not be seen so close together in public.

"Come away from the stalls, Agnes. We're getting in people's way."

A guildsman watched us move out into the open square. This was very awkward.

"I'm sorry I led Secretary Sculthorpe to the bread charity, but he gave me no choice. Susannah's left to have her baby and

Isobel's moved away, so I'm on my own now. Please come back and live with me."

"I'm sorry, Agnes. I can't."

There were tears in her eyes, "Please come and visit then."

How could I refuse her that?

Felde was walking up towards the Castle. I had missed an opportunity to confront him, but was pleased to have had the conversation with Agnes on the first day back. As I watched her move around the market afterwards, two older women turned their backs as she approached their stall. It was difficult for her in the city. I admired her resilience, but needed to concentrate on my apprenticeship and build my reputation. She was untrustworthy too. I had to move on.

Matthew and Eunice were pleased to learn that I was leaving Greestones. Eunice liked the comb, and the boys their picture book. We roared like Tower lions, chasing round the room. When the children had gone to bed, I talked with Matthew more seriously. "Having seen London, it's lost its allure. I would like to practise in Lincoln when I qualify."

"How long will this latest plan last?" he chuckled.

"I'm sincere, Matthew."

"I'm not surprised that you'd rather stay here, but will Geoffrey and Secretary Sculthorpe agree?"

"They won't have a choice."

"Give me some time to consider this and talk with Eunice. The workload is increasing. There may be sufficient patients for us both in two years' time."

A week later, Matthew beckoned me into the treatment room.

"Do you still want to work in Lincoln when you qualify?"

"I haven't changed my mind."

"As you know, this family is growing. Eunice and I have decided that we need to move to a bigger home."

"Knowing you, you'll soon have another baby," I laughed.

"We want to leave Lincoln," Matthew clarified.

I was taken aback by his statement, even more by what he suggested next.

"We'll stay here until you finish your apprenticeship, provided you promise to continue treating my patients when I've gone."

I made him repeat the offer, which seemed too good to be true.

"You have excellent skills and aptitude, plus a little more patience since you returned from London. I'm confident you'll do well."

"Thank you, Matthew. What an honour."

I thanked Eunice and the children too, drinking to the family's health several times, whilst acknowledging that I would miss them when they had gone. Eunice cried as she stirred the pottage. It would be hard for the Mobleys to leave, but this was another welcome opportunity for me. My new plan was working better than expected.

PAYING IN BLOOD

36

There were no more embarrassing doorstep rebuffs after my time away. Even those who lived in the highest streets welcomed me into their homes. I had learnt to keep my opinions to myself. Matthew was particularly pleased when some patients specifically asked to be seen by me.

My confidence grew throughout that spring. I delivered a baby, with minimal assistance, and correctly diagnosed gout and green sickness. Bishop Chaderton's skin problems improved with the warmer weather, but still wanted to continue my visits. When he warned me about pursuivants again, I did not tell him that I had met two.

Although I still hoped to find Crackleton later that year, I put Essex, Geoffrey and Bancroft behind me, to concentrate on my work.

My new rooms were larger and more comfortable than Greestones', with glass in all the windows, and a fireplace that caused fewer draughts. I missed Agnes and her cooking, of course, but the Hart was closer to my new home. I tried to put my former landlady out of my mind too.

As I reflected on my increasing success, I realised that my plan lacked a vital ingredient. A respectable physician would need a wife. Although I could not marry until I qualified, it might take several months to find a suitable woman, especially as Matthew kept me so busy.

Walking round the streets, I kept my ears and eyes open, mindful of the importance of making the right choice. Hopefully, I would find someone as agreeable as Joan.

Isobel had disappeared. She was too high-born for me to consider anyway. No-one at the bread charity would tell me where she had gone.

Matthew agreed with the need to marry, but warned against haste, "Don't assume that finding a wife will be easy. Our parents helped arrange our marriage. We both grew up in Lincoln, so knew of each other since childhood, but still relied on them for such an important matter. Love came later."

"Other parts of my plan are working, why shouldn't I find a woman too?"

"You can't marry before you qualify. Why rush?"

I should have listened to my master, who knew more about matters of the heart than me. Finding a wife was harder than I had thought. After weeks of futile searching, I returned to Michaelgate. Matthew refused to help, but Eunice agreed to make discrete enquiries on my behalf.

Following several more nervous weeks, she drew my attention to a handsome blond woman buying buttons on the High Street, "Do you know Jane Sudwell? Her husband died before you arrived in Lincoln. She has a small son called Piers."

"I met them once at the Smyth's home. Has Jane not remarried?"

"Not yet."

Other shoppers paid their respects to Jane, as she moved from stall to stall. She talked with some politely, not prattling on and on like Agnes.

"I've heard that Jane has German grandparents on her mother's side," Eunice added, "Would that be a problem to you?"

Foreign relatives might have limited Jane's appeal to others, but did not deter me. I was delighted that Eunice was suggesting such an attractive woman.

Fortunately, I did not have to wait long to meet her. Every July, the St. Anne's Guild organised a pageant to celebrate their saint's day. It was a dismal disappointment that year, but Eunice found an opportunity to introduce me to Jane on Castle Hill afterwards. The encounter was shorter than I would have liked, as Jane's son Piers kept pulling on her skirt. However, it was sufficiently pleasing to convince me to pursue her further.

As Jane and I both worked long hours, it was difficult to see her in the week. Each Sunday, I visited Lincoln's numerous churches, in the hope of meeting her there. The vicars read the Prayer Book in the same stupefying manner. Some altar queues were shorter than others, but I never saw Jane.

When Smyth returned from Broxtowe Hall, I spotted her at one of his open air sermons, listening intently to every word he said. More interested in learning about Jane, I practised delaying my arrival until his closing remarks. We would talk by the Pool when he finished, after his last "Amen".

Jane was a thoughtful, intelligent woman, with a direct approach the higher born often lack. Her smile was delightful too.

Piers, who was always with her, disliked long sermons too. When the floods receded, I offered to take him on walks along the Witham. Five years old and interested in everything, we picked medicinal plants by the waterside and counted ducks.

Grateful for the opportunity to listen to Smyth in peace, Jane gave me a pair of gloves as a present. I learnt that praising Piers was the best way to her heart. She loved the little boy and cared for him deeply.

"Piers, how much you've grown."

"What a bright intelligent boy."

"I expect you'll do well at grammar school."

I would need to take care of Piers if I married Jane. Hopefully, he would soon be outnumbered by Baxby children, who might have blonde hair too. I doubted I could love a child as Jane loved her son, but hoped I could bring them up well. Ours would not jump on visitors like the Helwys troop.

Although Jane's enthusiasm for religion greatly exceeded my own, by the end of the summer there was no doubt in my mind. I wanted to marry her when I qualified. Piers was always pleased to see me too. I was very fond of them both.

37

One Sunday when I arrived at the Pool, Smyth was concluding a sermon on the topic 'Jesus is priest and king'. Excited by what she had heard, Jane wanted to discuss this with me afterwards.

"Isn't this amazing? Kings and priests were distinct in the Old Testament, now Jesus fulfils both roles. He has authority in heaven and earth, and acts as intermediary."

Although this did not sound particularly heretical to me, I knew a man had been listening, behind a stack of crates. He left as soon as Smyth finished. I wanted to find out why he was there.

"Is Smyth a Puritan?" I asked Jane.

"Some people say he is. He's so knowledgeable."

"I'm afraid I'm in a hurry to get home today."

Jane sighed, "Jesus changes everything, the old covenant points to the new."

"Sorry, I have to leave now."

The man vanished through Stonebow Gate. Ignoring her pleas, I chased up Steep Hill, the incline no longer posing a problem to me.

My quarry slipped into the cathedral, using the cloister door. Was he a Church informer? I wanted to find out.

The Dean delayed me, discussing roof repairs, so by the time I reached the north east transept, the sneak had disappeared. I could hear Sculthorpe arguing with Chaderton through the gap in his door, "Fractious preaching is a crime. Can't we charge Smyth with that?"

"He's employed by the City not the Church," the Bishop replied.

"Why call Jesus a priest and king? How pointless! The Church provides enough priests and Elizabeth's our monarch."

"Smyth is a gifted preacher, and hard to replace. The law stipulates two for a city of this size."

"It states a maximum of two, none is quite sufficient. He sniffs around the margins of this city, like annotations in his Puritan bible. Can't we send him to the Bail for safe keeping?"

"As you sent the Crackleton woman? That wasn't your greatest success."

I gasped out loud at the revelation. Fortunately, the stone saints were well-anchored to their bases. Here was proof that Sculthorpe was implicated in Catherine's death. Despite his sanctimonious letter to her husband, the Secretary had sent her to the Castle where she died. My instincts had been correct. Bishop Chaderton confirmed that Sculthorpe had been lying all along.

I glanced up at the galleried walkways as I crept out through the nave, wondering what the cathedral ghosts had witnessed whilst Crackleton and I served overseas. Did Minster guards drag Catherine out? Was Pusey complicit? The locals said there was a secret tunnel beneath Minster Yard, which they could have used.

It was difficult to imagine what Catherine had done to deserve such treatment. Smyth antagonised the clerics with his preaching. She was just an illiterate peasant woman from an insignificant village. Sculthorpe rarely concerned himself with common folk.

There was another surprise that day. As I walked home along Eastgate, I heard faint footsteps, following behind. They matched my speed, stopped when I stood still. When I looked over my shoulder, there was no-one there. How strange! Sculthorpe could not have known I overheard his conversation. Who could be following me?

Having failed to lose the stalker in the lanes beyond Bailgate, I headed for the open ground which ran along the length of the Castle's eastern wall. It was the place where people gathered to watch hangings on the Cobb Tower roof above, but there were no crowds that afternoon. The area was suitably deserted, except for a few scrawny cats. This was my chance.

Removing my cap, I sprinted across the empty ground, trampling down the dandelions and dock weed, until I reached the far side of the Cobb Tower, an impressive speed given my earlier ascent of Steep Hill.

Hidden from view beyond the Tower, I tried to quieten my breath as footsteps approached and stopped close by. Good! My tactic was working. I put my cap back on, standing as tall as I could, to confront whatever ruffian was following me.

Surprisingly, I did not smell the foul perfume before I emerged, a musky, lemon stink. Julian Felde was standing before me, with his rapier drawn. The Crackletons' landlord was now menacing me. He wore a green cape, slightly less garish than his previous one, which matched his doublet.

"Mister Felde! What a co-incidence to meet you here."

"Good morning, Baxby. It's been a long time."

Felde must be doing well financially. He had a new rapier, considerably more expensive than mine. However, out in the open he seemed less intimidating than before.

"What brings you here?" I asked.

"I have two houses in Lincoln, plus land to the north of the county."

"How fortunate to meet you, you can tell me how Catherine Crackleton died. What did you do to her inside these walls?"

Felde looked puzzled, "I don't know what you mean. Please explain more."

"Catherine came to Lincoln to discuss her land. You were working for Sculthorpe. You must know."

Looking more perplexed, Felde stared up at the gallows on the roof, seemingly surprised to hear that Catherine had died in the castle.

"Why don't you tell me what you know, Baxby?"

"Do you take me for a fool? You enclosed the family's field-strips, then harassed Catherine's poor husband despite him only having one leg. Now you refuse to help again. Simply tell the truth."

Felde scoffed, "The truth! You are indeed a fool, good day to you."

That was all. He flicked his cape, before trotting off in the direction we had come, an unsatisfactory encounter.

As I watched Felde disappear, I realised how little I really knew about him or his true role. My suspicions about Sculthorpe had been vindicated earlier, but had I misjudged the Muster Lieutenant's deputy?

Since encountering him at the Haven, I had assumed that Felde carried the two letters from Lincoln on the Minster's behalf, therefore reasoned that he must have worked for Sculthorpe in some way. Perhaps the association between them was looser. If Felde was working for Sculthorpe, would he not have known more?

38

There was plenty to ponder on the walk home. When I reached my door, I remembered. How could I forget? I had promised to look after Piers that afternoon, while Jane visited her sister. Distracted by Sculthorpe's revelation about Catherine, I had neglected the woman I intended to marry.

Jane banged on my door the following morning. I had never seen her so cross. She would not let me give Piers a sweet. She wanted a serious talk, "I'm concerned by your behaviour, Baxby. Are you ill?"

"I'm very well, as always in your company."

"Please don't flatter me. That won't work."

Jane was a businesswoman, polite but to the point.

"Why do you keep disappearing? Why run away yesterday, after saying you would look after Piers?"

"I'm sorry, Jane. I was rude and forgetful."

"Why Baxby? Why? You arrived at the end of Preacher Smyth's sermon, then wouldn't stay to chat."

Jane made me return the gloves she had given me as a present. I did not want to part with them, but what could I do? Piers looked sad when they left. I had upset them both.

Mercifully, Eunice came to my rescue. After she explained the pressures of my work, we were reconciled two weeks later. Jane let me spoil Piers again, and eventually gave back the gloves.

The three of us spent more time outdoors, until the weather turned cold. We walked along the Dyke to Saxilby together, about five miles. Piers skipped along the bank, impressing Jane when he correctly identified medicinal plants. I taught him how to dry the plants and grind the seeds.

"Piers doesn't remember his father. Thank you for spending time with him."

Jane was always happy when Piers enjoyed himself.

Despite some difficult discussions about religion, Jane and I gradually grew accustomed to each other's company and habits. By Christmas, most friends assumed we would marry, when I qualified.

Matthew and Eunice kindly invited us to their cottage for a meal, delicious roast meats not pottage for once. Crammed on to the benches, I had never sat so close to Jane before, nor seen her so unguarded. It should have been a lovely occasion, but as I watched Piers playing with the Mobley boys and little Constance afterwards, I found my hands were shaking. Matthew put a hand on my shoulder and took me to the window, "Are you alright, Baxby?"

"I think the beer has affected me."

"That's unusual. Do you need fresh air?"

It was too misty to see the river and road, but I knew where they lay in the valley below. The view reminded me of Greestones and Agnes. I knew I had been cruel to her, and should treat Jane better. In particular, what should I tell her about my early life?

Jane had told me that her mother was born in a German city, and her father came from Kent. She knew nothing about my parentage or patron. Geoffrey regularly lied to women to gain advantage, as he did in his work. To my knowledge, he had never married, preferring temporary arrangements and encounters. I wanted to be more honest with the woman I intended to share my life with. Jane did not even know that I treated Bishop Chaderton, something she was unlikely to approve of. Criticising the Church hierarchy was one of her habits.

Feigning sickness, I returned home to Bailgate, disappointed and embarrassed by my behaviour. Jane and Piers stayed, and enjoyed the rest of their day with the Mobleys.

That night my old dream returned. Floating on the endless sea in the flat-bottomed boat, with no rudder, I could not prevent myself from following Catherine into the icy water.

I did not see Felde again that winter, and rarely bumped into Agnes. Pleased with my work, Matthew let me treat more patients on my own. I should have been delighted that my plans were working, instead I felt a gnawing unease, which worsened whenever I considered proposing to Jane. What was the matter with me?

I missed an opportunity to propose in the spring, when the two of us walked along the Fosse Dyke in beautiful weather. Jane's sister was looking after Piers. Why did I waiver? What was I waiting for? I had never cared about a woman like this. Having come so far, I did not want to lose her.

Patients started teasing me about weddings and babies, increasing my anxiety. The most annoying appeared in my dream. Although their fates varied, Catherine and mine remained the same, always falling in the water at the end.

Sculthorpe made matters worse, by reducing my allowance, and expecting me to account for every farthing I spent. He loved writing numbers in his books. I wanted to treat patients, not fuss with quills and ink. Trusting him less and less, I tried to verify everything he said with an independent source.

My patience shortened as the days lengthened, not just on account of Sculthorpe and Jane. Patients bombarded me with St. Anne's pageant nonsense too. Some grumbled that the July event was an unnecessary expense in austere times, others that it was a welcome distraction or good for trade. Some wanted bear-baiting or a dog-fight, rather than a procession.

"Everyone loves St. Anne's day," Chaderton laughed, "It's the highlight of the summer."

"Why do they all complain then?"

"It's part of the tradition."

A woman with boils wanted a play. She wanted to choose it, direct and pick the cast, even finding a role for me. How could I treat such stupid people?

"I won't visit that woman again," I told Matthew.

"Of course you will. She's a lonely lady who enjoys your company."

"I could treat three other patients in the time it takes to visit her."

"Try to be kinder."

Eunice calmed me down, with pottage on that occasion.

The woman's boil did not drain properly, darkened, and then turned yellow. When I called each day to dress it, she never stopped moaning about the pageant, from the moment I walked in the door until the time I left. She should have been more concerned about that protrusion, which was the worst I had seen.

Thankfully, Matthew took charge, applying a compress infused with herbs. When the inflammation subsided, he expected me to visit her again.

Although I tried to hide my tiredness, Matthew knew I was not sleeping well. The recurrent nightmare was affecting my concentration. He took me aside, after I accidently trod on a leech, "Do you still want to work in Lincoln when you qualify?"

I assured him that I did, despite my frustration with the St. Anne's tradition.

"Eunice is expecting again. Will you be alright when we leave?"

"I'm perfectly well," I lied.

"Why not propose to Jane before the pageant?"

I agreed that this was a good idea, and promised to take more care of the leeches.

When Sculthorpe told me that the Treasurer was refusing to pay my full allowance again, I confronted him in his lair, "How can you justify this?"

"The Minster is short of money."

"I've seen the buckets and leaks, but there's plenty of cash for vestments and silverware. Why can't you honour our agreement?"

"We must preserve the dignity of the Church."

"You pay for lavish entertainment of your guests. Look how many books you need to record the costs," I waved a ledger in front of him to illustrate my point.

"What are you doing?" he snatched it back, "Why should I listen to a minnow that Geoffrey trawled from a Boston drain?"

"Why should I believe a pig-bellied bigot, who sent a poor peasant woman to her death? A cleric who cares more about finances than Mister Buckler's murder."

The Secretary returned the book to its pile, before responding, "I have to follow procedures, Baxby. You don't understand the challenges we face, the costs, the casework, the precedents. How could a peasant boy? I've given my life for this Minster, as did my father did before me. You only care about your pay, an ungrateful goat devouring everything in your path, with no concern for the Church."

What a hypocrite! Sculthorpe was a petty clerk at best, possibly a shameless murderer, with no more respect for God than Geoffrey.

"Hidden in here, you don't see how common people suffer, fearful of informers every time they leave their homes, with no-one to speak on their behalf."

"Get out!"

"I'm leaving."

"Good."

I slammed the door behind me, but could still hear his rants.

The Dean met me in the cloisters, "Are you alright, Baxby? Try to be more patient with Reverend Sculthorpe. He has a very demanding job."

What about my needs? Sculthorpe was causing me hardship by cutting my pay.

PAYING IN BLOOD

London 1613

39

"That's enough," the vicar interrupts, "The Dean was right, you were too critical of Reverend Sculthorpe. Given his onerous responsibilities, I wouldn't be surprised if he made an odd mistake. I struggled to run a small parish which was short of funds."

Baxby does not respond, slower to anger than in his youth.

"And you had no evidence that the Reverend caused Catherine's death. He could have sent her to that castle to keep her safe, from Felde or someone else."

The printer nods, but is more interested in the story-teller himself. What was Baxby hiding from Jane? What did he dare not admit?

"I know nothing about church finances. Please can you tell us more about your background, Baxby? Did your family always live in Boston?"

Physicians grow accustomed to listening to patients, whilst disclosing little about themselves, but Baxby's reluctance started long before he picked up Lupton's saw. Growing up, he learnt to hide facts which might hinder his advancement. Recognising the trait, Geoffrey took solitary young men like Baxby, and trained them to be more guarded, to serve a higher cause. He understood the lure of adventure too, having travelled widely himself.

The printer persists, "Why did people in Boston dislike you? Did you do something wrong?"

Should he say? What difference can it make now?

"In their eyes I did, my father never married my mother."

"You're a bastard!" the vicar exclaims, "No wonder you struggle with religious belief. Bastards can't be part of God's chosen elect, although I've made money baptising those whose parents tried."

"I've lived with the shame all my life."

The vicar refuses to hear any more of Baxby's story that day, but relents when they have eaten.

Lincolnshire 1602

40

After visiting the play-obsessed boil-woman again, I raged at Matthew, "What is wrong with people in this city?"

He could see my fuse was burning short, feared I would explode.

"Come to Gainsborough with me," my master prescribed, "Smyth has invited me to accompany him there. The town needs a new physician."

"That's wonderful."

"We'll leave on Saturday."

"No, I'm pleased about the job, not the visit. I can't leave."

"Of course you'll go," Eunice intervened, "It will cure your awful temper."

Having heard about Gainsborough from Jane, I had reservations about the town. Situated on the River Trent, it suffered the afflictions of a seaport without the benefit of coastal fresh air. The gnats and tannery stench did not deter Jane from buying her leather there, but I was not eager to visit.

"Have you told him who lives there?" Eunice asked Matthew.

"He'll find out when he comes."

Matthew and Eunice seemed unnecessarily evasive which annoyed me. Many things did at that time.

Fortunately, Smyth had arranged for us to stay in the most prestigious property in the town. Standing in a prominent position overlooking the central square, Gainsborough Old Hall was even larger than Broxtowe. The owner Hickman and his elderly mother Rose lived in the east wing of the house, allowing the grand central hall to be used for civic events. Its sturdy roof beams resembled an upturned ship, a magnificent sight. The walls were decorated with colourful tapestries as befits a manor house.

PAYING IN BLOOD

"You can stay with us until you find a home of your own," Rose offered Matthew, "There's so much disease in the town, we're pleased you're willing to help."

"I have lots of children," he warned, "Two boys and a girl already, and my wife Eunice is expecting again."

"How lovely! Please bring them all. Stay as long as you wish. Children love running up and down our staircases, and through the interconnecting rooms. You can take them up the tower to see the view of the river too."

Rose's voice was soothing. The delicious meal improved my mood too. Leaning back on my chair, the roof timbers were disorientating, and Hickman's wine was strong. I did not notice another man had entered the room, until Matthew prodded me, "Baxby, I believe you've met John Crackleton before."

I nearly fell off my chair, when I saw my old Nieuwpoort comrade standing there, with a wooden leg and better clothes.

"Crackleton, I didn't expect to see you here," I rose to embrace him.

"It's a miracle I'm alive."

We might not have recognised each other if we had passed in the street. His hair was thinner but he looked better fed.

"What have you done with your beard?" he laughed, "Where has it gone?"

"A Boston barber shaved it off. Don't you remember seeing me, when I gave your letter back?"

Crackleton's memory was not as good as my own. However, I was amazed when he lifted a copy of Foxe's Book of Martyrs from a shelf, and started to read, rightly proud of his new skill.

"Mother Rose taught me. Mister Hickman has given me a job. I owe all this to them."

Crackleton read a chapter, about Wycliffe's followers who were burnt to death for reading English bibles, then crossed the room to show me how well he could move with his wooden leg. What a transformation!

I put my arm on his shoulder, "I'm so pleased for you."

"You saved my life. Thank you for trying to find out what

happened to Catherine too."

Smyth had informed them about my investigations.

"When I visited your village, I saw what your landlord did to the land. Catherine was brave to visit Lincoln to complain. I know she died in the Castle there, but wish I could find out more."

Rose smiled, "I knew Catherine's family many years ago. Thank you for making enquiries on John's behalf. The Church is powerful but the truth will prevail."

She had surprising faith, like Jane.

Later, I summoned the courage to ask Rose a question I was too nervous to ask when Crackleton was there, "Do you know what happened to Anna and John Junior? Did their father find them?"

"A neighbour asked us for help when Catherine died. My son smuggled them out, just before the Poor Law Commissioners arrived."

"Are they safe?"

"They live here at the Old Hall too. Poor John was so overcome when he found them, he couldn't speak at first."

After Rose signalled to a servant, two children came running in, healthy and full of life. Anna was smaller than her brother despite being older. She had dark hair, like Catherine's in my dream. Crackleton encouraged them to shake my hand, "This is my good friend, Mister Baxby. The kind man who saved my life by removing my foot."

There were tears in his eyes. I blew my nose to hide my own.

PAYING IN BLOOD

41

After an enjoyable evening reminiscing, I expressed my gratitude to Smyth and Matthew as we climbed a west wing staircase to our first floor room. The Crackletons slept on the ground floor, on account of his wooden leg.

When I blew the candle out, I expected to sleep well, warmed by the wine and comradeship. However, once the rest of the house was quiet, I heard movement in the room. Smyth and Matthew were putting their shoes back on, thinking I was asleep. The boards creaked as they moved towards the staircase. I found my own shoes and cloak, and descended too, carefully in the dark.

As Matthew unbolted the outside door near the kitchen, neither man spoke. This flight was obviously planned, my friends having secrets too. I had no idea where they were going, but lifted the latch to follow them out.

It was a warm and windy night. The fresh air cleared my head. Black clouds sped across the moon, giving intermittent light. My friends headed north, up the curving track on the right bank of the Trent. I was hidden a little way back.

Cows stood like ghostly sentries in the soggy meadows. A heron surprised me, taking off by the water's edge. Following its flight along the river, I saw a faint light ahead, dipping up and down. Hearing wash lap the banks, I realised a boat was coming across from Axleworth, near where the River Idle joins the Trent. Who would risk a crossing in the middle of the night? Axleworth was surrounded by waterways, but ferries only ran during the day.

Watching the mysterious boat, I missed my friends' fork into the wood. I returned to find them kneeling behind a small mound, below me in the bracken. The land fell away steeply in front of them, down to a wide pool. Its surface reflected the moonlight whenever the clouds dispersed.

Crouching behind a log, higher up the slope, it was hard to

keep still. The darkness seemed to amplify every sound.

"This is the place," Smyth told Matthew.

"Will we have to wait long? Are you certain that they'll come tonight?"

My two friends were hiding like me, waiting for the people in the boat.

Without warning, my log gave way. I slipped down the bank into Matthew, with a muffled yelp, catching his foot. He was more startled than hurt, "Baxby! What are you doing here?"

"I'm following you."

"Are you hurt, Matthew?" Smyth asked.

"I'm annoyed with my apprentice."

"You woke me when you left."

"I brought you to Gainsborough to see Crackleton. This has nothing to do with you."

"Don't worry," Smyth tried to calm him, "Baxby can be trusted. Keep down and watch what happens. He will find this interesting too."

Begrudgingly, Matthew inched along to let me hide behind the mound. When the moon re-appeared, we saw four people standing at the water's edge, with more emerging from the wood.

"Are they witches?" I whispered, knowing they convene with the Devil at night.

"No," Smyth replied, "Remember, neither of you can tell anyone what you see."

At least twenty adults gathered round the rim of the pool, including three dressed in white. The huddle started to sing. Their words were unintelligible, but the tune simple and reassuring.

"They're singing a psalm in a German language," Smyth explained.

"It's lovely, like a lullaby."

When the song ended, two men waded out into the water, followed by one dressed in white. They asked the white one a question, causing him to respond in a loud, defiant voice. I could not understand the language, but recognised the tone.

Astonishingly, the other two rocked him backwards, under the surface, seemingly to drown him. The singing recommenced as he bobbed up again, dripping and dishevelled.

"Jesus is Lord," Smyth translated, "That's what he said before they baptised him."

Witches do not make such statements of faith. We were watching Anabaptists, re-baptisers like the Dutchman on the *Mary-Anne*. God have mercy on our souls!

A pale-haired woman splashed into the pool next, her familiar voice answering the question, in English this time.

"Jesus is Lord."

It was Jane! Matthew pulled my head down as they submerged her, stopped me shouting out.

"I'm sorry, Baxby. I didn't know she would be here."

"How could Eunice recommend her? She's an Anabaptist."

"I thought this group only baptised foreign believers," Smyth apologised.

"They've baptised Jane! How could she do such a thing?"

I scrambled up the bank, then headed through the undergrowth, as fast as I could run. The heretics were too busy with their baptisms to notice me. The cows stood dumb, pretending nothing had changed when everything had. Jane was not the woman I thought she was. I could have married an Anabaptist.

It was spitting with rain by the time I reached the Old Hall but I did not care. I threw my boots at the wall, and pulled the blanket over my head like a child.

Although I did not believe in God, I would never betray my English birth-right like that. Was this a result of her German grandparents? I should have heeded the gossip. Distracted by the pageant, I had let my heart override my head. My friends had saved me from disgrace by showing me Jane's true nature. If I had married her, I would be shunned wherever I went. An Anabaptist heretic was worse than Agnes.

The squalls grew heavier outside. When Smyth and Matthew returned, soaking wet, I pretended to be asleep. The Preacher was coughing again.

42

The next day being Sunday, I stayed in bed later than the others, having no desire to accompany them to church. My mind kept returning to the moonlit pool, wishing Jane had stayed on the bank. I could not imagine the following week without her and Piers, let alone the rest of my life.

Rose was sitting alone by the fire when I went down. Although elderly and frail, she was good company. I was trying to gauge her age when her son crashed into the chamber, commanding a servant to saddle a horse. She clutched my arm for support.

Hickman came close, speaking slowly to ensure his mother understood, "Preacher Smyth has been arrested. Stay here with Baxby and wait for Matthew Mobley to return. I need to ride to Retford to send word to Thomas Helwys. Smyth needs a good lawyer."

"I'll pray," Rose nodded.

Understandably, I assumed that Smyth's arrest was linked to the scandalous baptisms the night before. If someone had seen me in the wood, I could be arrested too. Fortunately, Rose did not notice my hands were shaking.

When Crackleton returned from church, he told us that Preacher Smyth had led the service in the vicar and church warden's absence."

"Those two drink too much," Rose sighed, "John grew up nearby and attended Gainsborough grammar school. I'm not surprised he wanted to help."

I asked, "Was Smyth arrested because he preached in the church?"

"Yes, there was an informer in the service," Crackleton confirmed.

Thank God! Smyth's arrest was not on account of our nocturnal outing. My relief must have shown on my face.

Rose asked, "Are you smiling Mister Baxby? Do you understand how serious this is?"

PAYING IN BLOOD

"I'm sorry. It's such a shock."

As we sat waiting for Matthew, I tried to remember what Chaderton had taught me about ecclesiastical crimes.

"Did Smyth say anything controversial, Crackleton? Was he fractious? Did he cause affray?"

"He never opened the Prayer Book which surprised me. Everyone listened attentively to every inspiring word he said."

Another admirer! Crackleton seemed as enamoured by his sermons as Jane, surely an old soldier should have more sense.

Later, Matthew updated us, having come from the gaol where Smyth was being held. A magistrate arrested him for preaching without a licence, at the behest of an apparitor who claimed his was only valid in Lincoln.

"What nonsense! How can it be illegal for a Preacher to preach?"

Rose shook her head, "A group of Protestants met at my parents' home, when others fled into exile during old Queen Mary's reign. Imprisonment affected their health. I never thought I'd live to see this sort of persecution return."

Foxe's book sat on the table where Crackleton had left it, reminding us of the fate of former martyrs. If his cough worsened, gaol could kill him.

"Preacher Smyth is the one who needs our prayers now."

Matthew did not want to wait for Thomas to arrive. I assured Crackleton that I would do my best to find out more about Catherine, when I said good-bye. Matthew would not let us talk for long. As we rode home, he apologised for the night before.

"Jane's behaviour wasn't your fault, Matthew. I'm just relieved that I found out before I proposed."

"Don't be unkind to her, Baxby."

"Marrying her would end my career."

Although Matthew could not predict that Jane would be baptised, I was surprised that he had accompanied Smyth to the pool. Was he more sympathetic to heretical beliefs than I had realised? Why take such a risk?

Eunice was obviously shocked when Matthew told her. She kept stirring the pottage, but I could tell she was afraid. After several apologies for introducing us, she promised to speak with Jane on my behalf.

"Eunice, please can you let her know how much I regret this, but I know it is the right thing to do."

"Jane has done what she has done."

"Please pass my regards to Piers too."

"He's just a boy. He won't understand."

"What else can I do?"

Eunice made me sit down in the treatment room, "Listen Baxby. Don't mention this to Secretary Sculthorpe or anyone else at the Minster. Do you understand?"

"I would never do that. It would reflect badly on us both."

"It would reflect badly on us all. The Church might withdraw your funding. They could end your apprenticeship and medical career."

"I promise on my mother's grave. I don't trust Sculthorpe any more than you do Eunice, and want to protect Jane too."

A month later, Thomas Helwys secured Smyth's release, by producing a legal document which proved he was entitled to preach anywhere in the Canterbury province.

"Thomas knows influential people in London, and spent many hours investigating this," Matthew said.

The Preacher was fortunate to have such a friend. Geoffrey knew lots of important people in the capital, but was unlikely to dedicate himself to my cause in that way.

"Thomas has persuaded Smyth to stay at Broxtowe Hall, until he's well enough to preach again," Matthew said, "I'm concerned about his health. Smyth may have consumption."

"Is there a cure?"

"Joan will ensure he drinks the cordial I prescribed. Hopefully, all will be well."

Later, I learnt that the two friends grew closer during the

PAYING IN BLOOD

recuperation period, debating theological issues and radical ideas. The Church never apologised for the way the incarceration affected Smyth's health. Sculthorpe tried to have his licence revoked but failed.

Smyth returned to Lincoln even more determined to speak his mind. I kept away from his open air sermons, in order to avoid Jane.

43

The Guild announced that it would stage a bear fight on St. Anne's Day. The Sheriff let them use the Castle for a small fee. This would be an awesome event. Although people were familiar with baiting, few had seen two bears attack each other. The thrill of anticipation pawed down every street.

Agnes appeared on my doorstep a week before, asking me to accompany her. She had bought a new gown. It was hard for a woman like her at such a public event, regardless of what she wore. I would have been similarly shunned, if I had stayed with her or married Jane.

"I'm sorry, I can't sit with you, Agnes. I'll be a qualified physician soon. I need to guard my reputation."

She threw a shoe at a window on her way out, breaking a pane.

I had hoped the fight might tempt Isobel back to Lincoln. The bread charity deputy said she would never return, and told me to stop bothering him.

When Piers saw me on Steep Hill, I pretended to have forgotten about the fight, when everyone knew it was on Saturday afternoon. He concluded that I was ill, perhaps rightly. Thankfully, Jane was not with him at the time.

In truth, my mind was still troubled by the night in the wood. I found I could not dismiss my feelings for Jane any easier than Smyth could shed his cough. She tormented my nights, joining Catherine in my dream-boat, although she rarely fell in the water like us.

Matthew knew I was struggling to cope. Eunice fed me every day, concerned that I would not eat otherwise. They recognised the symptoms better than I did myself.

"Pay attention!" the boil-woman screeched, as the procession passed her window on Saturday morning.

"Aren't you excited like everyone else?"

"They should have staged a play not a bear fight."

"It's probably best that you stay home anyway, given your

condition."

"Oh no, I'm going this afternoon."

In truth, I was not surprised. Although sceptical and exhausted, I could not keep away either. As the Bishop had said, St. Anne's Day was the highlight of the summer.

I arrived early, to find families already claiming patches of grass in front of the castle wall. I bought a more expensive seat on the left, from where I could watch other spectators as well as the fight. Murmurs of excitement echoed round the ground, growing louder as the afternoon progressed. We heard dogs bark beyond the West Gate, but no bear growls yet.

The benches gradually filled, with the most prestigious taken by the Minster, Bail and City dignitaries. The St. Anne's Guild council took three rows. The Mayor sat in front, with the Sheriff, Lincoln's Members of Parliament and the county deputies, the Lord Lieutenant position still being vacant.

Julian Felde shook hands with the aldermen in the row behind, and kissed their wives' hands. When he sat down, he kept turning round to engage them in conversation. What a fuss! Felde liked to draw attention to himself.

Despite the distractions, the late afternoon sunshine helped me relax. Conversations around me merged into meaningless noise, as I dozed off.

When the bugles woke me, Jane was sitting in the front row in a bright green dress, with Piers, her sister and some female friends. I had forgotten how readily she laughed. The group were clearly enjoying themselves. If Jane had not punctured my plan, I could be sitting there with them now.

After the herald made an inaudible announcement, the Minster men processed in as they did for evensong, Bishop Chaderton, Secretary Sculthorpe, the Dean, Treasurer, Pusey, members of the chapter and choir, with their equally colourful wives. How different from Jane's friends in the wood. What would the clerics do if they discovered Anabaptists were re-baptising English women in their diocese? If they imprisoned Smyth for preaching, what could they do to them?

The castle hushed, it was time. As the handlers pulled the bears in on chains, their muzzles could not hide the size of their jaws and teeth. One raised his claws at the audience. A small child cried and had to be taken out, whilst others hid in their mothers' skirts.

The first bear was black with a pale snout. He was impressively large, but lumbering and old.

"May I present great Angus ..." shouted the crier.

Everyone cheered until he added, "... from Scotland."

Oh no! Learning that the fiercer looking bear was foreign, some queued to change their bets. We only stopped booing when the crier presented his sand-coloured rival.

"And the English bear Solomon."

No-one let the second bear's smaller frame influence their opinion. We cheered as his handler brought him past, naturally supporting the English one. The guildsmen adjusted the odds.

"These bears are hungry and eager to fight," the crier assured us.

"Solomon! Solomon!" the chant went up, as they prepared the ring.

Felde was turning round again, talking with wives. Piers was transfixed by the bears, in the front row next to Jane.

Solomon started well, standing high on his hind legs to roar at the sky. The sound reverberated from his tree-trunk throat, causing a flock of birds to fly off the Cobb Tower roof. Solomon's frame was larger than I had thought, his jaws stronger.

"Solomon!" we cheered.

Both bears were keen to make the first blow, snarling at each other in front of the Bishop and Dean. Whenever Solomon raised a paw, the crowd applauded. Can you imagine our satisfaction when he drew blood first? Angus skulked off to lick his wound.

"Solomon!" spectators were on their feet.

However, our favourite did not follow up on his early success. He failed to exploit his advantage when Angus fell over a rope, taking a rest instead. The handler braved the ring to prod him, without success. Losing interest, both bears sat down to scratch themselves.

Those on the grass lost patience first. The tone turned nasty, there being a lot of money at stake.

"We came to see a fight."

"Why doesn't the Scottish bear go **** himself?"

Taking charge, the Sheriff sent lads into the ring with firewood to pile near the bears. Solomon gave half-hearted chase to one, momentarily enlivening the crowd. Then, as we waited for the flames to take hold, someone let three fighting dogs into the ring. As they ran round the perimeter, baring their teeth, the grass erupted in cheers.

"Dogs, at last!"

"Dogs know how to fight!"

"Dogs are better than bears!"

Common people always want the dogs to win in bear baits, delighted whenever smaller creatures topple a larger beast.

This was more exciting. Would the fires work? Would the bears fight each other or the dogs? Solomon clawed Angus' ear, causing blood to spurt out. Angus injured a dog, who limped off trailing a leg.

"Solomon!" we shouted.

Everyone was watching the action not the sky. As Solomon lunged forward again, it began to pour with rain. Poor Lincoln, lucky bears! The finest gowns were ruined, revealing more when wet. Some women screamed, others laughed at the ridiculous scene. A blacksmith hit a guildsman, demanding his money back. The Sheriff argued with Solomon's handler as he pulled the bear away. The Treasurer and St. Anne's Grace-man were drenched debating pageant finances. Sculthorpe tried to shelter the Bishop under his enormous clerical cloak, with little success.

Few noticed Piers in the front row. Turning round, the little boy slipped on the wet bench and fell into the ring, his body disappearing from view. I could not see what was happening fully. Jane caught his ankles, tried to pull him back without success, then screamed for help.

Matthew and I converged from opposite directions. The Bishop's group obstructed his route, so I arrived first. A dog had sunk its teeth into Piers below, refused to let him go. No wonder Jane was screaming, what mother would not?

Breaking a piece of wood from a bench, I clubbed the dog on the head. It relinquished its grip and slinked away. Matthew was beside me by then. We pulled Piers to safety, laid him down on another bench.

"Piers! Piers! It's Baxby," my voice became more desperate, "Wake up!"

Matthew and I tried to stem the blood, while Jane's friends held her back. She was hysterical, screaming, the noise was unbearable.

"Concentrate, Baxby," Matthew urged.

When he caught my eye, I sensed his fear, as great as my own. Neither of us noticed the Minster party coming towards us. We were in their way as they tried to leave.

Sculthorpe demanded, "Let the Bishop through! He's getting wet. Have you no respect for the Church?"

As some tried to shuffle aside, Jane opened her mouth. Her friends did not stop her. I was too far away.

"What respect have you?" she screeched, "Clerics should set an example, caring for others rather than themselves."

Foolish woman, why did she speak out? Even a distraught mother cannot insult a bishop. A constable dragged her away at Sculthorpe's insistence.

I called out, "Jane!"

She shouted back, "Look after Piers."

Agnes helped Matthew carry the little boy to the Mobleys' cottage. I was too shaken with emotion and rage.

PAYING IN BLOOD

44

Piers did not respond well to our initial attempts to save his life. His left arm was torn above the elbow, his chest was worse. We could see the fang marks where the dog had held him fast. Matthew took me to the treatment room to discuss the boy's condition.

"If we remove his arm, it could hasten his death from the chest wound," I said.

Matthew agreed, "We can't take that risk."

"He may not last the night."

Matthew nodded, but wanted to check before we returned to the others, "Did you tell Secretary Sculthorpe about Jane?"

"About the baptism in the wood? No, of course not. I'm not heartless. I'll ask Sculthorpe to release her in the morning."

I had not mentioned the baptism to anyone, too scared on account of my own reputation and her safety. Although I could not marry her, I still cared about Jane and was terrified by her outburst.

"Regardless of what Jane's done, she should be here with Piers now."

"Don't worry, Matthew. I'll do what I can."

"I'm sorry I doubted your word. This is ghastly for us all."

We applied a herbal balm and waited. Agnes, Eunice and Piers' aunt took turns to sit by his bed.

Next day, Sculthorpe's mood was worse than the weather. I found him in his lair, thumbing through books with an ecclesiastical lawyer.

"Insulting a bishop only carries a fine?" he raged, "That disrespectful woman should hang."

"We must be seen to follow the Canon. Everyone sympathises with her. Her boy was bitten by that dog," the lawyer replied.

"A stupid child!"

"This must be upsetting for the Bishop," I interjected, "Shall I visit Mistress Sudwell and see what I can learn?"

"That's a good idea. The delinquent's being held in the Cobb Tower dungeon. See what you can do."

Unaware of my attachment to Jane, he took pleasure in knowing that I would have to enter that pit.

Piers was breathing gently when I returned to the cottage, with friends and family gathered round, listening as Preacher Smyth read a psalm.

Matthew led me back to the treatment room and confirmed, "The boy will pass away soon. We've done all we can."

"Sculthorpe's given me permission to see Jane."

"Good, try to check her condition, and tell her that Piers is peaceful. Remind her that we all rest in the hands of the Lord."

Matthew sounded like a preacher now, affected by Smyth's teaching too.

The Castle Hill cobbles were wet and dangerous, but my heavy heart slowed me more than the polished surface. Although Matthew had taught me how to break bad news to patients, how could I share this with someone who had been so close?

A smartly-dressed gentleman blocked my entrance to the Castle, arguing with the guard on duty there. Ill-mannered and obviously agitated, he kept rubbing his cane on his leg.

"Don't you know who I am? I have Privy Council friends."

The gate-keeper replied, "I'm sorry Sir Selwyn, I have my orders. Please move aside."

The belligerent continued, "You're holding another woman in the Cobb Tower, so could benefit from my skills. I served with Topcliffe in the Tower, the best in the country."

"I'm not at liberty to discuss the prisoners, Sir."

I would never have guessed the profession of the man in front of me. Torturers look the same as everyone else.

Fortunately, the Sheriff arrived to deal with the disturbance. I held up my papers for the guard to see. As he led me along the perimeter wall, I pretended to know Selwyn, in order to find out more, "What is Sir Selwyn doing here? I've only seen him in

London before."

"He's retired to Lincolnshire."

"Did he torture the previous woman who was held here?"

"Someone let Sir Selwyn into the Castle when the Sheriff was away, a terrible mistake in my opinion. Although there was no evidence that he touched her, I think the shock was too much. She was clutching her belly, as if in pain, and died a few days later. I had to clean up afterwards."

"Secretary Sculthorpe mentioned her earlier."

The guard wiped his brow, "He couldn't have known Sir Selwyn would visit, but he shouldn't have sent Catherine here. This is a difficult job. I don't enjoy my work anymore."

Sculthorpe did not kill Catherine, but left her unprotected when he sent her to the Castle. How could I tell Crackleton that?

"Don't let anyone know that I talked about a prisoner," the guard made me promise.

Although deeply shocked by his revelation, I did not have time to consider it further, given my more immediate concern for Jane. The Sheriff had tightened security since Catherine's incarceration, but she was not safe. I needed to find a way to get her out, without alerting Sculthorpe or his spies. Piers might die before nightfall. I still held hope for Jane.

45

The stink of excrement and rotting flesh overpowered my nose, before we reached the Cobb Tower door.

The guard apologised, "We delayed two executions until after the bear fight. These vagrants have been chained here for weeks."

In the poor light, I did not spot the two men, shackled beyond the roof ladder, until a rat scuttled over one's foot. I clutched my handkerchief to my face, knowing gaol fever is spread by bad air, a foul lingering death.

"Jane Sudwell's in the dungeon below. I'll tie these two outside, then bring her up for you. The rain will wash them down."

Angelic whispers seeped up through the grate in the floor. She was praying beneath me.

"Jane! It's Baxby. The guard will bring you up so we can talk."

"How's Piers?"

"He's at the Mobleys' cottage, with your sister and Preacher Smyth."

When she emerged, it was hard to believe that this was the successful businesswoman I had hoped to marry. Jane appeared to have shrunk overnight, with matted hair that looked more white than blonde. Her green dress was filthy and torn.

"Have they hurt you?"

"No, please tell me more about Piers."

I made her sit on the ladder rung and catch her breath, before telling her the tragic news.

"Sadly, Piers' condition has worsened. Matthew expects him to pass away soon. Preacher Smyth is saying all the right prayers."

Jane did not respond immediately. She sat on the ladder, looking straight ahead, lost in thought.

Remembering Matthew's words, I added, "We all rest in the hands of the Lord."

Jane turned towards me and nodded. Looking into her eyes, I

grasped her pain, but not her anger and residual determination. Jane had inner strength. She maintained the glove business when her husband died and looked after Piers alone. Confused by grief myself, I did not realise.

After sitting in silence for some time, Jane did two surprising things. Firstly, she pulled a small book from her under garments to give to me.

"Baxby, please take my Geneva Bible."

It was a pocket-sized edition, like those Captain Atherton smuggled into the country on the *Mary-Anne*. I opened the front cover and saw the wood-cut picture of people by the sea. Jane quoted the surrounding sentence from memory.

Fear not, stand still and behold the salvation of the Lord.

She must have read those words many times to recite them so easily.

When I looked down at the picture again, Jane made her second move. I do not know how she climbed the ladder so quickly. One minute she was there beside me, the next her bare feet disappeared above my head. I was too slow to respond. By the time I climbed the ladder to the Cobb Tower roof, Jane was already tottering on the battlements.

"Come back. It's wet. You could fall."

"Keep away from me."

The wind caught her hair and skirt. There was nothing to block its path. Only the cathedral spires and tower were higher than us. St. Hugh's statue stared across the rooftops in displeasure.

"The clerics are heartless hypocrites. Sculthorpe wants me dead."

Gripping the gibbet upright, Jane twisted round, pointing at the cathedral with her other arm.

"What do you care about women like me?" she screamed across the gap.

"Hold on, Jane! Don't do anything stupid. The punishment's only a fine."

"Baxby, you don't know how deep their hatred runs. In their eyes, I'm an Anabaptist heretic ..."

"No, Jane!"

"... but I won't give them the satisfaction of watching me burn."

Jane threw herself over the edge. She jumped off the Cobb Tower roof before my eyes.

"Jane!"

I touched the hem of her dress as she went over, understanding the truth at last. How slow I had been. Although I disliked Jane's foolish foreign beliefs, I loved her all the same, just as my mother loved me when I was young, despite my misdemeanours. True love was not conditional on behaviour. It was surprisingly easy to love her.

As the Minster bell started to toll the hour, I hid Jane's bible in my pocket to stop it getting wet.

"What's happened? Where's Mistress Sudwell?" the guard emerged on the roof

I pointed to the edge, telling him that she had jumped. He looked over first, gripping the gibbet pole as Jane had done. It was twelve o'clock.

By the time I took my turn, her shattered body had drawn a crowd. Jane lay on the spot where I had confronted Felde. How long ago that seemed. How foolish I had been back then. Now Jane had gone. When people started looking up at the roof, I retreated back out of sight.

"They'll blame me. I'll lose my job," the guard trembled.

"You're a good man. It wasn't your fault."

"I didn't want her to suffer alone, like that Crackleton girl. I thought your visit would help."

Peering over the edge for one last glimpse, I devised the story.

"When I examined Mistress Sudwell, I found she was suffering from temporary uterine madness, which explains her overpowering strength. We couldn't stop her running up the ladder and jumping off the roof. Temporary uterine madness must have been the reason she insulted the Bishop too."

"You're a physician. You understand medical matters more than me."

"Can you repeat what I said?"

"Jane Sudwell had temporary uterine madness. We couldn't stop her jumping off the Cob Tower roof."

My diagnosis secured Jane's reputation and the guard's job. Sculthorpe and the Sheriff wanted lots more detail afterwards. Minster and Bail could conspire, when the need arose, but expected separate reports. I spent hours stirring pottages of words for them both. Looking back, I do not know how I managed to write at all.

Piers died at noon, the same hour as his mother. Agnes took me aside, after the funeral cart had taken the bodies away

"I found these in Piers' pocket," she said, placing a bunch of dried leaves in my hand.

They were from plants that I had taught Piers to pick. I shut the door of the treatment room and howled.

KAREN HADEN

London 1613

46

Baxby produces a small book from his pocket, carefully unwrapping the scrap of Gainsborough leather that has protected it for years. The book is his only remaining possession now. His physician's robes and licence lie in a chest in Spitalfields. Matthew uses his instruments in his absence.

After wiping the well-travelled bible on his doublet, Baxby shuffles across the stone floor. Extending the chain to its full length, he passes the book to the printer to see. The name *Jane* has faded, but the words she quoted in the Cobb Tower remain clear. Wintry sunlight from the south window illuminates the illustration and surrounding text.

Fear not, stand still and behold the salvation of the Lord

The printer admires the quality of the wood-cut picture of Moses standing with the Israelites. They are waiting for God to part the Red Sea, to rescue them from the Egyptian chariots.

"I printed wedding pamphlets with a beautiful wood-cut picture of Princess Elizabeth in a wide gown and ruff, resembling portraits of the late Queen. It sold well but the detail was not as good as this."

"Why are some verses under-lined?" the vicar asks, when he takes his turn.

"Jane marked some of her favourite passages. I didn't notice at the time."

The vicar disapproves, "Bibles belong in churches. People should not write in them."

His view of the Christian book is very different to Jane's.

PAYING IN BLOOD

Lincolnshire 1602-1603

47

With Matthew and Eunice's help, I survived the last months of my apprenticeship by concentrating on my work. The boil-woman still moaned about bears, but I no longer cared. My mind often wandered back to the moonlit pool in the woods. Although Chaderton told me the Church's Articles prohibited Anabaptism, I felt it was unlikely that he would have burnt Jane for heresy. Other churchmen might have. She was more afraid of them than death itself.

Eventually, Jane stopped appearing in my boat dream, but Catherine remained. I still wanted to know the circumstances of her death and Mister Buckler's murder, but did not have the confidence to pursue this as before.

The Mobleys held a small celebration at the Hart when I qualified. Matthew made a speech and gave me two leeches as presents, the first I owned myself. When I thanked my friends for their kindness, I acknowledged his role in my success. My excellent master taught me so much, about medicine and more beside. For all Sculthorpe's shortcomings, he could not have chosen better.

After we had both drunk a considerable amount, Agnes took me aside to tell me she was going to move to Gainsborough too, "Susannah isn't well, and needs me to help her look after her son Toby. Sculthorpe's found a new cleaner to live at Greestones, a younger one."

"I'm pleased for you."

"Thank you, Baxby. Isobel's found me a position in the kitchen at the Old Hall."

"Mister Hickman and his mother Rose are kind people, who will look after you."

"Isobel said that too."

"And you won't have to do Sculthorpe's bidding anymore."

"Good luck, Baxby. I hope everything works out well for you."

I was surprised that she was leaving, but not concerned at the time. Moving amongst my friends in my new physicians' robes, I had no idea what Sculthorpe was plotting next.

After Agnes and the Mobleys left Lincoln, Smyth was stripped of his preaching position and banished from the city. It happened quickly, so there was no time to talk with him before he left. I received a letter later saying he was safe at Broxtowe Hall, where Joan and Thomas Helwys were looking after him again.

Then I started hearing rumours that my job was not safe. Patients grew concerned about the implications for their health. With Matthew gone, they did not want to lose me too. Some thought Sculthorpe was jealous of my popularity, that he wanted a nephew to take my place. I knew he blamed me for the criticism he received following Jane's death. The Secretary found fault with everything I did, no longer showing the slightest begrudging respect for my now considerable skills.

"God help Lincoln with you as physician, now Mobley has left. I'll travel to Stamford if I sneeze."

I enjoyed my appointments with Bishop Chaderton, but missed my friends who had moved away, even Agnes, astonishingly.

Sculthorpe grabbed my arm one morning in January. He had been lying in wait behind the cathedral's great west door.

"Baxby! Where have you been? Sir Julian Felde needs your help immediately."

"*Sir* Julian?"

"He's been knighted recently. He needs you to treat the tailor in Silver Street. It's an emergency."

The Secretary was more civil than he had been for weeks. Although I doubted his concern for the tailor's welfare, I responded to the request as any physician would.

When I reached the tailor's shop, the door was open. The poor man lay on the floor inside, clutching his right ear. Felde rose from his seat in the far corner to shut the door, blocking my exit.

PAYING IN BLOOD

Despite the odd circumstances, I asked the usual question, "How can I help?"

Felde replied, "This man has a pain in his ear."

After making the tailor tilt his head towards the light, I spotted the tiny object in his ear canal. It was difficult to retrieve, even using my smallest forceps. After several attempts, I showed them the little bead resting in my palm.

"How did that get there?" I asked.

Neither would say. Felde helped me tidy up and paid generously. Gratified to leave with such a full purse, I was looking forward to a meal.

A small child stopped me at the corner of Silver Street, begging me to treat her mother. Having visited the family's hovel before, I knew they would struggle to pay, but followed her down to the Pool, reasoning that Felde's money was ample for the day.

The girl's mother lay on a pile of straw, wheezing. Suspecting consumption, I opened my bag to find a potion and could not believe my eyes. There was a bundle of ten or more Martin Marprelate tracts inside, neatly tied with ribbon. Felde must have put them there during the extraction, there being no other explanation. My heart thumped even harder, remembering the Martin Marprelate on Mister Buckler's beam.

Could the idiot have put the bead in the tailor's ear too, a crass thing to do? Knighthoods were not given for basic common sense. This was a trap. Felde was trying to incriminate me. Sculthorpe would never believe my word against his.

Fortunately, there was a small stove in the home. With trembling hands, I stoked the embers, burnt the tracts, one by one. It took an age, but my patient was too ill to notice, and her daughter too young to understand. I left a potion, without asking for payment. Surprisingly, the woman recovered later.

The Secretary was waiting with two constables in Castle Square. Refusing to arrest me there, they marched me through Exchequer Gate to avoid the growing crowd. Gargoyles and statues watched the proceedings instead.

"Open your bag!" a constable demanded. "The Reverend needs

to see what's inside."

I pulled my sleeves back, to prove I was not hiding anything there, placed the bag on the flagstones and unfastened the clasp. Sculthorpe grinned as he bent over to peer in, then snorted when he only saw medical instruments and potions inside. He shook the bag upside down, showering its contents on the ground, but found no incriminating tracts.

Emboldened, I fought back, "Why did you demand my arrest? I've served you loyally for years."

"I received intelligence in good faith."

"Your so-called intelligence was clearly wrong. What will Geoffrey say?"

"We won't mention this to him."

"You ordered my arrest. I will mention this to him. The matter cannot rest."

"You're correct," he spat, "I'll ensure that."

Had Felde and Sculthorpe conspired against me, albeit unsuccessfully? The nature of their relationship remained unclear. Someone must have printed the Martin Marprelate tracts that Felde placed in my bag. They could have originated from the same source as the one on Buckler's beam. I did not doubt that Felde could buy tracts from a printer and kill, but was guild rivalry a feasible motive?

Sculthorpe did not speak to me for a month afterwards, but kept his word. He did not let matters rest. The Secretary spread malicious rumours, gradually turning patients against me. They kept cancelling appointments and delaying treatment. The Dean no longer wished to discuss building repairs. The new cleaner ran away when she saw me by the Galilee Porch. The Treasurer thought I had defrauded the Church.

When I could no longer afford my rent, I had no choice but to leave the city. Sculthorpe had won his battle to remove me, but where could I go?

I sent a letter to Matthew, then regretted it. The Church's tendrils stretched in all directions, so could intercept post.

PAYING IN BLOOD

Matthew replied saying there were insufficient patients for both of us to work in Gainsborough, but he would send word if the situation changed. Hickman corresponded with business associates across the country, so could convey letters securely.

With nowhere else to turn, I sought Geoffrey's help again. Sculthorpe gave me papers and sent me back to London. To his credit, Chaderton did not appear to believe his lies and was sorry to see me go, "You've been the best physician I've had."

"I will miss my visits. You've taught me so much."

"We may meet in London when I'm there."

I hired a horse, rode down the Fosse Way to Newark, and on to the capital. At least it was not snowing this time.

KAREN HADEN

London 1613

48

The printer commiserates, "Secretary Sculthorpe shouldn't have forced you out like that. However, pay is better in London and the weather kinder too.

"It felt like failure at the time. I didn't forget my promise to Crackleton. Catherine still appeared in my dream."

The three men listen to the cries of a boatman, calling passengers on the quay below. When silence returns the printer asks, "Did you see your friend again? Did you find out what happened to his wife?"

"Matthew wrote to me when a position became available in the village of Scrooby, near his Gainsborough home. That was after Queen Elizabeth's death."

"How foolish we were to imagine life would improve afterwards," the printer laments, "We printers expected more freedom, but the Church tightened its control. I was arrested for adding a table to the Book of Psalms, which helped people find their favourites. What harm did that cause?"

Many groups were disappointed when King James succeeded Elizabeth, including Puritans. A thousand signed a petition, calling for an end to popish practices in the English Church, but Kings James re-enforced the Act against them instead. Bancroft was always at his side, spreading fear of the threat.

After his promotion to Canterbury, Archbishop Bancroft devised an oath forcing Puritans to break cover. Hundreds lost their livings in his purge. He strengthened the Church's web of informers and prosecutors to catch the rest.

"This is a good point to break," Baxby says, "I'm tired and need to sleep.

His cell-mates recall Queen Elizabeth's reign, with fondness they would have scorned at the time.

PAYING IN BLOOD

Wednesday

Lincolnshire & Nottinghamshire 1606

49

Matthew helped secure my new position in the village of Scrooby, which straddled the Great North Road, a few miles west of the River Trent. Its previous physician had died unexpectedly, producing a vacancy I could fill.

Despite the weather, my new Nottinghamshire home looked charming. The cottage was larger than I had expected, with a thatched roof and a soggy garden sprouting beans. As I lifted the latch on the garden gate, a skinny young man opened the front door to welcome me inside.

"Good afternoon, Doctor Baxby. I'm Nicholas Barton, your new servant. Come in out of the rain. Let me take your bags."

"I'm pleased to meet you, Nicholas. Matthew sang your praises in his letter."

"I worked for your predecessor. Thank you for letting me stay."

After several years in London, I was pleased to return north. It was satisfying to think I would live in such a house, with a servant of my own. Also, Matthew had told me that there were plenty of patients in Scrooby and the surrounding countryside.

Ushering me into the main room, Nicholas took my cloak and hat, and hung them to dry near the stove. There was an additional small room downstairs, with a narrow bed.

"That's where I sleep," Nicholas pointed, "There's only one problem with this house, as you'll see when I show you upstairs. The thatched roof keeps leaking. However, it's a large room. The previous physician always found somewhere dry to position his bed."

There were a number of half-filled buckets, but plenty of space for the bed and cupboard. Looking out the window, I admired the view of the forest, which extended beyond the garden to the east.

"Scrooby Manor owns that hunting forest," Nicholas informed me, "Can you see the red brick building through the trees"

"It looks a large estate."

"There's even a moat, but you can't see that from here. A servant girl told me that a King wanted to buy it once."

In addition to hunting rights, I imagined the Manor's location would have attracted the King too. A staging post on the Great North Road could provide useful intelligence.

"You'll meet its owner Postmaster Brewster soon," Nicholas continued, "Matthew Mobley wants you to treat a member of his family. He'll explain more when he comes here tomorrow."

"I'm looking forward to seeing Matthew again. Thank you for organising all this."

I was tired after my journey, but pleased to have left London. Nicholas told me he had left Yorkshire to look for work there, but only travelled as far as Scrooby. He cooked a meal, then chattered about his childhood as we sat near the stove.

The sound of rain drops in the buckets did not stop me sleeping that night.

My old master Matthew looked no different. It was wonderful to see him when he called. He shook my hand and admired my robes.

"You look well, Baxby. How are you settling in?"

"It feels good to be back. Thank you for sending your letter."

"It was sad to lose the previous physician so suddenly, but I was delighted when you accepted the post. Scrooby will appreciate your skills."

"I'm hoping to save to buy a horse."

"Any sign of a wife yet? Were there any women in London?"

"Too many. You weren't there to help me choose."

"I don't know what you're waiting for. You're getting older. Do you remember Agnes from Lincoln? I have something to tell you, but don't know how you'll respond."

"Please speak openly, Matthew. You always can with me."

PAYING IN BLOOD

He made me sit down, then appeared lost in thought for some time. When my servant Nicholas disappeared into his room, I sensed something was wrong.

"Sadly, Eunice died in childbirth, a horrendous delivery. I blame myself, although there was nothing I could do. The baby died too."

I found the news hard to believe. Eunice had always been there, cooking, chatting, making guests feel at home. Childbirth always carries risk, but Eunice seemed so strong.

"Matthew, how could you cope? She was so good with the children too."

He hesitated before replying, "I married again, that's how I coped. I hope you won't mind."

"Mind? I'm pleased for you. In fact, I'm relieved to hear it."

"Agnes nursed her sister through her illness. She looked after little Toby when she died. I knew she would make a good mother to the children."

"Agnes! You married Agnes?"

"And she can't have children herself. That's a god-send, I have enough."

"But you can't ..."

I stopped myself in time. How inappropriate to question Matthew's choice. Why not marry Agnes? Because she was too low-born for him? Because she spied for Sculthorpe? Because she had slept with me? Of course not, I did not own her.

"But you never liked Agnes," I said instead, "You were relieved when I left Greestones."

"She has changed. We all have."

"I'm pleased for you, Matthew, truly I am. Congratulations! I'm pleased for the children too."

"John Smyth lives at the Old Hall now, along with other former clergymen who refused to sign Bancroft's pledge. They've had a big effect on Agnes, me and your friend Crackleton too. They're wise, godly men."

"How are they all keeping?"

"Smyth's cough improves a little occasionally, but never goes away."

"It might be more awkward to meet Agnes again."

"Don't be silly Baxby. She's a different woman now. Hopefully, you're older and wiser too."

Certainly, I was an older, experienced physician now, but still had a lot to learn, including the truth about Catherine's death.

PAYING IN BLOOD

50

Matthew had prepared a list of patients for me to visit. William Brewster's son Jonathan was at the top. I was intrigued by Scrooby Manor and happy to visit the family first. Matthew told me that Brewster might want to ask me some questions. The postmaster was thorough and concerned about security.

The next day, my servant Nicholas insisted on showing me the way, although it was a simple route. The drawbridge lowered to reveal an impressive cluster of red brick buildings around the central courtyard, all protected by the moat. There seemed to be ample space for several families to live in comfort, plus plenty of ponds, barns and outbuildings.

A servant led me to the main chamber, where Brewster's wife Mary was sitting with their son Jonathan. Nicholas slipped away as soon as we arrived, saying he would accompany me home later.

Mary Brewster greeted me, "Thank you for visiting Mister Baxby. I hope your journey from London wasn't too exhausting."

"You have a magnificent home."

"My husband William inherited the postmaster position and tenancy from his late father, after working for a Privy Councillor. We're pleased you've come so quickly. Jonathan is unusually hot, and keeps being sick."

The boy, who was taller than his mother, looked pale and weak.

I asked him, "How long have you been ill?"

"For two days," his mother answered, "He hasn't eaten anything unusual or breathed any bad air."

"Is that true?" I asked Jonathan.

He took some time before admitting, "I fell in the moat."

"The moat!" his mother exclaimed, "How did you do that? Why didn't you tell us before? What will your father say?"

However thorough Brewster might be administering the mail, it was hard to control a lad of that age. Nevertheless, moat water was unlikely to contain anything poisonous or otherwise life-threatening. I found a potion to settle Jonathan's stomach, telling him to be more careful. If he was not better in a couple of days I would return to see him again. Mary Brewster was grateful to me and cross with Jonathan.

As I prepared to leave, she asked, "Could you stay a little longer? My husband would like to meet you too."

"It would be an honour, Mistress Brewster."

"I'll show you to his office."

She led me down a long narrow hall, furnished with sturdy oak furniture, including several bookcases. Obviously, the Brewsters liked to read. I wondered whether they bought illegal books, as I believed John Smyth and Thomas Helwys had done in London.

William Brewster was sitting behind a large oak desk, covered with letters and packages. He slid them into a box with his arm when he saw me, his stern eyes barely looking away. The postmaster was smartly dressed, with a sensible beard and balding forehead. I felt more nervous in his presence, than I had for some time.

"Mister Baxby, how good of you to treat Jonathan. Thank you for agreeing to see me too."

"How can I help?"

"I need to ask you a few questions, a standard practice for which I apologise. Although your friends have vouched for you, there are a few points I need to check. Handling mail carries risks, as I feel certain you will understand."

"There's no need to apologise, Mister Brewster."

"Thank you. My father, who was postmaster before me, taught me not to compromise. Let's start at the beginning, were you born in Boston?"

"I lived with my mother in a small hamlet nearby. When she died, the Red Lion landlord Edmund Sibsey looked after me, until his cousin introduced me to a man called Geoffrey who became my patron.

"Ah Geoffrey. It's been difficult to find information about him. What is his full name?"

Brewster must have made enquiries, with limited success.

"He preferred not to use it, to protect his clients I believe. He told me this was common practice amongst those in his business, so I never knew."

"And what was his business exactly?"

"Geoffrey found work for unemployed young men like me. He arranged my apprenticeship in Lincoln."

"With Secretary Sculthorpe?"

"Yes, little happened there without his approval."

"I've heard that Sculthorpe works for Archbishop Bancroft now. How did Geoffrey react when you told him you were taking the position here?"

"I didn't tell him. I haven't seen Geoffrey for a long time. Working as a physician in London, I was able to support myself."

Brewster knew more about my past than I expected, but did not appear unduly alarmed by my answers.

"Your friend John Crackleton told me you speak Spanish."

"After arranging lessons, Geoffrey employed me as an interpreter at the Capture of Cadiz, but I can't remember much now. Don't worry, I don't work for papist foreigners. I killed the last Spaniard I met."

Brewster smiled, the questioning complete, "Thank you. Please accept my apologies again. Guy Fawkes' plot has made us more cautious. There are so many informers these days. Welcome to Scrooby. We're glad you've joined us here."

Having previously worked for a Privy Councillor, he knew the importance of security. His questions seemed reasonable in the circumstances. Brewster had satisfied himself that I was not a threat.

As I stood to leave, he confided, "I was concerned about your servant Nicholas when he first arrived from Yorkshire. He said he was on his way to London to look for work, then showed no interest in travelling on. Later, I discovered he was more interested in our servant Margaret Deryngton than spying on the mail. He's talking with her in the buttery now."

"He's been helpful to me."

"Margaret Deryngton is a sensible girl too. She lives with her mother in Mattersey. Let me know if you have any concerns. You're always welcome here."

He retrieved the box of letters as I left the room.

I was grateful for Brewster's offer, and Nicholas' assistance too. It would have been harder to settle in without the postmaster's warm welcome and my servant's cheerful willingness.

Nicholas accompanied me to other appointments during that first week. In addition to cooking my meals, cleaning the cottage and emptying buckets, he introduced me to a thatcher who agreed to come and fix the roof. As I had already arranged to meet Crackleton at Matthew's house that day, Nicholas offered to show me the route to Gainsborough and then return to assist the thatcher afterwards. Although anxious about meeting Agnes, I was looking forward to seeing my old friend Crackleton.

In some ways, Nicholas reminded me of myself when I was younger, eager to work and find his place in the world. However, he showed more patience than I had at that age and was besotted with a girl.

Sitting by the stove on Nicholas' day off, I reflected on my good fortune. My predecessor's unexpected death had been my gain. Although the locals were saddened by his loss, they were friendly towards me, and complained less than patients in Lincoln.

PAYING IN BLOOD

51

Matthew and Agnes lived in a three-storey oak-timbered house, overlooking Gainsborough square. Their home was spacious and comfortably furnished, with a view of the Old Hall, and a separate side room for Matthew to treat patients.

"I was wrong to question your choice of town," I acknowledged, "Gainsborough suits you Matthew."

"Have you met William Brewster yet?"

"He's a fine gentleman with an exceptional manor house. Does William Hickman still own the Old Hall?"

"Yes, Agnes is visiting Rose there today. She's at least eighty years old, an amazing lady."

Agnes would love talking with Rose, in front of the Old Hall's enormous fire-place, surrounded by sumptuous furnishings and tapestries, a remarkable turn of fortune for her too.

Matthew offered me a drink while we waited for Crackleton to arrive. It seemed strange watching him pour, as Eunice had always done that before. Reminiscing about Lincoln together, we heard a terrible noise above our heads.

"It's the children," Matthew apologised, "I told them to stay on the top floor with our servant, but they've ignored me."

"Your boys behaved well in Lincoln. How many have you now?"

Matthew laughed, "These aren't all ours. The oldest three Helwys children are staying with us."

"Those youngsters were unruly when I stayed at Broxtowe Hall, so I'm not surprised they're making such a din. Will they be here long?"

Matthew closed the door, before sharing the troubling news, "Thomas is on the run. He has left the country. Joan is hiding locally with their smallest two. We have the loudest three, and another couple the rest. The Helwys family no longer own Broxtowe Hall."

"What do you mean? The family has owned Broxtowe for generations."

"Thomas had to sell the estate quickly to avoid confiscation. You mustn't talk to anyone about this. Do I have your word?"

"Of course you have, Matthew. What crime has Thomas committed?"

"Thomas is wanted by the Church."

"How ridiculous! The deanery must have made a terrible mistake."

Matthew shook his head, "No, this isn't a deanery matter. The High Commission Court in York has issued a warrant for Thomas' arrest."

By a strange twist of ecclesiastical geography, Nottinghamshire, on the west bank of the Trent, is governed by the Church's York province, whilst Lincolnshire, to the east, is governed by Canterbury. The acclaimed lawyer Thomas Helwys, who I once wished to emulate, was wanted by the second highest Church court in the land, charged with Separatism.

"The family stopped attending their parish church after Thomas defended local Separatists in court, then the Church came for him. If they trap him with theological riddles, or torture him, he could burn for heresy."

Separatists were more radical than Puritans. No longer believing it was possible to purify the English Church, they met separately in homes instead. Archbishop Bancroft detested them even more.

"Why didn't you tell me before?"

"Brewster wanted to question you first. He's one of the leaders of our group. It is even a crime to shelter a Separatist. This is dangerous for us all."

If they could target a man of Thomas' stature, they could come for anyone.

I hesitated, almost too nervous to ask, "Are you and Agnes Separatists too?"

"Yes, but we don't use that term. We call ourselves believers, like Jesus' followers in the bible. We meet at the Old Hall."

PAYING IN BLOOD

"Whatever word you use it is a serious offence,"

"The English Church is beyond reform, the rot has set too deep. Fortunately, we're relatively safe here. Our apparitor left some time ago and our vicar is often drunk."

"Smyth was a Puritan when he preached in Lincoln. Is he a Separatist now?"

"Yes, he knows the bible so well, as does our other ex-cleric John Robinson who you should meet."

I was shocked to learn that Matthew and Agnes would join such a group, endangering themselves and their family. They were foolish to think they were safe in Gainsborough. Archbishop Bancroft would not spare them if caught.

When Crackleton limped up the garden path behind the house, it was good to see him moving so well with a stick. We embraced, and shared another drink while Matthew supervised the children upstairs. Crackleton told me his own were well, and good company.

"How are you finding Scrooby?"

"I think it will suit me well. I even have a servant called Nicholas."

"I work for John Robinson now," Crackleton beamed, "Although he's younger than Pastor Smyth, he's written as many theological books. I help prepare his manuscripts."

"Isn't Robinson one of the leaders of the Separatist church? Are you a Separatist-believer too?"

"Yes, he helped me understand it all. John Robinson is a very patient man."

What a transformation! Crackleton's believer-faith was more surprising than his earlier ability to read. Matthew had been interested in religion before, but Crackleton was as clueless as me.

"If you come to the Old Hall on Sunday, you can meet Robinson and his wife Bridget. They had to leave their Norfolk vicarage when he refused to sign Bancroft's pledge, so live at the Old Hall like us."

"That's a kind invitation but …"

"Although Rose Hickman is too old to attend services, you could see her there too. Rose has told me things about Catherine's family I never knew before. Her mother had a relation who worked at Lincoln Minster, a second cousin or similar."

"Did Rose say what the cousin did or how long he worked there?"

"Rose is very old and sometimes confused, but thought he worked in the library."

"The library is fairly close to Sculthorpe's office. If Catherine visited her cousin there, she might have seen him too. Have you told anyone else? Do your children know?"

"They've seen their mother's grave, but know nothing more."

"I think that's wise. What we don't know we can't divulge. There are so many informers these days."

"There's another thing," Crackleton added before leaving, "A gentlewoman in our believers-church would like to meet with you. Do you know Isobel? She said she remembered seeing Catherine in Lincoln and would like to speak with you."

"Isobel managed the bread charity. Will she be at the service on Sunday?"

"I believe so. Your servant Nicholas can bring you with him."

Nicholas was a believer too. They seemed to be everywhere, all taking an enormous risk. However, I was delighted to hear that Isobel wanted to speak with me. Crackleton confirmed that she had not re-married.

Matthew, Agnes, Crackleton and Isobel, what a reunion!

PAYING IN BLOOD

52

Having previously lost hope of seeing Isobel again, it was surprisingly hard to wait until Sunday. Now appointments took longer too, as Scrooby-believers emerged from their fox-holes wherever I went. Brewster was the only local gentleman in their group, most were simple folk who liked to talk a lot.

Nicholas caught his head on a spar when helping the thatcher on my roof. As blood ran through his hair, both men insisted on praying. The thatcher was a believer, another one.

From my room, I looked out across the hunting forest, anticipating my visit to the Old Hall. I was excited about seeing Isobel again, but concerned by the circumstances. What would the believers' service be like? How had they attracted so many?

Dawning bright at last, Nicholas led me along the path through the lush forest on that memorable Sunday morning. A damselfly flittered through the dappled shade, as if intoxicated. Deer bolted into the greenery. We met the thatcher and walked the last section together. I did not know what to expect, but sensed their excitement.

The crowd at the Old Hall seemed similarly roused when we arrived, the mood resembling that before a bear fight rather than a service. Although the tapestries and banners still adorned the great chamber walls, the Hickmans' furniture had been replaced by rows of wooden benches around a central table. Noisy families crammed on to them, whilst those at the back shouted to make themselves heard.

I counted over eighty adults in total, including the Crackletons, Mobleys, Smyths and Brewsters. Believer-fever had spread through north Lincolnshire and Nottinghamshire like a virulent disease, its 'victims' as numerous as the gnats. The leaders had found a new way of meeting together which the locals found appealing. Although not a believer myself, I found I was not completely immune.

Smyth did not hide in a vestry beforehand, nor process into the chamber with a line of grumpy choristers. Instead, he walked around the circle, shaking adults' hands and laughing with the children.

"Welcome to our believers' church," he bounded across to greet me, still looking slightly incongruous in his overly large preaching gown, "Newcomers can feel shocked at first, not realising that the Greek word translated as 'church', originally meant 'gathering' not 'building'. That's what we're doing here, gathering together in Jesus' name. Please let me know if you have any questions afterwards."

It was good to be back among friends, but strange to see Agnes sitting with Matthew and all the children, four Mobleys, three Helwys and Susannah's son Tobias. After waving, she sent Matthew to sit with me, a reassuring presence.

Isobel arrived alone, a little late and flustered. No longer wearing her expensive necklace and ruff, her neck rose from a simple collar instead. A young man gave her his seat. She did not notice me.

The room quietened when Brewster moved to the central table. He explained that Pastor Smyth would lead the morning service that day. John Robinson was attending to important business elsewhere, but should return in time for lunch and the afternoon discussions. This was going to be a long day at the Old Hall, hopefully one with an opportunity to talk with Isobel.

After Smyth opened the service with a prayer, they began to sing psalms. Male and female voices rose in haunting harmony to the timbers above. Their soothing melodies reminded me of the moonlit night when Jane was baptised, but the words were intelligible this time. Although I grew accustomed to other aspects of the believers' worship later, I always liked the singing best.

•

After the meal, Agnes found me loitering near the kitchen servery, where I had hoped to meet Isobel.

"Baxby, I'm so pleased to see you again. Isn't the Old Hall

beautiful? There are two enormous spits in the kitchen and a separate buttery."

"You look well, Agnes," I mumbled in reply.

"Moving to Gainsborough saved me. I looked after Toby when Susannah died. Isobel found me a job. Matthew asked me to marry him, thinking I would be a good mother for his children. Me!"

"I'm not surprised, and am very pleased for you both."

"I did many wrong things in the past. The believers have helped me change."

"Did you spy for Sculthorpe in Lincoln?"

Agnes lowered her eyes, "He expected me to pass on information about guests. That was why I visited his lair so often. You were one of the better ones."

It would not have been fair to press her further. Agnes had a new life now. Instead, I pointed to a window.

"Greestones was very draughty I recall. Do you have glass in all your windows now?"

"Every one of them," Agnes started to cry, "The believers have been so kind to me. I'm trusting God will forgive me too. "

Agnes' tears mixed joy and relief. I passed her a handkerchief.

"I didn't think this sort of life was possible for someone like me. The children keep me busy but I thank God every day. I couldn't have any of my own."

Agnes had always seemed adrift like me. Neither of us had parents to help us navigate our journeys into adult life, a 'sea' where others owned the charts. Agnes did not want to spy for Sculthorpe, but he gave her no choice, exploiting any weakness. I had been cruel to her myself.

"I must ask your forgiveness, Agnes. I shouldn't have moved out like that, when you were missing Susannah."

"You were kinder than many. I forgave you long ago. Jane was a lovely lady and you needed to qualify."

"I was very sorry to hear that Susannah passed away. Does Toby understand?"

"He has a piece of his mother's hair to remember her by. He's too young to ask questions about his father yet. I will protect him as far as I am able."

"Toby's lucky to have you. Let me know if you need help. I was orphaned myself, although not at such a young age."

Agnes sniffed, "Thank you. Do you remember Isobel, who arranged for Susannah and me to come here? She's busy in the kitchen, but would like to talk with you after the afternoon speakers."

"How long will that take?"

"It can be hard to predict, as there may be several, complementing or even disagreeing with the morning sermon. Can you imagine that happening in a parish church? Sometimes we hold a business meeting instead, where all believer-members are allowed to speak and vote. We make big decisions together like that. I've spoken at one myself."

Agnes had done well. The encounter proved easier than I had feared.

PAYING IN BLOOD

53

The afternoon did not follow the typical pattern Agnes had described. Before the first speaker started, a dishevelled man hurried into the chamber. As he took Brewster aside, Matthew whispered that this was John Robinson. Not wearing a cassock or gown, it was hard to imagine he was once a clergyman. The room quietened, sensing the two leaders were discussing a serious matter.

Moving to the centre of the room, Robinson gripped the table as he made his shocking announcement, "As many of you know already, the High Commission Court issued a warrant for Thomas' arrest, since when his wife Joan has been hiding with their two youngest children."

People murmured in agreement around me. Agnes hugged the small Helwys child on her lap.

Robinson continued, "We were wrong to think that Joan's hiding place was safe. She was arrested last night, and taken to York gaol."

"And the babies?" someone asked.

"They're with her in the cell."

A tanner swore, a young mother fainted, as a sharp pain speared my chest. The child on Agnes' lap hid her face in her bodice. Her siblings sat frozen as stone.

The couple treated me with kindness and respect during my stay at Broxtowe Hall. They had already lost their home, now Joan had lost her liberty too. How could this be justified? The York High Commission had issued a warrant for Thomas' arrest not hers. Could a gentlewoman survive in prison?

As Smyth and Robinson led prayers, I studied Isobel again. Although she did not sob like other women, her bottom lip trembled when her eyes were closed. I did not understand my true feelings at the time, but knew I did not want to lose her again.

The believers started singing, quietly at first, then with increasing confidence and volume. Brewster prayed, followed by

Robinson and a woman sitting at the back. Other voices spoke in turn. I felt disorientated, not knowing what would happen next.

Smyth read a passage from the church's big Geneva Bible, spread on the table in the centre of the room, then invited the believers to say the words of their covenant together. All rose in silence, waiting to recite words they obviously held dear

We as the Lord's free people
join ourselves by a covenant of the Lord
into a church estate
in fellowship of the gospel
to walk in all his ways, made known and to be made known
according to our best endeavours
whatsoever it should cost us

Heaven help them all! This was an alternative covenant as outlawed by Bancroft, the first time I heard one. What would the Archbishop do if he knew? I remembered his probing eyes in the Russell Chapel, his grip on my arm. My friends might promise to continue 'whatsoever it should cost', but did they really understand the risks? If the High Commission Court could imprison Joan in York, were any of them safe?

Relieved when the service was over, I headed outside for fresh air. Isobel found me by the door near the kitchen, the one which Smyth and Matthew used on the night of Jane's baptism. There were many things I wanted to say, including questions about Catherine, but at the time I was distracted by the terrible news.

"It's a delight to meet you again, Lady Isobel. I didn't know if you'd remember me."

She smiled, "Of course I do. After Reverend Sculthorpe interrupted our conversation, we didn't have another opportunity to speak."

"I went back to the bread charity several times, but never found you there."

"Sculthorpe interfered with my work, so I had to move away. Lincoln wasn't safe, and now we've learnt that Gainsborough isn't safe either. I'm so worried about Joan."

"I am too. Do you know how they found her? Did someone

betray her?"

"I can't imagine anyone doing that. We all loved Joan."

Isobel brushed some hair from her face. Her hands were more worn than before but still graceful.

"Agnes told me that you moved to London. Why did you return? Did you miss the Lincolnshire rain and mud?"

"I missed them both. I'm glad to be back, especially now I've seen you."

Although obviously anxious, Isobel's generous smile radiated warmth and grace. Neither of us mentioned Catherine Crackleton that afternoon.

As Nicholas and I left the Old Hall later, we saw a man carrying sticks from the churchyard to add to a pile in the square.

"That's the church warden," Nicholas informed me, "I wonder what he's doing."

This was the first time I had seen such a heap, but guessed correctly, "I think he's building a bonfire, ready for the Gunpowder Plot anniversary."

"We're a long way from London. Why is he building one here?"

"King James expects every parish to remember the fifth of November in that way."

Nicholas asked, "Did you watch Guy Fawkes' execution when you were in London?"

"I saw his head on the Bridge afterwards, and watched the death of a co-conspiring priest."

Of course, not all English Catholics handle explosives, neither do Separatists, but that did not stop the Church persecuting all those it disagreed with.

"At least it's not raining," Nicholas observed, "So the buckets won't need emptying today."

It had been a tiring day, but I did not sleep well that night or the following ones. Joan Helwys appeared in my boat dream, alongside Catherine, admonishing me for not doing more to help.

54

Given the risk, it was not surprising that Brewster posted sentries whenever the believers met. I volunteered to join the list, alongside Nicholas. As a mere sympathiser, I was happy to take my turn, letting true believers worship and debate in the great chamber as they wished.

On the Sunday when Thomas Helwys returned, I was on duty up the Old Hall tower. It was an ideal vantage point, with views over the town, the quay and the meadows. Barges left at high tide as usual, carrying goods downstream to the Humber, but I was uneasy.

Thomas had acknowledged me by touching his brim, before I climbed the stairs to my post. Deep in conversation with Smyth, there had been no opportunity for me to talk with him. The believers finished dinner early, impatient to start their business meeting, excluding sympathisers on this occasion.

Late in the afternoon, at my sentry post up the tower, I watched a rider dismount on the far bank of the Trent and catch the ferry across. The thick-set man walked with purpose, continually looking around. His expensive beaver fur hat showed he was not local. He carried a pistol and sword.

Suspicious, I called down for Brewster in the meeting below. Joining me up the tower, we watched the beaver hat cross behind the bonfire mound and disappear into the churchyard.

I asked, "Do you recognise him?"

Brewster shook his head.

"Could you ask the church warden or vicar? Is there someone you trust?"

"I keep away from all churchmen. They question my whereabouts on Sundays. I can't keep paying the fines."

A little later, we watched the stocky man retrace his steps, re-cross the river and gallop west. He did not look up at the tower, or pay attention to the Old Hall otherwise, but Brewster was clearly concerned.

I asked him, "Do you think he's heading for York? Could this be connected with Joan's arrest?"

"I'll go down to tell the meeting. This is a worrying sign."

I was worried too, the hounds were closing in.

After the meeting ended, Smyth called everyone into the crowded chamber. Isobel was at the front with Agnes, both with children on their knees. Crackleton beckoned me across, to where he was sitting near the back. When I asked what the meeting had discussed, he would not say.

Everyone fell silent, as Thomas moved to the centre. Despite all that had happened to him and his family, he remained calm and dignified, a commanding presence alongside the more diminutive Smyth.

Disappointingly, Thomas did not report news about Joan, nor explain the purpose of the meeting to those of us who were absent. Instead, he read some words from the big Geneva Bible.

For where two or three of you are gathered together in my Name, there I am in the midst of them.

Smyth addressed us next in his authoritative voice, "Never forget the promise that Jesus made to his followers, to be with us whenever we meet in his name. Whenever, wherever, whoever, this promise makes us a church."

Several believers echoed "Amen."

"The bishops think it's their job to interpret the bible. They try to control the presses, attempting to limit our access to books, but they cannot contain the truth. We are 'the Lord's free people'. We meet together in his Name, interpret the bible for ourselves."

The believers rose to recite their covenant again, more soberly this time. I could sense the nervousness in their voices, without knowing the precise cause. What had they agreed that afternoon? Smyth prayed for God's protection over all the group's future plans, but gave no clues. It was frustrating to be excluded in that way.

After the meeting dispersed, I found Matthew waiting for me by the door. He shook my hand firmly, reminding me that he was very pleased with the way I had settled in. Although seemingly wanting to say more, he moved away when he saw that Isobel was waiting too. She suggested we walk along the east bank of the Trent, so we could talk privately. I was pleased with the opportunity, without understanding her urgency.

Sometimes looking back, I struggle to believe such an afternoon was possible. Memories and dreams can mingle in our minds, to contort and trick us. But Isobel remembers the walk too, a gentle route which followed a loop in the river.

The air was fresher outside the town, and the meadows spotted with medicinal plants. I plucked a couple of interesting ones, explaining their use. Isobel listened, but seemed more subdued than usual. Like the others, she refused to tell me what the business meeting had discussed. She wanted to tell me what she remembered about Catherine Crackleton instead.

"I found her quivering in the bread charity yard, after one of Buckler's deliveries."

The murdered baker was one of Isobel's suppliers.

"He liked to make a show of generosity towards the poor, but I don't think that was the reason he came. I think that Buckler was spying for Reverend Sculthorpe."

"Spying on you?"

"Sculthorpe disapproved of my charity work. Buckler's death made me more suspicious than I was before."

"Did you give Catherine one of Buckler's loaves?"

Isobel smiled and shook her head, "Catherine wasn't hungry. She wasn't one of my customers. I brought her inside because she was frightened and cold in the yard. Whilst we were drinking, she told me that she was expected to perform errands for her landlord, without saying what that entailed."

Felde could have forced Catherine to follow Buckler to Isobel's yard, but why would a landlord do that? Foolishly, I told Isobel how he had hidden Martin Marprelate tracts in my bag. Understanding the implications, she stopped and gripped my arm, "Baxby, promise me you'll be more careful another time. They could have hanged you like the authors, or burnt you as a heretic."

"I agreed to treat a poor patient at Brayford Pool afterwards, so was able to destroy the tracts in her stove, before Reverend Sculthorpe could find them."

"Your heart is good. God bless you."

She seemed short standing so close to me. Her hat had slipped on her hair again. I was concerned that I had upset her.

"Don't worry, Baxby. Everything will be alright."

How could I know what she meant? As we walked further along the river bank in silence, I commented, "You seem quieter today."

"It's difficult doing something that feels right, but which carries great danger. Baxby, whatever happens, I won't forget you."

Isobel confused me. What was she talking about? Separatist-believer faith or love? Surgical procedures are dangerous, but it clearly was not that. In what circumstances was Isobel likely to forget me? I did not want to lose her again. Somehow, I summoned the courage to stop and face her, holding her hands in mine, "Isobel, I will never forget you."

In that moment, my lowly origins seemed less important than when I had been with Jane. Isobel smiled, without trying to move away.

Disturbed by a commotion on the far bank, we both turned to see a wild stag bounding towards us from the wood. Although not full grown, it was a magnificent beast. Three lads were running behind in pursuit, brandishing vaulting poles.

"Poor creature," Isobel exclaimed.

The stag was quick, but I assumed its pursuers would trap it at the river. However, after pausing on the opposite bank to stare at us, it threw itself into the water with an enormous splash. Isobel and I looked on astounded as the deer washed downstream past us, struggling to swim. Astonished like us, the lads stood watching as the stag disappeared, before trekking back to the wood. Although they could swing across ditches on their poles, the Trent was far too wide.

"It will live," Isobel concluded, "There are shallows downstream and the tide is out."

There were so many things we could have talked about. How different it might have been. I had not felt like that with a woman for a long time. The London ones were different. I kept Jane's bible in my pocket, but no longer felt the same pain.

PAYING IN BLOOD

55

When I returned from visiting my patients the next evening, I was shocked to find Agnes under my porch. It was a long way for her to walk alone, especially as the skies were threatening rain. If Nicholas had been home, he would have taken her in, but my servant rarely worked on Mondays. He was visiting Margaret Deryngton and her mother in nearby Mattersey. Poor Agnes had been waiting outside in the cold.

"Baxby, I'm sorry to surprise you like this, but I need to speak with you."

"Come in, Agnes. You must be freezing cold."

I found a blanket, and tried to light the stove while she shivered on a stool, chilled through. It would have been easier if Nicholas had been there.

"Does Matthew know you've come here?"

"He thinks I'm visiting a sick cousin nearby."

"What will she say?"

"She doesn't exist and will die soon enough. I haven't got any uncles or aunts or cousins. I needed to speak with you."

"It will be dark soon, Agnes. I don't think you should stay. You're a reputable woman now."

"Baxby, this is important. It can't wait."

"But how will you get back tonight?"

"Matthew doesn't expect me home until tomorrow. He has help with the children, which was difficult to arrange."

This was an awkward situation. Why had Agnes done this? What could not wait until Sunday? I managed to find some cheese and bread. Nicholas would have prepared the food more quickly. Did Agnes know he did not work on Mondays?

Once she had warmed sufficiently, my former landlady talked about the Minster men in a way she never had in Lincoln. Definitely, Agnes had changed. She was a little plumper too, married life appearing good for her health.

"Do you remember the cloisters in the cathedral?" she asked.

"They were beyond the north-east transept door, near

Sculthorpe's lair."

"In the summer before you came to Lincoln, Secretary Sculthorpe found Catherine Crackleton in the cloisters after one of Buckler's visits."

I nearly knocked her off the stool in surprise.

"Catherine was in the cathedral? Agnes, tell me more!"

"I'm sorry I didn't say before. Please forgive me."

"Don't worry about that. Tell me now!"

"Secretary Sculthorpe paid the baker to inform. His guild connections were useful."

Agnes confirmed what Isobel suspected.

"I should have told you earlier. I was frightened of Sculthorpe, but never let it show."

"I was scared of him too. What else do you know? Why was Catherine there?"

"I think she was hiding in the cloisters, but I don't know why. Catherine was just a country girl, with no business to be there."

"Does Matthew know you saw her?"

"I haven't told him. He doesn't need to know. That's why I've come in secret today."

"I won't mention it, so don't worry on that account. What did Sculthorpe do when he found Catherine?"

"I heard a cry, when I was cleaning in the Angel Choir, then squeezed through to watch from behind a shrine with a good view of the transept."

"Is that where you were hiding when we first met? You appeared in front of me with your broom suddenly, causing me to think I'd disturbed a ghost."

"You soon discovered I wasn't one."

"Please tell me what happened next."

"Catherine's bonnet fell off as Pusey dragged her to Sculthorpe's lair. She was tiny with long dark hair. He was shouting awful words, worse than the names they called Susannah and me. My life is very different now."

"And you did nothing to stop them?"

"What could I have done?"

I shook my head, knowing it was true. We were powerless

against Sculthorpe back then. Catherine was a victim, as were the rest of us, albeit to a lesser extent. Joan had warned me to be careful, now she was a victim of the Church herself.

"Could you hear what they were saying?" I asked, remembering the split in the door.

"Secretary Sculthorpe was fretting about money. I heard him mention Bishop Bancroft too. His assistant Pusey thought they should report the incident to Bishop Chaderton, but Sculthorpe said he didn't trust him. What a thing to say about a bishop!"

"Chaderton is one of the best I believe."

"In the end, Secretary Sculthorpe decided to lock Catherine in the cell in the west wall."

I had visited the building every week but never knew of its existence. She told me it was common practice in the past. That was the oldest part of the cathedral.

"Catherine had dropped her bag in the transept. I slipped away when I heard Pusey offer to search for it. He might have heard me, my breathing was so loud."

Agnes clutched the blanket closer. She had obviously been terrified, but brave to do what she did.

Agnes slept in Nicholas' ground floor room that night, curled up in her blanket on top of his bed. The thatched roof was still leaking, so she was safe from the weather too. When I woke in the morning, she was getting ready to leave.

"Is there anything else you remember? Have you thought of anything overnight?"

Agnes looked up, and smiled at me, "There is one other thing. Isobel likes you. I don't know how you managed that."

"Are you certain?"

"I have lied about many things in my life, for which I am ashamed, but I would not lie about that. Isobel is a wonderful woman, don't let her down."

"I'll walk with you to the river. I have a patient nearby."

"It's best that I go alone. Thank you for your hospitality."

Agnes was resilient. She always had been. The difference was that I respected her now.

56

The following Sunday, Nicholas barred my way when I tried to leave for Gainsborough, saying the Old Hall was not safe anymore.

"I know, that's why we stand guard each week."

"No, this is different Baxby. We will meet at Scrooby Manor today."

How peculiar! Nicholas would not say more as he led me down the lane.

"Has this got something to do with Joan's arrest?"

"Possibly, please hurry up."

Nicholas seemed anxious, as Isobel and Agnes had been when I talked with them. Instinctively, I touched Jane's bible in my pocket, feeling something was wrong. We passed the entrance to the hunting forest. This Sunday would be different from previous ones.

The drawbridge lowered and closed again behind us. A couple of ducks flopped into the moat. There was no servant to accompany us this time, nor signs of life. When we entered the main chamber, we found the others sitting in silence, on benches arranged as at the Old Hall. The room felt empty, even though at least thirty adults were there. Most lived in Scrooby or close by, the Robinsons and Crackletons being the only two Gainsborough families present. Where were the Mobleys and Smyths? Where was Isobel? Crackleton studied the floor in front of him. I could not catch his eye.

Heads turned as Brewster rose to address us, speaking slowly and deliberately, "Everything went smoothly. Our Gainsborough friends boarded the ship near Hull. They have escaped without incident. Bancroft's pursuivants cannot hurt them now."

Bursts of gratitude rose from the benches, exhalations of relief. My neighbours, who knew about this plan, had been waiting for news. I could scarcely believe what I heard.

PAYING IN BLOOD

"Let's thank God and pray for safe passage across the Narrow Sea, which is unpredictable at this time of year," Brewster continued.

"Unpredictable!" I blurted, unable to control myself, "The Narrow Sea is treacherous."

"I'm sorry Baxby," the post-master replied, "We know this is particularly difficult for you and other sympathisers who weren't present at the meeting last week, but the risks were too great. Our friends didn't have licences to leave the country. Thomas made the arrangements, and secured funding for the voyage."

That is what the believers decided when I was on sentry duty up the tower. What madness possessed them? No-one is allowed to leave the country without a licence, a civil crime not an ecclesiastical one.

"Where are they heading? Can I know that?"

Several Scrooby-believers spoke, relaying reasons they had used to convince themselves that this was a good idea, "To the Dutch Republic."

"The official Church is more tolerant there."

"They can meet in freedom, safe from spies."

"Free to speak the truth."

"Worship as they choose."

"Others have already established an Independent church in Amsterdam."

They did not convince me that this was not a reckless desperate act.

Matthew, Agnes, Isobel, Thomas, Smyth and the rest had gone, without saying good-bye. Isobel and Agnes contrived opportunities to talk with me before they left, knowing they might never have another chance. Catherine and Jane died in Lincoln. Joan was imprisoned in York. Now they had been forced to flee, a thought too much to bear

My friends might be dead already, perished at the bottom of the merciless Narrow Sea, including the children. Matthew and Agnes found a new life after losing loved ones, now the Church had taken this away.

KAREN HADEN

I sat alone by the main chamber fire, while the others held their service. Even the psalms could not lighten my mood, I scarcely heard them. Refusing to give up, the believers repeated their covenant, including the line
Whatsoever it should cost
Please God not their lives! Don't let them drown at sea.

I was too overwhelmed to eat the excellent meal that Mary Brewster and her servants had prepared from the Manor's estate. Crackleton managed to tempt me with some wine, then brought Robinson over to sit with me by the fire.

"I can't imagine how it must feel to learn like this," Robinson said, then waited in silence until I was ready to speak.

I found myself asking, "Why did they flee? Why take such a risk?"

He asked if he could tell me a story, a favourite one which I subsequently heard several times, "Once there was a wonderful house, where the generous landlord provided for all his tenants' needs. Food, drink, furnishings, they took them all, enjoying his gifts, whilst never enquiring after the landlord himself. They never knew him.

"Do you mean that God is like that landlord?"

"Yes, and our bishops are like the tenants. They have many magnificent cathedrals and palaces, but miss knowing God himself. They don't experience his gracious love in that way."

Certainly, I had never heard a Church cleric speak about God in such personal terms.

"True faith resides in the heart," he continued, "We believe Jesus is with us whenever we meet. We acknowledge this truth in our minds and feel his presence in our hearts."

Archbishop Bancroft would disagree, but why persecute kindly men like Robinson with such ferocity? He seemed genuinely concerned about me. His eyes were always smiling, even when his mouth was not.

Still struggling to believe my friends no longer lived across the

PAYING IN BLOOD

Trent, I visited Gainsborough square on the fifth of November in an attempt to convince myself. Seasoned tanners and other townsfolk squashed into the square for the Gunpowder Plot anniversary. I wrapped a scarf around to hide my face and mitigate the smells.

As darkness fell, the vicar lit the bonfire with a tipsy hand. I jostled for position, cheered like everyone else. The smoke kept the gnats away. There was no doubt that believer-fever had dissipated too. The Mobleys' house and the Old Hall stood in silence, watching the proceedings. My friends' words burnt in my heart as the flames roared up.

"Try to be more patient Baxby." Matthew had taught me more than medical matters.

"When two or three meet. That's all we need." How could the Pastor believe such a thing?

"The believers have been kind to me. I'm trusting God will forgive me too." Agnes needed heroic trust to cross the Narrow Sea.

"Whatever happens, I won't forget you." I could never forget Isobel.

"Were there any women in London?" Matthew had asked. There were none like her.

I did not see the beaver-fur man in the square, the churchyard or at the quay. He must have completed his work in the town and moved elsewhere, hopefully far away.

KAREN HADEN

London 1613

57

The printer shakes his head, "If the bonfire wasn't enough to convince you of your foolishness, I don't know what would. Those so-called believers had no common sense. Now, I'm less certain about you."

The vicar bristles, "Foolishness indeed! That was flagrant criminality. Despite your previous trespasses, and those of your mother, I thought you had more decency and reverence. It isn't surprising that the women and Crackleton were hoodwinked by fanatics. A physician like Mobley should have known better, so should you."

"I was distraught at the time," Baxby replies.

"And why trust anything Separatists said? They obviously had no regards for the basic tenets of the Church, nor those who administered its sacraments. I think they lied about Secretary Sculthorpe. Why would he imprison Catherine as they alleged? Maybe bastards are more easily misled."

The three prisoners listen to the sound of bells in the distance, a reminder of the world beyond the walls. The vicar and printer still hope to be released in time for the royal wedding festivities.

"Do you want me to continue?" Baxby asks, when the bells stop, "Or does the sin of my birth nullify the rest of my life?"

The vicar pretends not to hear, but the printer urges him on.

"I've more to confess, far worse. The believers were kind, beyond all deserving, especially mine."

PAYING IN BLOOD

Lincolnshire & Nottinghamshire 1607

58

Mercifully, the Robinsons and Crackletons stayed behind, so John Robinson could complete his manuscript. Scrooby Manor was large enough to accommodate them all, and Robinson's numerous theological books. He had even more than Brewster and Smyth.

The bonds between us grew stronger, after the Gainsborough-believers left. Crackleton became like a brother to me, Robinson a trusted friend. I do not know how I would have survived without them both. They tried to revive me as we drank Brewster's beer, by his enormous fireplace, but my distress was rooted deeper than they knew. The Church's power was growing, mine seemed to be ebbing away.

I found it difficult to settle at night, with conflicting thoughts in my mind. When I did sleep, I often drifted into my familiar boat dream with Catherine. Its frequency grew as did my anxiety. I kept Jane's bible in my pocket, stared at the pictures sometimes.

Although Crackleton told me not to worry, I felt I had failed him too. I had discovered that Sculthorpe imprisoned Catherine, and sent her to the Castle where she died, but still did not know why. John Robinson said I had done well in the circumstances, but it felt like unfinished business nevertheless.

The Scrooby believers elected Robinson to be their new Pastor and Brewster as their Elder. Both leaders grew in stature as the weeks progressed. I admired them both.

Robinson was an ordinary yeoman's son, from the nearby village of Sturton-le-Steeple, who had been fortunate to gain a good education. He could explain Separatist beliefs in ways that were easier for uneducated people to understand, and was always willing to answer questions. With the older Smyth gone, he seemed to gain confidence with every sermon he preached.

William Brewster was more like a militia sergeant, his sermons accumulating military metaphors and illustrations as the weeks progressed. More practical than Robinson, he prepared us for the battles ahead. The Brewster's ward Bradford shared a similar temperament. Their eldest Jonathan was more hesitant.

Brewster continued to take responsibility for security matters, often discussing them with me. I was impressed by his thorough approach. One Monday, he called me to attend to his servant Margaret Deryngton who had been hurt in the hunting forest. The brave girl was dripping blood on the buttery floor, whilst trying to calm the cook.

I asked, "Did someone hit you?"

"No, I fell whilst running away from a man who approached me on Mattersey Bridge, when I returned from visiting my mother. I know the forest paths so lost him easily."

I knew the route too. The wound did not look serious, a small facial tear that would subsequently swell to an ugly black balloon before mending. Margaret breathed more slowly. She was a sensible girl and reliable servant.

"Did the man say anything before you ran away?"

"He wanted to see you Mister Baxby."

"How strange! Did he wear a beaver hat or fancy cape?"

"Neither, he wore ordinary clothes and carried a spade. He said his name was Grey."

"Do you know this man, Baxby?" Brewster probed, "Is he one of your patients?"

"Not to my knowledge. I'll make enquiries, try to discover more."

Brewster was always vigilant, knowing spies could hide like moles underground. The danger diminished when the Gainsborough-believers left, but had not disappeared. I made sure that Grey posed no threat to the others.

At Christmas, Brewster announced that our Gainsborough friends had arrived safely in Amsterdam, warming news in the depths of winter. However, chilling rumours started to whistle up the Great North Road. The Canterbury and York Archbishops had joined forces against the Separatist threat. They wanted to eliminate us.

We panicked when a horseman arrived at the Manor gate, commanding Brewster to lower the drawbridge. Fortunately, it was just his landlord who had come to collect the rent.

Believers in other towns faltered, returned to the English Church. Elder Brewster and Pastor Robinson steadied our nerves. They said that Jesus never promised his followers' lives would be easy, but would always be with us whatever befell. We must keep trusting Him, like his early disciples in the bible.

The winter grew colder than any of the oldest believers remembered. The moat froze over enabling us to walk across. The icy conditions continued well into spring. Neighbours died. The record price of bread was partly to blame, although we distributed what food we could.

Nicholas caught a chill, while out shovelling snow, but fortunately recovered. Margaret Deryngton's mother could not leave the house for weeks, on account of her swollen legs. I struggled to reach patients at remote farms. We lost believers along with the rest.

The following summer was inexorably hot and dry. Plague struck Retford and took twelve more lives. Crops failed and the price of bread rose higher than the official rate. The whole country worried about the freak weather. News pamphlets prophesised doom. Crackleton did not expect such a strong reaction when he showed me one.

"What's up, Baxby? Are you ill?"

I pointed to the page with the wood-cut picture, before letting the pamphlet fall on the floor. Crackleton shouted to Pastor Robinson to come quickly.

I stuttered, "The picture! What is it?"

Crackleton picked up the pamphlet and read the paragraph beneath, summarising the contents for me, as I had once summarised Sculthorpe's letter for him.

"A tidal wave swept up the River Severn. It washed away villages in Somerset, before flooding the cities of Bristol and

Gloucester. Hundreds have died."

The picture was terrifying, like the sea in my recurrent dream. Livestock and possessions struggled in the water. People clung to branches but could not save themselves.

"It's my dream," I spurted, "The view from my flat-bottomed boat."

"What are you talking about?"

Pastor Robinson tried to help but could not understand, "Have you dreamt about this flood? Have you had some sort of premonition?"

"I'm surrounded by water in my dream, stretching in all directions like the flood in the pamphlet."

Crackleton studied the picture again, "My friends told me there were bodies in the sea like this, at Nieuwpoort where Baxby removed my leg."

The pamphlet did not seem to bother him, in the way it bothered me. When he tried to show me the picture again, I spun my head away. Pastor Robinson hid the pamphlet out of sight, and asked, "Can I pray for you, Baxby?"

"Show him your bible," Crackleton said.

I held Jane's Geneva for Pastor Robinson to see, "A friend in Lincoln gave me this before she died. She was an Anabaptist."

"Anabaptists have some disturbing ideas, but it's a lovely little bible. Do you read it often?"

"I look at the pictures sometimes."

Opening the cover, Pastor Robinson read the words Jane had quoted in the Cobb Tower

Fear not, stand still and behold the salvation of the Lord.

"Why not start to read it too? The underlined verses may help. Sometimes, Jesus can seem more approachable in the bible than in church services."

It was a strange remark. However, as the year progressed and the danger increased, sometimes I took the Pastor's advice. Staring at Jane's underlined verses, I wondered why my friends were so convinced by God's presence, when he seemed remote to me.

PAYING IN BLOOD

59

The comet appeared soon after the pamphlet, low in the sky at first. It rose until its plume crossed the whole night sky, an awesome sight and fearful portent, one that was impossible to ignore. No-one in Scrooby had seen a comet before.

Tracts implored the nation to turn from its wicked ways or perish. This was God's judgement upon us. Some believers feared the world would end. Brewster and Robinson preached a calmer response. We must keep trusting the bible's promises, and Jesus' presence with us.

Poor Brewster faced a further dilemma, as his wife Mary was expecting their third child. She might lose the baby or even her life. The due date had already passed when we heard of a specific threat to our hitherto secluded lives. A sympathiser rode up from London, interrupting our service, to tell us the terrible news. The High Commission Court at Lambeth, the foremost ecclesiastical court in the land, had issued a warrant for Robinson and Brewster's arrests.

We needed to act quickly. Pursuivants could arrive at the gate, at any moment, to carry our Pastor and Elder away. Some believers had already sold possessions, fearing this day would come. Our leaders had dispatched their treasured books to safe houses in another town.

Now, Brewster sent word to Thomas Helwys in the Dutch Republic, requesting his help. We needed money and advice, events were moving fast. Although the believers tried to trust God, we were all terrified.

Brewster called everyone together, including sympathisers this time. The meeting was a sombre but moving occasion. After Pastor Robinson's introduction and other contributions, Crackleton spoke from the heart, "This church is my life, my hope. Where would I and my children be without my believer-brothers and sisters? We might be beggars or dead in a ditch. Whatever else we decide today, please can we stay together, that is my plea."

As darkness fell, the believer-members voted to flee the country, as the Gainsborough-believers had done the year before. In truth, they had little choice. If Robinson and Brewster escaped or surrendered, the rest of us would be rounded up by the Church.

Hopefully, Thomas would be able to secure a ship, although he had not yet replied to our request. The success of the Gainsborough congregation was cited. In comparison, we were ill-prepared and winter was approaching.

A week later, we heard word that pursuivants were travelling up the Great North Road from London, with a cart. No longer able to wait for Thomas, we had to flee. With the women's help, I tried to induce Mary Brewster's labour. Who could blame the baby for its reluctance to enter the world?

We heard that the pursuivants' cart had broken down, delaying them in Stamford, which gave us a few more days. As we tried to induce Mary again, I could not stop myself from thinking about poor Eunice. Mary must survive this labour. We had lost too much already.

When I sent Margaret Deryngton downstairs to pray, she found Brewster physically sick with worry and called me down to treat him.

"I feel so guilty," our leader confessed, "They're all suffering because of me."

"Sir, you can't falter now. The others don't blame you. They need you to stay strong."

I was trying to convince myself as much as Brewster, aware of my own inadequacy. After passing him a potion to settle his stomach, I downed one myself before returning upstairs. He remained in the great chamber, pacing its long length, until he heard the baby's cry.

"It's a girl!"

How we cheered! I am surprised the pursuivants did not hear us in Stamford. Brewster ran up the stairs.

"Have you chosen a name?" I asked.

PAYING IN BLOOD

"Her name is Fear. Although we face great dangers, we are not afraid. Some may not survive the journey, but we will keep trusting God. We will walk in all his ways, whatsoever it shall cost."

Mary was too tired to talk. The women behind me said, "Amen."

The name Fear was apt. Fear could be ignored for periods, while busy, but then came back.

I struggled to decide what to do. Should I flee with my friends? It was hard to analyse the options, let alone decide. I doubted Geoffrey would offer another post in London. If I hid locally, how would I survive once my friends had left? The pursuivants might come for me too, a fate too awful to contemplate.

Although the thatcher had done his best to patch my roof several times, the cottage would never be water-tight unless the whole roof was removed and replaced. Likewise, it seemed that none of us would ever be safe whilst Archbishop Bancroft ruled the Church. His pursuivants would not give up until they had caught their quarry.

After a particularly anxious night, when Geoffrey, Crespin, Sculthorpe, Felde and the beaver-hatted henchman invaded my dream, I made up my mind. The likelihood of my believer-friends reaching Amsterdam was poor. Few would wager on them even reaching the coast. However, they had come to rely on me, and I was desperately concerned for them all.

Perhaps more surprisingly, I had increasing respect for their cause. Having witnessed their sincerity and appreciated their care, I wanted to protect this fledgling community as much as I wanted to protect Fear.

I decided to accompany my believer-friends as far as Boston, help them find a ship and then decide what to do next. I slipped my physician's licence and *Richard II* pamphlet in my bag. Jane's bible was already in my pocket, with the money I had been saving to buy a horse.

60

We left Scrooby Manor when Fear was two days old. I watched William Brewster place his resignation letter on his desk for his landlord to find. He was leaving the family home and position he had inherited from his father, a poignant moment. The former Privy Councillor's clerk was now a fugitive from the law.

His son Jonathan stayed behind to raise the drawbridge, whilst the rest of us crossed the moat for the last time. The ice cracked as he slid across, which did not bode well for the Lincolnshire ditches ahead. His mother screamed as we hauled him up. Mary was weak from her labour and frequently crying. We wanted her to ride the thatcher's donkey, but she was determined to walk, carrying baby Fear.

The donkey transported our food and blankets. After the cook won her argument with the thatcher, it also carried her pot. He carried his tools. Pastor Robinson strapped the church's Geneva Bible to his back. Margaret Deryngton brought her mother, whose legs were now well enough to walk. There were forty-eight of us in total, including the children.

Scrooby Manor stood in proud isolation as Brewster prayed. Our beloved sanctuary, which had witnessed many solemn gatherings, would not do so again. He asked God to lead us safely to Boston and find a suitable ship. As we bade the Manor farewell, the clouds cleared sufficiently to reveal a first star.

I found it hard not to cry as we set off, having grown fond of the red-brick house and the warmth I had known there. Padding through the private forest, I remembered the first Sunday when Nicholas showed me the route to the Old Hall. My heart ran free that day as I watched a damsel fly. Now, every twig-crack alarmed me. I imagined pursuivants hiding behind every tree. Once Archbishops hunted wolves and wild boar through those trees, ·now the Church was hunting us instead, intent on eradicating Separatists.

PAYING IN BLOOD

The moon illuminated our path to the bridge at Mattersey. Mary Brewster slipped and refused to move, having not been in her right mind since giving birth. We could not prise baby Fear from her arms, however much we tried. Two of the family's servants eventually helped her across.

Bradford and Jonathan went ahead to check the lane. They returned in a state of alarm to say that they had seen a rider there. We sheltered in a black-water ditch, until we were certain that the rider had gone. It was difficult to keep the donkey still. Jonathan was the only casualty though. He was soaked when he stumbled on a body, under the ice in the ditch, a grim discovery.

As the group's physician, I naturally took charge, pronouncing the man long dead. Pastor Robinson said a short prayer, and we set off again, more mindful of the risks of travelling in winter. Light snowfall slowed our progress, covering the tracks we had made.

The crumbling causeway at Littleborough was the most obvious place to cross the Trent. Bridget Robinson's brother and Sturton cousins were waiting to help us, but took a long time, refusing to overload their boat. At last, we said our good-byes.

Regrettably, the smaller ones refused to walk from then on. My allotted child grew heavier with each step. As the older folk slowed, the line of believers stretched out across the frozen fields, following Brewster and the donkey.

When Crackleton caught me in conversation, I was grateful for the distraction, "Do you think you'll see Isobel again?"

"It's a long journey, and much can happen on the way. We walked along the Trent together before she left, but I'm not certain of her feelings."

"I'm surprised she likes you," he teased.

"I'm surprised you're so blunt."

"You haven't seemed happy since she left."

"I've been worried since Joan's arrest. The couple let me dine with them like a gentleman at Broxtowe Hall. Now their home has gone and gaol is no place for a woman."

"Did you see the dungeon in Lincoln Castle, where Catherine was held? What was it like?"

I shook my head, unwilling to describe its horrors. We walked in silence, to the edge of the field, before he spoke again, "Isobel is an attractive woman, and you have good prospects, a physician's licence and two good legs."

"It's more complicated."

"I'm not surprised you've been downhearted since she left. Anna and John Junior are wonderful children, but I still miss my Catherine."

Matthew was able to marry again after his wife died, Crackleton did not.

Brewster planned to avoid Saxilby and cross the Fosse Dyke further west. Crackleton surprised me when we were trying to find the path, "Catherine lived in Saxilby at one time, before her mother came to work at our manor house."

"Was Catherine born in Saxilby then?"

"If I knew, I've forgotten. Catherine had a better memory than me."

I had assumed Catherine's life was as limited as her husband's. If she lived so close to Lincoln as a child, she was more likely to have the confidence to travel there later. Also, Crackleton seemed to have relied on his wife more than I had realised.

The cold made it hard to think clearly, and Crackleton was slowing. It was difficult enough to cross the frozen countryside with two legs, so I did not question him further. The more I learnt about Catherine, the more I wished I could have met her.

PAYING IN BLOOD

61

The stragglers were able to catch up when the vanguard reached the Fosse Dyke, the mud and slush very different from conditions on the late summer's day when I walked along with Jane and Piers. Bradford gripped the arms of the weakest, to help them down the ditch. Nicholas pulled them up the other side.

Now, each traveller stood and stared, shocked to see how close to Lincoln we had come.

The cathedral loomed ahead on the hill, in the first flush of dawn, like a cat waiting to pounce. Its spires pierced the pink sky, dominating the valley, a fearful distraction. Sculthorpe had moved to London, but I still imagined him there, sitting at his desk.

Margaret Deryngton's mother needed to rest, on account of her swollen ankles. The poor lady said that she would be the first one caught if the pursuivants spotted us. In truth, none of us were strong enough to outrun those horsemen. The others did not realise how capable they were.

As the sun came up, we scurried into the relative safety of a bramble-edged wood, collapsing exhausted. Despite Margaret's protests, I forced her mother to dip her ankles in a freezing cold stream, an act of medical cruelty that enabled her to walk again the following night.

Many had never slept in the open before. Huddling close to keep warm, we managed a few day-light hours. Mary Brewster still clutched baby Fear, a respectable gentlewoman sleeping like a common vagabond.

Crackleton used my leg as a pillow, so it was numb when I woke. The thatcher snored but no-one commented. There were bigger problems to worry about.

How splendid to cross the flat expanse of the upper Witham valley on the second night! For a few miles, I forgot the dangers we faced, bewitched by its beauty. The moonlight reflected on the frozen pools, as we strode beneath the canopy of stars stretching to every horizon. Bold constellations marched overhead, with countless tiny companions, ideal conditions for clandestine travel.

The hunter Orion rose in the east as we neared the Fosse Way, warning us of the risks ahead. If the pursuivants had turned off the Great North Road at Newark, instead of riding on to Scrooby, they could be very close to us now.

Nicholas and I went ahead to check that the main road was clear. Straining my eyes in the darkness, I imagined phantom horsemen riding up the thin straight line from Newark, thought I heard their hooves.

"Come on," Nicholas complained, "You're staring at shadows. The pursuivants will have passed the cross-roads long ago and be nearing Scrooby now."

"We must be vigilant."

I stood guard with my rapier, as the others crossed behind. Archbishop Bancroft's men might appear from the darkness. I wanted to defend my friends.

"What will one sword achieve?" Pastor Robinson asked as he crossed, "Pursuivants hunt in packs."

"If one eavesdropping peasant says which way we went, in order to fill his stomach, they'll be back on our trail again. It only takes one Judas."

"Informers are always listening. Danger lies close by. We're dependent on the goodwill of others every day. It's just more obvious at times like this."

"Aren't you scared?"

"Of course I'm scared, but I also try to trust the Lord's enduring providence."

"I don't find that easy."

"Me neither. I need to practise constantly."

It was too dark to see his face, but I expect Pastor Robinson's eyes were smiling even then.

Although too tired to talk, we felt safer once we had crossed the Fosse Way. Only a hooting owl disturbed the peace, as we crossed the valley floor and climbed the ridge. Brewster pulled the donkey up first, then led us across the empty moor. Clouds gradually covered the stars but he knew where to go.

Our leader had arranged for us to stay in a sympathiser's barn, at the end of a rut-strewn track. Sleep came easily once inside its walls, feeling more secure than we had for weeks. Exhausted and aching, we forgot what we had left behind and what was yet to come.

The yeoman owner and his family took an enormous risk on our behalf, as sheltering Separatists was a punishable offence. They let us rest in the barn for a whole day and night.

The pause gave me an opportunity to treat the sick and suffering. Crackleton's stump was sore but not bleeding. The thatcher had a raspy cough. Margaret Deryngton's mother agreed to raise her feet on the bean sacks, having stopped arguing with me by that stage. To everyone's relief, I also persuaded Mary to release her grip on Fear. Bridget Robinson fed her while I checked the baby's health. Little Fear appeared to be thriving, a miracle in the circumstances.

It was a remarkable achievement to reach that point, one my believer-friends attributed to the goodness of God. Our yeoman host let us arrange his bean sacks in a circle, in order to hold a thanksgiving service. Separatist-believers do not need a proper building to worship.

During the service, Pastor Robinson baptised Fear in the traditional way, stroking her head with water, in the name of the Father, Son and Holy Spirit. Robinson had performed the ceremony many times, but as he no longer held a clergyman's licence, this baptism was an illegal act. The baby slept throughout, unaware of the significance.

Afterwards, Brewster preached, "God blessed us with stars to guide us and good people to help us on our way. We thank Him, and thank our generous host for this barn. His son Elias has agreed to be our guide for the rest of the journey, an answer to prayer. Elias knows the best route to Boston. We've sold the donkey and bought vaulting poles to help us cross the ditches and dykes ahead. Listen to our guide tomorrow, do whatever he says, without arguing or muttering. God will bring us through this watery wilderness, lead us to a new home."

Someone clapped, others joined in, the noise growing steadily. Brewster rested on a sack, clearly relieved himself. Like me, he knew the causeways were treacherous to the uninitiated.

When silence returned, he continued with the travelling theme, "Last night, we crossed the straight Fosse Way, which ancient pilgrims used when travelling to St. Hugh's shrine. They knew where they were going, in a literal and spiritual sense. Our route meanders more, through fields and marshes and woods, but we are pilgrims too, travelling to freedom in Amsterdam.

A stillness settled, as Pastor Robinson read psalm one hundred and seven

They wandered in the desert and wilderness and found no city to dwell in,

Hungry and thirsty, their souls fainted within them,

Then they cried to the Lord in their trouble and he delivered them from their distress

He led them forth by the right way to a city of habitation.

A woman started to sing the refrain and others joined in

They cried unto God in their trouble, and he delivered them from their distress

"Remember this psalm, when your legs are aching and your shoes are sodden," Brewster concluded, "We are pilgrims on God's journey. He will bring us through."

Then, one by one, the believer's called out honest and earnest prayers, many believing, against the odds, that the group would reach Amsterdam. Was there a possibility of seeing Isobel again in exile, a fragile hope that I could start my life anew? Nervously in the next silence, I uttered my first prayer out loud, "God, please show us the way to go."

The barn service was a significant milestone for me, a turning point. Since my mother's death, I had felt like a wanderer. Cadiz, Nieuwpoort, Lincoln, London, always moving on. During that service, I made an important decision, not where to go but who to go with. I chose the Separatist side in my internal battles, hoisted my flag up their mast. These people were my friends. I would stay with them, never work for Geoffrey again.

However, I also felt guilty, different from the others since birth. I had accepted their kindness, but not fully embraced their faith nor their desire to know God. They accepted me as their physician, without knowing how I felt inside. Pastor Robinson was the most compassionate man I had known, but I could not talk with him.

I admired our leaders more each day. Brewster led us on with fortitude and courage. Robinson soothed tensions between us, tackling each hardship with prayer. Our young guide Elias knew where sympathisers lived, but many were too poor to provide enough food. The children moaned when hungry, which was particularly difficult for parents to bear.

Crackleton relied on others for support, struggling to walk in the wet. Margaret's mother was hampered by her ankles, the thatcher by his cough. At times I doubted whether the cook would last the journey. We had to carry her on a make-shift stretcher towards the end.

Nicholas and Bradford were indispensable, assisting the youngest and oldest along. The children enjoyed using the poles, more adept than the older ones whose nervous attempts provided amusement. When the thatcher got stuck in the mud, Brewster refused us permission to search for his lost tools. Ducks splash-landed through the drizzle, as he urged us on towards our goal.

Brewster paid Elias his last instalment at Tattershall, as I knew the route from there. St. Botolph's tower beckoned over familiar fields, where I had played as a child. The wind picked up, but we reached the Red Lion before the rain set in.

London 1613

62

Baxby pauses. Telling the story of the escape from Scrooby has affected him deeply. He tries to explain the decision he made, "When the Gainsborough-believers left, I was pulled apart, like someone tied to the rack. My loyalties stretched, I didn't know which way to turn. In the barn service, I made the decision to stay with my courageous friends. They were honest pilgrims, trusting the God they professed, simple folk with kindness in their hearts."

Brewster's band forged a new form of pilgrimage for the modern age. Rejecting external definitions, they constituted themselves. Declaring 'we the Lord's free people' as the basis for their covenant, they found a new freedom for the soul. Gainsborough, Scrooby and Boston were oblivious to their historical significance.

Archbishop Bancroft recognised the threat. His pursuivants were closing in.

PAYING IN BLOOD

Lincolnshire 1607-1608

63

Cellars make poor living quarters, especially in Lincolnshire where the ground water is high. Foul street water seeped into the Red Lion cellars, but at least we were protected from the downpour outside. Generous as ever, Sibsey offered us rooms at a low rate, but it was safer to hide underground.

Unfortunately, Brewster and Bradford shunned my old friend's advice about the voyage, having already found a captain who was willing to take us across the Narrow Sea. Captain Atherton would have been a safer choice.

That night Sibsey pleaded with me in the kitchen, "Atherton's due back in three weeks. Can't you persuade your friends to wait for him?"

"They've made a down-payment on another boat and won't listen to me."

"Baxby, your hands are shaking. Who are these companions? What trouble are they in? All sorts of people escape through here, but I've never seen so many at once."

"They're wanted by the Church. Brewster knows what he's doing. He worked for a Privy Councillor."

"He didn't work for one in Boston. Things are different here. Why not return to Geoffrey in London? He has always helped you before."

"I'm not a boy anymore. You trust people too much."

"I trust Atherton, who knows these waters better than anyone. You might be able to get a job in Boston, the town is kinder now."

"I'm leaving with my friends. It's the right thing to do."

Sibsey was correct to be concerned though. He was trying to help.

Waking early, I regretted our disagreement. Once we set sail, I might never see Sibsey and the Red Lion again. To make amends I decided to help him in the kitchen. He only had one servant to help him serve breakfasts. The others had left to find work in London.

Coming up from the cellar, I was surprised to hear Sibsey talking with another man, whose voice sounded familiar but was hard to place. Through the key-hole, I could only see his back which was turned towards me.

"I have orders from our Lord Lieutenant," the visitor said, "A gang of foul traitors are at large in the countryside. They left their Nottinghamshire base some days ago, heading for the coast. As an inn-keeper you must be extra vigilant."

"Am I in danger here?"

"The miscreants spread alarm wherever they go. Keep all your doors and shutters locked."

"Thank you for warning me, Sir Julian."

It was Felde. I had not seen him since he placed the Martin Marprelates in my bag. His cape was a sensible shade, and I could not smell any foul perfume. What was he doing in Sibsey's kitchen at this inopportune moment?

Felde continued, "You must report anything suspicious to the magistrate Horace Methering, who will keep me informed. Don't tell anyone else."

Well-respected throughout the town, Methering had been the town's magistrate for as long as I could remember. Why would he assist Felde? To emphasise his point, he added a customary threat, "Remember, Mister Sibsey, the Lord Lieutenant can revoke your licence whenever it pleases him."

When unsuspecting Sibsey opened the cellar door to fetch a drink, I grabbed his arm and tried to push him back, "Felde hid Martin Marprelate tracts in my bag in Lincoln. He'll hide some in your kitchen if you don't return quickly. You can't trust him."

"What are you talking about Baxby? I've met Sir Julian at the guildhall."

"You've been there?"

"Don't look so surprised. The guildsmen have invited me to

their forthcoming feast. Let me through."

We could hear Felde moving around the kitchen. I assumed he was hiding tracts there.

When Sibsey reopened the door to tell me Felde had left, I was shaking from top to toe.

"You look half-dead, Baxby. Come and have a drink."

"No, we mustn't sit down. We must search the room for illegal pamphlets."

After poking around the fireplace, I crawled under the table.

"What are you doing son? Have you gone mad? All this believer-business seems to have affected your mind."

Sibsey lost patience when I emptied the pockets of his pink jacket, which was hanging on the door.

"Stop, Baxby! Stop now. Sir Julian is a good friend of Horace Methering. He works for our new Lord Lieutenant."

"He's cunning. Someone must have told him that we were here."

"That's unlikely. Boston is discrete and values its independence. Are you certain that you want to leave with this Separatist sect? Our new Puritan vicar is very popular and seems godly enough to me."

Unusually, the town was allowed to choose its own. I did not share Sibsey's faith in Felde or others in the town, but could not find tracts in the kitchen, nor elsewhere in the inn. When Sibsey calmed me down, he tried to persuade me to wait for Atherton again.

64

Brewster and Bradford had confidence in the captain they had found, the rest had faith in them. Having come so far, what could go wrong now? Sibsey hid his concern when we left the Red Lion, just before dawn. We would board the ship at the Haven, and sail on to the Boston Deeps. White clouds raced towards the sea, promising a fast crossing.

As the wind propelled us along the Witham bank, my friends were excited and eager to embark, a colourful pilgrim-procession crossing the pale landscape. Most were cheerfully unaware of conditions at sea. They chatted about where they would sleep and what they would eat. Crackleton told them about the woman who lost her bonnet, when we returned from Nieuwpoort, lightening spirits more.

Following the route of a line of geese, taking advantage of the wind, I spotted three masts on the horizon downstream, and pointed, "There's our ship. She's anchored at the Haven, as the captain promised."

As the others saw her too, hallelujahs mingled with children's laughter. How joyful we all were! Brewster tried to quieten us, but his voice betrayed his own relief. Our ship was ready and waiting for us. The tide was rising up the mud banks, we would be on our way to Amsterdam soon.

When we reached the Haven ferry point, Brewster stopped to count us, checking everyone was there. He made us shed surplus possessions, including the vaulting poles which we would not need anymore.

I could see that the ship was old, her sails ragged. Captain Atherton kept the *Mary-Anne* in better repair. While Pastor Robinson led the last prayer together on English soil, I climbed a mound to get a better view, the vantage point from which the Muster Lieutenant and Felde had watched the militia disembark.

Back then, the Haven was noisy and crowded. Today the cottages were dark, the inn shutters were closed. Why was it so quiet? Where was everyone? Something felt wrong.

Looking back, I wish I had trusted my instincts. Even more, wish I had heeded Sibsey's advice and persuaded the others to wait. We put too much faith in that captain and his ship.

"Come on Baxby," Crackleton called, "Don't you want to sail to Amsterdam? You'll be left behind if you don't keep up."

Pastor Robinson's prayer had been shorter than usual, impatient to board too.

A rowing boat was making good progress towards us from the ship, with three men on board. The passengers stayed in their seats for the return journey, which was unusual, but not sufficiently to alert me at the time.

Brewster needed to pay the captain, so we had agreed that he and his family should board first. There was space for the cook and thatcher too. The oarsman helped them all into his boat.

As they set off, the rest of us shouted encouragement from the shore. It was difficult to wait for our turns. Why weren't there more rowing boats today? I remember my relief as I watched William transfer to the ship, but that feeling did not last long. Soon after he disappeared from view, we heard a thud on deck.

"Take your hands off my husband," Mary screamed.

A voice boomed out, "I am arresting you in the name of His Majesty's customs officials."

What was happening? In the confusion I had no idea. Something was very wrong, but it was impossible to see from the shore. Mary Brewster had a better view in the rowing boat. One of the men pulled her back as she tried to climb the rope ladder on to the ship.

"Mother! Father!" Jonathan and Patience cried, as the rowing boat rocked precariously.

I was particularly concerned for baby Fear's safety, and the others who were still unwell.

Then Brewster appeared at the rail, waving his arms, "It's a trap. The captain's double-crossed us. Get away! Save yourselves while you can."

Someone hit him, and he fell back on the deck. What a

disaster! We had been tricked by that captain, who never intended to take us to Amsterdam. Constables had been hiding on board, waiting to arrest Brewster once he had handed the money across. All our efforts had been in vain.

Those in the rowing boat were already lost. Could the rest of us escape? Children were crying, some adults close to panic.

We saw two constables, running towards us, along the bank, from the direction of the inn.

Bradford took charge, directing terrified families back to the ferry-point. Margaret Deryngton supported her mother and Crackleton. Bridget Robinson made the older children help the younger ones, whilst her husband prayed the Lord's Prayer, in an increasingly breathless voice. All followed Bradford back along the path, as best they could.

Re-enlisting Nicholas into my service, the two of us moved to the rear of the group. I passed him my dagger, and drew my rapier blade, essential tools in London proving useful in Lincolnshire now. We were able to hold the constables off for long enough to allow our friends to reach the ferry.

Whilst Robinson helped the first women and children on board, Bradford hammered on the owner's door. He tried to negotiate a rate, but was unlikely to succeed, as most of our money was in the pockets of that double-crossing captain.

Momentarily distracted by Bradford's efforts and too slow to react, the constables dodged past us, heading for the boat, "Stop in the name of King James' customs officials! Stop the boat!"

The ferryman stood rigid, uncertain what to do initially. When he realised his boat was low in the water, he tried to pull the nearest believers back, "Get out! You're sinking my boat!"

The constables closed in, ordering everyone to line up on the bank.

Nicholas and I moved quickly once we realised we could not help our friends any more. Picking up the discarded vaulting poles, we headed out across the marshy field, not daring to look back. Behind, we could hear Pastor Robinson leading the group in song.

PAYING IN BLOOD

65

After squelching through fields of bean stalks and cabbage husks, Nicholas and I reached a section of solid causeway near Fishtoft village. The constables were too busy with the others to care about us.

After sleeping in the open, we crept back to the Red Lion in the morning, using a roundabout route. The magistrate Methering was remonstrating with Sibsey in the courtyard, so we kept out of sight.

We learnt that the whole town knew we were missing. Boston gaol was in need of repair, so our friends were being held in St. Mary's Guildhall. The men were confined to the cells, the women to the hall above, grossly inadequate for such a large group. Nicholas wanted to plan a rescue mission, but I advised caution.

When Methering left, we slipped into the stables where we were able to speak with Sibsey briefly.

"You must hide," the landlord was adamant, "Boston doesn't agree with this incarceration. The guildsmen have filed complaints. They need to use the building for their banquet."

"But the pursuivants will arrive soon."

"Don't worry, Boston will solve this problem, and that wicked captain will never anchor here again."

Sibsey instructed us where to go, having found a safe house a full day's travel away. Using our precious vaulting poles, we were exhausted and wet when we arrived. After using the codeword Sibsey had given us, our former guide Elias opened the door.

The wind dropped and the murk returned. Lying on our stomachs in our hiding place, Nicholas and I could watch the weather, through a grating near the floor. The room was cramped and dingy, but far better accommodation than our friends' in Boston guildhall. In addition to feeding us, young Elias kept us informed of developments there.

Methering secured the release of the women in the poorest health first. Margaret Deryngton, her mother, the cook, Mary and Fear were moved to safe houses elsewhere.

"Have the pursuivants arrived in Boston yet?" I asked Elias.

"They are still in Stamford. Their cart has a broken axle, which will take some time to repair."

A fortunate coincidence or deliberate damage, I neither asked nor cared. It was enough to know the remaining captives were safe from Archbishop Bancroft's henchmen for a little longer.

Time passed slowly in our refuge, snow began to fall. Elias would not let us outside in case we were seen. It was hard to be so inactive, and dependent on him and unknown others for support.

Nicholas read my *Richard II* pamphlet several times. Having never been to a theatre, he was fascinated by the play.

"Henry was accused of being a traitor, then became King. We've committed minor crimes in comparison. Perhaps the Church will change its mind about us," he reasoned.

"There are different rules for kings and commoners like us. We must wait for spring."

Even Atherton would not cross the Narrow Sea during the winter.

Elias informed us when Crackleton and the rest of the women and children had been released, assuring us they were all hidden safely nearby. Most townsfolk were sympathetic to our plight, not just because they disliked customs officials.

"What about the pursuivants?" I asked again.

"Clever Sir Julian has delayed them with obscure legalities. Leaving the country without a licence is a civil offence, a customs charge. Your friends' so-called crime has nothing to do with the Church."

"Julian Felde? You must be mistaken. Why would he do that on our behalf?"

PAYING IN BLOOD

"He will have his reasons."

It was hard to reconcile this breakthrough with the Crackleton's unpleasant landlord. Felde remained an enigma, a puzzle I needed to solve. I had assumed he worked for the Church, but if Elias's assertion was true, I might need to reappraise by theories, not something I wished to do.

Growing more anxious and confused as our seclusion continued, I read the underlined verses in Jane's bible, although they brought no relief

Fear not, stand still and behold the salvation of the Lord which he will show to you this day

Great are the troubles of the righteous but the Lord delivers them from all

In addition to my troubling boat-dream, sometimes disturbing images appeared in the daytime too. I never told Nicholas. Sometimes we keep secrets, fearing rejection if others find out. The strength of the bond is critical, only the tightest knots hold. The believers were the most likely people to accept me regardless, but I did not unburden my soul.

Nicholas found consolation in his faith, continuing to believe we would leave soon. His cheeriness seemed illogical in the circumstances, but he helped to keep me from despair.

When we learnt that Brewster and Robinson were the only remaining prisoners in the guildhall, I still doubted that we could escape.

Then Elias made an announcement, "Someone else is coming. Someone with money. We've got to move your friends on. Boston is splintering under the strain."

The next day, when we heard the code-word and opened the door, a different, taller figure was standing there. He ducked to clear the lintel and sat on our only chair. Praise God and all his angels in heaven above! Thomas Helwys had returned to England to rescue us. I leapt across the dirt floor to shake his hand. "How wonderful to see you again, Sir."

He looked no different despite his travails.

"I'm very pleased to see you both. When we heard about the arrest warrant in Amsterdam, we were beside ourselves with worry. I came as fast as I could, sadly not fast enough to find you safe passage with a trustworthy captain before the winter. However, I'm formulating a new plan now."

"Thank you, Sir. It's so good you've come back. How is everyone in Amsterdam?"

"They're all well, except for Pastor Smyth whose cough has not improved. Matthew Mobley has found work on the islands, where most of the immigrants live. Isobel's hoping to set up a new bread charity soon."

Elation! My friends were alive and undeterred in Amsterdam.

"And your wife Joan and the little ones?" I asked.

"Thank you for remembering them in your prayers. Joan is still in York."

I sunk back, shaking my head, on hearing that disappointing news. How could the Church continue to justify her imprisonment?

"God willing, she will be released soon. Firstly, we need to move you to another safe house. The people of Boston have been remarkable, but can't sustain this level of support for much longer. There's room where the Crackletons and Deryngtons are staying, further north. I'll engage a reliable captain in the spring."

"Thank you for coming back to save us, Thomas. Please take this money I was saving to buy a horse."

"I appreciate your contribution. An official called Sir Julian Felde, who I believe you know, has also promised funds."

"I'm afraid you can't trust Felde. He planted Martin Marprelate tracts in my bag in Lincoln, endangering my life."

"I'm very sorry to hear that, but people can change. Sometimes our enemy's enemy can act as a friend."

"Please be careful, Sir."

PAYING IN BLOOD

66

One morning in the safe house, Nicholas and I were woken by the sound of horsemen outside. Peering through the grating, we saw two dismount in the yard. Although not Bancroft's pursuivants, I was appalled to see stocky men I had hoped never to meet again. The beaver-hatted man was accompanied by Sculthorpe's assistant Pusey from the Minster, an inauspicious pairing that caused me to fear the worst.

"We need to search these buildings," Pusey called out.

There was no reply. We did not know if Elias was nearby.

"We come with authorisation to search your buildings."

Nicholas had not shared my disquiet initially, not recognising either man. I could see he was shaking now, even indefatigable Nicholas.

My own feelings were those of resignation, only a miracle could save us. We had survived the worst of the winter, the days were lengthening again, but we would be captured now.

Before the men could secure their horses, another figure appeared from a door in the building opposite, in a black cloak and capotain hat.

"What are you doing here?" his voice was deep and familiar.

"We need to search these buildings, in the name of the Church."

"These lands belong to Robert Cecil's estate. Lord Salisbury, the King's Secretary of State, does not take kindly to those who trespass on his land."

Our protector was Julian Felde. If he had not spoken, I would not have guessed. Felde was standing up to the intruders on our behalf, a miracle indeed! Would they take heed?

"If you don't leave immediately, Lord Salisbury will inform His Majesty. Neither of you will walk again after spending a night in the Tower."

As we waited nervously, militiamen emerged from the stables nearby to help convince the pair.

Re-saddling, the beaver-hatted man replied, "Archbishop Bancroft will hear about this. We'll return."

Nicholas and I hugged each other once we were certain they had gone. He talked about guardian angels and answered prayer. To me, it seemed equally remarkable that Felde should have saved us from inevitable discovery.

"It's time to leave," Felde told us, "You're no longer safe here and neither am I. My men will take you to another safe house."

"Have William Brewster and Pastor Robinson been released from the guildhall yet?"

"Yes, it won't be long before you see them again, but there's no time to talk now, Baxby. You must go."

Elias took the vaulting poles, knowing we would not need them again, but refused to say more as we climbed into the cart. The snow was starting to thaw.

Nicholas was very excited, predicting we would sail to Amsterdam soon. Help could come from unexpected sources. If Felde could defend us, perhaps others would too.

Felde's actions that day convinced me that he was not working for the Church. In the weeks that followed, I tried to make sense of everything that happened to Catherine and Buckler in the light of this revelation. Perhaps Felde had killed the Buckler after all, for reasons other than personal ambition. Some things began to make more sense, but I still found no peace.

The Crackletons and Deryngtons had passed the winter together, in a cramped farm-house, without knowing its location. Even Anna and John Junior had been blind-folded on the journey, a precaution in case any of us were caught. Sheltering Separatists was still a crime. We never knew the names of our kind, brave hosts.

It was reassuring to find our friends in reasonable health, given all they had been through. Margaret Deryngton had continued to enforce my instructions with regards to her mother's legs, and re-dressed Crackleton's stump. Also, she had supervised a small service each Sunday since their release from Boston guildhall, not something I had thought a woman could do. We let her continue, incapable of doing this ourselves.

There was plenty of time to reminisce with Crackleton. By the end of our time there, the others could have recited the stories themselves. However, I was pleased to find a quiet moment alone, to explain my latest theories about Catherine to him, "I think your former landlord Felde may have murdered the baker Buckler, after making Catherine track his movements. He could have made it a condition for keeping your land. That's how spy-masters work. They exploit whatever they can."

"Spy-masters!"

"Sorry, that wasn't the right word to use. Felde could have used Catherine to find the best place to murder Buckler."

"Do you think that sounds better? Accusing my wife of spying for that cheat? Anyway, does it matter now? Catherine's gone and we're stuck here."

Crackleton threw his crutch at me but missed. Nicholas calmed us both down. We played with the children later, so Crackleton could get more rest.

67

In early spring, we were blind-folded and loaded into another cart. The driver deposited us in empty scrubland, near the Humber estuary. He pointed to a narrow track that we should follow, before abandoning us there. Apart from a few ponies huddled beside a stunted bush, there were no other signs of life.

Although we could not see the sea through the mist, we could smell it. Could this be the day? Did we dare to believe? Little Anna Crackleton gripped my hand tightly, her nails digging into my palm.

Traipsing along the tuft-path, we saw a tall man ahead, looking out to sea through an eyeglass. John Junior recognised him first, "It's Mister Helwys. He must have found a ship to take us to Amsterdam."

I cautioned, "Let's wait and see."

On a clear day, this would have been a good place to embark, with no cover for ambushers to hide. Today, anyone could be lying in wait in the fog. I grew more anxious with each step, praying this was not another trap.

A herring gull squawked overhead, reminding me of my experience in Minster Yard. Why was I being so foolish? I needed to keep walking. Filled with dread, my legs were reluctant to move.

"Are you alright?" Crackleton asked twice before I replied.

"It's been a long time since I've seen the sea."

"You can't have forgotten what it's like. Hurry up! You're getting left behind."

Nicholas came back to help me carry my bag to the grassy mound, where Thomas explained, "I've chartered a single-masted Dutch hoy, anchored out in the estuary. Brewster, Robinson, Felde and the other Scrooby men are on board already, having trekked through the night to reach this spot. The captain will send a rowing boat to fetch us soon."

Thomas must have noticed my apprehension, "Don't worry, Baxby. Sir Julian has checked the captain's credentials, and the weather should be better at this time of year."

PAYING IN BLOOD

Naturally, I worried. Relying on Felde in such a way, allowing him to join us, seemed utter madness. Previously, I had thought Thomas to be a good judge of character. However, there was little I could do, and did not wish to alarm the others. Thomas was insistent that this plan would work.

As the mist began to clear, I spotted our ship through Thomas' eyeglass. She looked small but sturdy enough. Please God, do not let us fail again. As a rowing boat was lowered down the side, Nicholas waved his arms above his head, then ran down to the silt beach. I kept checking the scrubland behind us, still fearful.

The Scrooby women were due to arrive on a coal barge. Hiding with us, Margaret Deryngton and her mother were able to come in the cart, but the other women had further to travel. Their boat would sail directly to the hoy, where we would all be re-united and sail to Amsterdam, all except Joan.

"I can see them," Margaret spotted the barge first.

Thomas took charge of the eyeglass to monitor its position. Progress was slow. There appeared to be at least sixty women and children on board, some taking numerous belongings with them. We shouted, but they could not hear us.

As our rowing boat negotiated the channels through the mudflats, Nicholas waded into the water. Margaret and Thomas helped the rest of us down the bank. I was the last one to be pulled on board.

My friends assumed I was anxious because I could not swim. In truth, I was filled with deeper dread. Reeds brushed against my legs, reminding me of the bodies at Nieuwpoort. Assuming this was another trap, I could not stop shaking with fright.

Half way out in the estuary, we could see the women's plight. Their barge was stuck in the mud at the water's edge. Their skipper yelled at the largest, trying to force them out. Brewster's old cook threw her pot in the water, without effect. Children were perilously close to the rim.

The oarsmen brought our little boat alongside the hoy, enabling us to clamber on board. The other men were already pressing round to watch, their wives and children unable to hear their advice.

Then letting out a startled cry, Thomas passed the eyeglass to me. What now? Company, I spotted them too. Six horsemen were riding along the coastal path, towards the women's barge. As they galloped closer, I could see the soldier's muskets and swords.

How could this happen? What could this mean? Had Bancroft contrived to arrest us at this late hour? If so, why target the women and children rather than the men?

Spotting the women's barge, the soldiers made their way down to the mud. We stared as they dismounted and tested its solidity. One shouted at the women, beckoned them across. It was unbearable to watch the catastrophe unfold.

Frantic men paced the deck, demanding the captain let us return to the shore. William Brewster had to be forcibly restrained, when he tried to re-lower the rowing boat. Jonathan nearly fell overboard. It was amazing no-one was hurt. However much we pleaded, the Dutch captain would not let anyone disembark. He refused to risk his ship. The hoy needed to sail on the tide.

We could hear the children sobbing, but there was nothing we could do. Their barge was sinking lower. The first woman to step out sunk to her knees. How could we be thwarted a second time? We must have been betrayed.

Felde was on the hoy as Thomas had predicted, standing slightly apart from the other men, in a thick cloak fastened tight to keep out the cold. Although he did not acknowledge me, I know he saw me board.

As Thomas took him aside to talk, Felde kept shaking his head. He did not believe what was happening either. They tried to convince the captain to delay, but without success.

When the sails were ready, he gave the word to raise the anchor. The soldiers were forcing the women out of the barge. Loving husbands and fathers shouted in vain, as they witnessed the horror unfold. The wind caught the hoy's sails. We were off, leaving the women and children to their fate.

Whatsoever it should cost? Why them not us?

PAYING IN BLOOD

68

When we could no longer see the speck on the horizon, the men broke down and wept like women themselves. Battle grief was nothing compared to the anguish of husbands and fathers who feared they would never see their loved ones again. Their loss reminded Crackleton of his own. I put my arms around him and his children, letting him sob into my chest, "Catherine!"

Felde was watching us from the bow. How could he stand there gawping? He was complicit even if he did not kill Catherine himself, having taken the family's land and home.

Staring out to sea, I pondered her fate again. Catherine, why did you die? I tried my best to find out, but ultimately failed you.

My mother was poor and sick, a fatal combination I had seen many times since. Why do poor lives matter less? I saw her lying on her sick-bed again, and the earth they made me throw in the grave. If I believed in God before, I stopped believing then.

I think Lupton died because he could not bear to operate again. Who could blame him for absconding? The kindly surgeon was ill-suited to such a hellish place.

Jane chose to take her own life, rather than suffer at the hands of the Church. She was an Anabaptist, so could expect no mercy on earth. Her death remained tragic as did Piers'.

The baker Buckler was murdered, his life brutally stolen from him, after he had filled his ovens.

What about Essex? No-one should die like that, but it is still hard to know the true reason. Bancroft, Cecil and Crespin each had their own accounts. We all adapt to gain advantage, lie to each other and ourselves.

Lost in thought, I was slow to realise the growing violence of the weather. Felde was sick over the side, others doubled over. Waves rarely bothered my stomach, but I knew how serious storms could be.

The wind and rain grew stronger throughout the day, blowing us off course. The crew lowered the sails to protect them. The captain said he could do no more. We were at the mercy of the storm.

Margaret Deryngton helped me bandage a bleeding leg, when someone fell on the treacherous deck, whilst Nicholas tried to calm her mother. She had never even seen the sea before leaving Scrooby, now she witnessed its horrors. The crew found buckets, bailed water with our strongest, as the storm grew worse.

Waves rose to heights I had never seen before, our ship was too small for such weather. How could we survive? As night fell, Jonathan admitted what we all feared, that the women were the fortunate ones after all, for we would surely drown.

The crew lashed us to the woodwork to prevent us washing overboard, then we could only pray. Our prayers grew more ragged with every passing hour.

In a storm, time is not measured by the bells of a church or the hands of a clock, but by the deathly pitch of the ship. We crashed down to be drenched, in freezing despair, only to rise in hope again. The hope was the worst part, knowing we were destined to repeat the cycle again. How much more could we endure?

Each feared death in their own way, the others never guessing the depths I reached. How could they suspect? Geoffrey taught me well, not to let my feelings show, but I could no longer pretend to myself.

The storm unleashed a tidal wave of guilt and shame, that I had hidden from others, rarely admitted to myself. How foolish to think I could escape. My sins caught up with me, uninvited and unannounced. I had betrayed the kindest people I had known.

The women sinking on the mud-flat, Joan wasting in gaol. Faces accused me in the tumult, Jane, Piers and Essex's rolling head. Their mouths moved in agreement, telling me that I should drown. My heart was rotten, as black as Crackleton's discarded foot. A hellish death was fair punishment for my iniquity.

My recurring dream had been prophetic and profound,

confirmed by the pamphlet in Scrooby. I deserved to drown, as the inevitable consequence of my crimes. I had followed Catherine over the side many times, sinking into icy darkness. Nothing should stop me now. I must leave this world, as she had, whatever waited beyond.

As I struggled to untie the knot that bound me to the ship, I remember hearing Pastor Robinson's voice, muttering words from the psalm

They cried to the Lord in their trouble and he delivered them from their distress

KAREN HADEN

London 1613

69

Baxby is physically exhausted, dripping with sweat. The printer shuffles over whilst the vicar looks on puzzled. The story-teller is not a ghost. He did not die at sea. After regaining some composure, he reads the stormy verse of his favourite psalm from Jane's bible

They that go down to the sea in great ships and occupy the great waters, see the works of the Lord and his wonders in the deep.

For he commands and raises the stormy wind and lifts up the waves so they mount up to heaven and descend to the deep, so that their souls melt with trouble.

They are tossed to and fro and stagger like a drunken man and all their cunning is gone.

The others wait in silence, expecting to hear how Baxby survives the storm. He pauses, then fills a dark hole in his tale instead.

"I wanted to start my life afresh in Amsterdam, but found I needed to confront my past."

"Now you're talking in riddles," the vicar complains.

"It is the way with spies. Nothing is as it seems, the truth is always hidden. I can't hide it any longer," Baxby confesses, "I was a spy. I spied for the Church."

The others do not respond, so he repeats his admission, "I am deeply ashamed that I spied for the English Church."

"Many people welcome a small reward for passing information," the printer seeks to reassure.

"I wasn't a casual eavesdropper, Bancroft paid a good salary."

"Typical bastard behaviour!" the vicar explodes. Then panics, worried that he has incriminated himself during their conversations.

Baxby smiles, "Don't worry, I'm not spying now."

Questions form in the others' minds, have they missed important clues? Was something missing all along? Baxby seemed obsessed with informers, but that was only prudent. If they had been more careful, they would not be shackled alongside him now.

"How can we trust anything you say?" the printer poses.

"I have no reason to lie now. I'm telling an honest story."

"Were you spying on Agnes, when she was spying on you? What a pair!"

"No, I was part of a new prized group, funded by Bancroft, who needed to know where Bishop Chaderton's loyalties lay. I reported to Sculthorpe, once a week in his lair, when I collected my pay. By the time I met Jane, I was already questioning everything he said."

Baxby's skills and aptitude had been recognised. He could not have escaped if he wanted too. The opportunity to treat Crespin in the Tower was not part of the original plan, but confirmed his suitability, propelling him to the capital sooner.

The story-teller returns to the time he left Lincoln, after qualifying as a physician.

KAREN HADEN

London 1603-1606

70

Sculthorpe gave me papers and instructed me to meet Geoffrey at court. London was awash with rumours about the Queen's health. Everyone expected the city to riot. Patrols roamed the streets, with extra checks at the gates causing tedious delays. No-one could stop the speculation though. Elizabeth still had not named a successor.

After battling my way through the crowds to Richmond Palace, the gatehouse guards refused me entry, even though my papers were correct. They had orders not to let anyone in or out. The reason was self-evident, although no-one dared breathe the words. The Queen was dying inside.

With nowhere else to go, I found a few vacant inches of wall and settled down for the night. My furs were warmer than my neighbours' clothing, but I could not sleep. The smell of Jane's gloves reminded me of her, whenever I shielded my face from the cold.

Restless and uncomfortable, the sound of a horse's hooves woke me in the early hours. Money changed hands at the gatehouse, before the guards let a rider out. Having witnessed their disregard for orders, they had to let me through too. I bobbed under the portcullis before it re-shut.

Inside, the grounds were deserted and the Palace doors locked. Crouching down behind a hedge, I tried to formulate a plan. How could I find Geoffrey? Where was he likely to be? The solution came in an unlikely form. A slight figure exited a side door, and tripped towards me through the formal gardens, before stopping to piss on a flower bed.

"That's for Essex," he aimed at a bush close by.

My former patient Crespin was seemingly taking an enormous risk.

PAYING IN BLOOD

I filled my lungs and lowered my voice, "Crespin, what colour is that?"

"Who's there? The roses are red and white in summer."

"I meant the urine. Is it purple?"

My inflection faltering, he recognised my voice, "Baxby! I never expected to see you again."

"What will the Queen do if she sees you?"

"Elizabeth collapsed on cushions some days ago and passed away this evening. She will never authorise another execution."

"Was her piss really purple? Did you ever find out?"

He shook his head, "Her physicians are blaming her rotten teeth, an unusual cause of death. Elizabeth's medical secrets will be buried with her in Westminster."

"What about her successor? Did she choose one?"

"Apart from her ladies-in-waiting, only Cecil, Whitgift and Bancroft were with her when she died. They insist she signalled for King James to succeed her, just before she breathed her last."

Whether that was true or not, no-one else could argue otherwise. England's fate was decided. She would import a foreign King next, at least one with several children to avert the need for such uncertainty again.

I will never forget the scene in the grand chamber that night. Colourful clerics, lords and ambassadors clustered on the marble tiles. Ladies whispered behind their fans, while City dignitaries shuffled back and forth. All were dwarfed by the palace proportions and enormous tapestries. Everyone was waiting for the Great Council to complete its business, behind the door at the far end of the room. A new assembly of statesmen was governing the country in the absence of a monarch.

"They're compiling a proclamation to be read at Whitehall at dawn, no doubt arguing over its contents," Crespin explained.

I found it hard to believe they would spend hours fine-tuning a statement, but he assured me this was a highly prized skill amongst the country's most powerful politicians.

"Will Londoners accept its authority?" I wondered, "People

have stock-piled weapons."

"Cecil has taken precautions. He's sealed the gates so that no-one can leave the Palace before him."

When I told him that I had seen a horseman gallop off earlier, Crespin was visibly shocked. Hurrying off to let Robert Cecil know, he negotiated his way past the guards on the door with a smile and a wave.

Geoffrey looked unusually crumpled when I found him on an upstairs window bench. His hair was greyer and curling the wrong way for once. He knocked a weighty box of papers on the floor, but refused to let me help him gather them up.

"Alexander, I'm pleased to see you again. Lincoln's loss is our gain. You wanted to work at court, now your wish has come true."

Despite his smile, I could tell that he was worried.

"What is happening? Who is in charge?"

"The last few weeks have been a nightmare. Bancroft visited Scotland, then sent me up there with his negotiators, refusing to believe that any members of my team were trustworthy enough. I choose carefully, but Bancroft would not take any unnecessary risk. It's a ridiculous distance and the weather was grim. Coming from the coast, I prefer to travel by sea, not balance on horses for days."

Previously, Geoffrey had told me that his father built boats in Kent, but I knew little else about his past.

"After Elizabeth flopped on cushions, Bancroft sent a daily courier to Scotland. Cecil was sending his own, neither knowing how long she would last. Fortunately, Whitgift persuaded her to move to a royal bed, for a more dignified end. Then Cecil's Great Council was a nasty surprise. Our team worked hard preparing for this, but he moved quicker when Elizabeth died."

Geoffrey had rarely divulged so much detail about his work before. He was clearly stressed by the demands of recent days.

"What do you want me to do?" I asked.

Geoffrey's familiar smile returned, "Listen out for problems that we could exploit. Fortunately, councillors seem to be an unhealthy breed."

"I'll see what I can learn."

"One more thing, I saw you talking with Crespin earlier. We think he may be working for a Privy Councillor. Continue to build the friendship, which may prove useful, but don't trust him. We're still trying to confirm the chain of command."

In those precarious days after Elizabeth's death, nothing was straightforward.

71

Londoners stayed indoors to avoid succession riots, then were relieved by their absence, and in good spirits until James snubbed the city by taking weeks to journey south. Dignitaries flocked north to swell the travelling court. Crespin took a pair of velvet slippers as presents. Bishop Bancroft went too, on Whitgift's behalf, hoping to encourage more haste.

Left in charge of an increasingly angry capital, Cecil promoted the new King's book *Demonology* in his absence, a disturbing read. James was a foremost expert on the subject, having personally thwarted the Devil's tricks. I watched Shakespeare's *Macbeth* at the Globe which took a similar theme.

As witch-fever gripped the city, London talked of little else. The Great Council acquiesced to demands for extra patrols after dark, and the risk of rebellion passed. *Demonology* was an effective distraction. Cecil was good at his job.

Eventually setting up residence in London, King James became the centre of our universe, around which the sun and political planets swirled. The coronation was a great success, with the newly anointed King particularly grateful to his Archbishop. However, this did not stop Geoffrey fretting that the Church was losing power to Cecil.

Bancroft was not complacent. Ever mindful of the Puritan threat, he decided to secure England's Episcopalian future by waging war on his enemies' greatest weapon, the Geneva Bible itself. Copies kept flowing on to the streets, sowing dissent.

The Bishop sought to supplant the people's favourite with a new Authorised Bible of his own, a scholarly English translation, without annotations or other insidious inventions, purporting to explain the text. Common people must be dissuaded from reading the bible themselves. The Church should be the sole interpreter, on the nation's behalf.

For his plan to work, Bancroft needed to be seen to have the broadest possible backing for his scheme, so he put his spy-network to work. We helped him identify compliant scholars who would translate the ancient Hebrew and Greek to his liking.

When Geoffrey explained the Authorised Bible operation, I did not realise how many others were involved. It was a massive undertaking of national importance, with funding to match. Bishop Bancroft brought Sculthorpe from Lincoln to assist with administration, but kept a tight grip on the operation himself. I saw the Secretary soon after he arrived, writing notes in a little book.

For my part, I was assigned a number of clerical targets, and expected to report to Geoffrey each week. Unsurprisingly, Bishop Chaderton was on my list, along with potential rivals for the future Archbishop position.

Geoffrey was complimentary whenever we met, impressed by my medical skills and ability to elicit conversations on relevant topics.

By the time King James convened the Hampton Court Conference, we had sufficient intelligence to control the guest-list. Unsurprisingly, it delivered a strong mandate in favour of retaining bishops in the English Church. The event was hailed as fair, open and consensual, such was Bishop Bancroft's success. He would oversee the new Authorised Bible translation committee. A small number of Puritans were allowed to speak on the last day. The King's attention had returned to hunting by then, so they were largely ignored.

When the whole team was invited to a generous banquet afterwards, I realised the true extent of the Authorised Bible operation. My co-workers filled three long tables in Bancroft's great hall, devouring pheasant, peacock and swan, adorned with sugar-plums, washed down with six different wines. Geoffrey told me that the Bishop had escaped an austere upbringing by joining the Church, so liked to display his wealth in this way.

Fellow diners kept coming up to shake my patron's hand. He seemed to remember all those he had recruited, or perhaps he just gave that impression, with his fulsome smile.

As Bishop Bancroft watched proceedings from the top table, it was hard not to stare back. His forehead was more wrinkled than I remembered, but he wore the same style of pointed cap.

Sculthorpe sat to Bancroft's right, enjoying his meal, until the Bishop leant across to whisper in his ear, whereupon he fumbled through the pages of an enormous book.

The room went silent as the Secretary rose to his feet, "How fortunate we are to have a godly churchman such as Bishop Bancroft who takes the Puritan threat seriously. Archbishop Whitgift is often ill and relies on him more than any other prelate ...."

Geoffrey pulled me up to join the applause as the Secretary finished his introduction. The enthusiastic chaplains opposite us were the last to sit down.

Bishop Bancroft stood next, his familiar staff in his hand, "Sadly, My Lord the Archbishop of Canterbury is too ill to attend in person today. In his absence, I want to thank you on the Church's behalf. Soon England will have a new Authorised Bible translation, a noteworthy achievement of which we should all be proud."

Geoffrey did not need to instruct me to stand to clap this time. No-one dared to stop until Bancroft waved his rod in the air for silence.

The Bishop continued, "Be assured the King, sharing our aims, will show no mercy to Puritans. Let me read what His Majesty said at the Hampton Court Conference."

Sculthorpe pushed the book across so he could read the quote.

I will make them conform themselves, or else harry them out of the land, or else do worse.

Bancroft's smile was more unsettling than his scowl. When he restored silence, his next quote was even more astonishing, his accent becoming more pronounced as he lifted his arms to recite

No bishop no king.

The cry went up from the tables

No bishop no king. No bishop no king.

The chaplains opposite jumped to their feet and cheered.

Bancroft burst forth, "Our godly King can trust his Bishops. There'll be no annotations or such connivance in the new Authorised Bible. We'll clean the Puritan filth from this land."

We kept thumping the tables long after Bancroft sat down.

No bishop no king.

I had a terrible headache the following day.

72

Basking in Hampton Court Conference glory, Bancroft moved ever closer to the King, even recommending the new Authorised Bible bear his name, a stylish touch. His rival Cecil gained ground by giving the King credit for foiling the Gunpowder Plot, but the Archbishop remained a formidable presence.

I missed Fawkes' execution. Geoffrey invited me to watch the death of a co-conspiring priest the following spring. We had an amazing view from St. Paul's roof, flanked by clerics. The crowd crushing round the scaffold in the Yard below, did not know we were there, perched like birds along the roof edge.

Absorbed by the excitement, I did not study the stocky man, with a thick neck, who moved to Geoffrey's right. After the priest was hung and quartered, he waited behind as the clerics filed down the steps. When we were the only three remaining on the roof, Geoffrey introduced him, "Baxby, thank you for all your hard work. I wanted to let you know that I've been promoted, so you'll need to report to Leonard Redfern from next week."

"But ..."

"I trust Redfern's judgement and will pass instructions through him. Obey him just as you would obey me."

Redfern wore an expensive hat made of soft beaver fur. I disliked him from the start, but there was nothing I could do. Geoffrey had made up his mind. I followed the pair of them down the spiral stone steps while they gossiped about people I did not know.

By that time Crespin was one of the King's gentlemen, James presumably appreciating his company as Essex had before. We continued to meet occasionally, sometimes taking the ferry to Southwark. He was a useful source of Whitehall gossip, one that I was reluctant to lose.

After taking responsibility for my supervision, Redfern forbade me from seeing him. Geoffrey would not listen, saying he was too busy to intervene, "I would love to be able to keep meeting, as we did before, but promotion brings new responsibilities. Try to be patient with Redfern, he's still learning how to manage the team."

"When can I see you again?"

"I'll let you know, when things are calmer again."

How strange that I should miss my old patron, after complaining for so many years!

Having become convinced that the King pissed purple urine, Crespin sought my opinion, "Do you think King James might suffer from the same royal disease as the late Queen?"

"Some illnesses are common in particular families, but I've never heard of such a case."

When Redfern found out that I had seen him again, he called me to his office, "What is up with you? You must follow orders if you want to keep your job."

He gave me a new list of lower ranking clerics to treat, a clear snub, then berated me in front of a fellow physician. Although I maintained a professional disposition throughout his rant, I was livid. How could Geoffrey let this blockhead be in charge?

One evening, Crespin knocked on my door, insisting I let him in. He lifted the hat he was holding, to show me the specimen bottle beneath.

"Come inside before anyone sees you. Why have you brought this here?"

"I'm worried about His Majesty's health. You must test this sample. We may be able to help him."

He was taking an enormous risk, as was I by association. The liquid was dark, but was it purple? There was not enough light to be certain. After he left, I separated it into three vials and found the relevant page in my medical book, ready to experiment in the morning

Redfern banged on my door before breakfast, "Baxby, let me in! I need to see what you're doing in there."

Surrounded by the evidence, I could only deny the donor.

"I was testing my own urine," I maintained.

"I don't believe you. You're not stupid. A specimen bottle went missing from the King's bedchamber yesterday."

Physicians use them all the time, a theft was impossible to prove.

Redfern detested me as much as I detested him. I swore at him in front of a lady-in-waiting, after he gave my best patients to other physicians in the team. He called me to his office again to explain, "We've found a new assignment. You'll be deep undercover this time, back in more suitable territory for you. We need you to infiltrate a fanatical group whose extreme ideas are threatening the peace in Lincolnshire."

"Will I treat Bishop Chaderton again?"

"No, commoners this time. A Gainsborough physician called Mobley has heard that you're unhappy here. You will take the place of a deceased colleague in a nearby Nottinghamshire village, a good base to spy on despicable radicals, either side of the Trent."

"Has the Archbishop of York agreed to this? Nottinghamshire is in his province."

"I can't discuss that. This is particularly sensitive work. The fanatics move back and forth across the border, between Canterbury and York, an administrative head-ache for us. You're the right man for the job. Don't fail this time, Baxby. This is your last chance."

Redfern gave me the name of my local contact and arrangements for handing over my current list.

When I found out that he was reducing my pay, I tried to find Geoffrey again, but Sculthorpe ambushed me instead, "Harry them, Baxby! Heed Archbishop Bancroft's words! Separatist scum are even worse than Puritans."

I rode up the Great North Road to spy on my former friends. When Nicholas welcomed me to my new home in Scrooby, he showed me the leaking thatched roof. It proved difficult to fix, as was the personal tribulation I would face.

PAYING IN BLOOD

London 1613

73

The printer raises his hands in despair. Having grown fond of the physician, he is more disturbed by Baxby's revelation than the vicar chained opposite, "How could you spy on your friends like that? William Brewster was right to be concerned about security. You should have told him everything."

"Redfern was the man in the beaver hat who crossed Gainsborough square, when I was on sentry duty up the Old Hall tower. My contact didn't warn me that he was coming. It was a nasty shock."

"Your deception is a nasty shock for us. You lived two different lives at once. What could be worse than betraying your friends?"

"I revealed Joan Helwys' location to my contact, a greater sin."

"How could you do that? Joan was a lovely lady. She welcomed you to Broxtowe Hall."

"I didn't betray her intentionally, but that made no difference. I deserved to die in the storm."

Baxby faced a deep dilemma when he discovered that Redfern's so-called fanatics were the kindest people he had met. He avoided his contact for weeks after Joan's arrest, but could not escape from the guilt.

KAREN HADEN

Narrow Sea 1608

74

Abandoning my attempts to untie the sodden cord, which bound me to the wood, I listened to the wind, rolled with the ship. Down for a soaking and up again, periodically released from the salty depths to steal another breath. Having lost awareness of all else, I threw my head back and screamed to the darkest clouds
Deliver me from my distress
When no-one else could save me, I called on the Separatists' God for help. The ship plunged again. I cried out again as she rose
Deliver me Lord
A monstrous wave shocked me to my senses. Through dripping hair, I saw the others suffering too. Brewster gripped Jonathan and Bradford. Robinson's lips moved in perpetual prayer. The thatcher's body hung lifeless at the base of the mast. Crackleton tried to shield his children, like a mother hen with chicks. How could young ones witness this? Even the Turkish sailors wept for strength to hold the ropes.

While I was marvelling at their courage, a momentous wave washed Julian Felde towards me, without warning. I do not know how I found the strength to catch him in my frozen arms, sodden and spluttering. Somehow, I managed to secure the rope ends around his waist. Felde was alive but only just.

I do not know why I saved him. Whatever Thomas believed, in my eyes Felde was an evil landlord, who did not merit effort from me or anyone else. Exhausted and gasping for breath myself, some uninvited instinct must have possessed me in the madness of the storm. Felde hung on the rope with me, as the waves crashed over the ship.

Lord deliver us all.

Eventually, the storm moved on, leaving the ship to settle into a more restful rhythm. My old flat-bottomed boat took its place as I slept, drifting on a milder sea. Jane sat serenely on a sack in the stern, singing the psalm. She replaced Catherine in my dream, but never moved towards the side.

Then they cry unto the Lord in their trouble and he brings them out of their distress,
He turns the storm to calm so that the waves are still.

We drifted on, peacefully in my dream. Jane's voice was sweet and soothing. Her bible was still in my pocket. It would have drowned with me if I had untied the rope.

Reluctant to wake, a strange cry brought me back. The look-out was pointing ahead, whilst shouting down to the deck in Dutch.

"It's Norway," Thomas translated, the only one of us who understood the language, "The crew have never been blown so far off course before."

We saw a strange new world of mountains and snow in the distance. The huge peaks dwarfed any I had seen in England or Spain, although still a long way away.

Felde must have released himself while I was sleeping. We surveyed each other in disbelief, astonished to have survived, let alone in such a way.

The crew reset the sails for Amsterdam. We were on our way to dry land again. People cheered and hugged each other, even Thomas Helwys briefly. How wonderful to be alive! Each breath was more precious than treasure, the laughter of friends more melodious than the best musicians.

With my fingers still too numb, Felde untied the knot which bound me to the ship. He tossed the frayed remains overboard, as I took my first steps on the strangely level deck.

"Thank you, Felde," I coughed.

"No, I need to thank you for saving my life, Mister Baxby."

What could I say? So much had happened since the day he placed Martin Marprelate tracts in my bag.

"Did you really help Thomas arrange our escape," I asked, eventually.

"I paid a considerable sum, and previously helped your friends when they were imprisoned in Boston Guildhall."

Felde's eyes were red and sore, but I could see he was trying to smile.

"I kept the pursuivants in Stamford while the Privy Council discussed your case. The only time Scrooby has been on the agenda, to my knowledge, a quaint name for a village."

I had refused to believe Sibsey when he told me that Felde was our ally, even though I could not find Martin Marprelates at the Red Lion.

However, that was not the time to question Felde further. Pastor Robinson was leading songs of praise. Jonathan and Bradford chased each other round the deck. Nicholas and I swung Anna and her brother round, before collapsing in a dizzy heap. Crackleton slipped when he tried to dance with Margaret's mother, neither complaining about their injuries. Margaret helped them up whilst Felde found beer.

The crew helped us bury the thatcher at sea, our only loss. I do not think the poor man's heart was strong enough to take such a battering. Nicholas was particularly upset, the two having spent many hours together, including several on my roof. We gathered for the small remembrance service on the deck.

After thanking God, Brewster praised the crew's skill and bravery too. Only the captain understood English. The other Dutch sailors stood reverently in the circle with us, leaving the Turks in charge of the ship. Felde stood there too, bowing his head, a sight I never expected to see. The Turks prayed to their God later, when we had finished our service. They believed in divine deliverance too.

PAYING IN BLOOD

75

As others were preparing to sleep, I moved to where Felde was folding blankets he had previously hung out to dry. I had tried to rehearse what I would say to him, never imagining that it would be like this. The words left my mouth, without the anger I expected. Perhaps the storm had washed it away, or I was too tired.

"Thank God, we both survived the storm, but you have serious questions to answer. You tried to kill me in Lincoln, by putting Martin Marprelate tracts in my bag."

Felde stopped folding the blankets, and took his time to answer, seeming surprised, "Come, come, Baxby. Your recollection is wrong. I regret my actions that day, but I didn't try to kill you."

"Sculthorpe would have killed me, if he had found the tracts there."

Felde shook his head and almost seemed amused. This was not funny. Was he trying to provoke me?

"Dear me, no. Sculthorpe wouldn't have killed you. I thought you understood him better than that."

I knew him well, having worked with him for years.

"He was easily riled, never let matters rest."

"That's true, but you must also know that Sculthorpe followed orders, and Archbishop Whitgift's were clear."

"What orders? What are you talking about?"

"Whitgift expected Sculthorpe to report every Martin Marprelate sighting to Bancroft, who then had to investigate promptly on the Archbishop's behalf. There were such sightings in Lincoln, as you know."

"I found one on the baker Buckler's beam. Are you trying to tell me that Bancroft visited Lincoln because of Whitgift's rule?"

"Sculthorpe always did what he was told. Bancroft travelled to Lincoln whenever a tract appeared. It worked every time."

When the pursuivants told me about their journeys north with

Bancroft, I had naturally assumed that the deaths were their primary concern. Even now, I was reluctant to believe Felde's reasoning.

"But you killed the baker Buckler and nailed a tract to his beam. There's blood on your hands Felde."

The accusation came quietly without venom, not retaliating as I once would have done. Naked and heart-felt it was more affective.

Felde nodded once, before replying, "Buckler threatened to tell Sculthorpe."

"You killed him?"

"I panicked."

It was true. Felde was a murderer.

"I have my own reasons for leaving England. I'm not proud of what I did."

His ascendency was over. He could never return to England given his confession.

As I waited, wondering whether he would explain more, the planet Venus appeared ahead, shining brightly as she rose on her strange journey round the earth. Catherine had joined me in my dream, night after night, now Felde stood with me on the hoy's deck, staring at the planet. It was time to ask him about her, "What about Catherine Crackleton? You stole the family's land and made her run errands, whatever that means."

"I'm truly sorry, Baxby. Catherine helped me uncover the truth."

"Sculthorpe abducted her in the cloisters, then moved her to the castle where she died. If you sent her to the Minster, you are culpable too."

"Helwys told me that Catherine was your friend's wife."

"Why? How could you?"

"To me, Catherine was just a country girl who was useful for a while. Her death was very unfortunate."

"Unfortunate! What are you inferring? Catherine's death was tragic, utterly tragic. How can you dismiss her so? Two children lost their mother. Crackleton has never remarried, still missing his wife. What did you do to her? Admit your crimes!"

"Catherine wasn't part of my original plan. Blame Sculthorpe or the Sheriff, not me."

His attitude betrayed him though. He hung his head in shame.

"You nailed a Martin Marprelate tract to Buckler's beam, and put a pack in my bag. Did you plant one on Catherine too?"

"I asked her to follow Buckler."

"To spy on him?"

"I wouldn't use that word. I just needed Catherine to confirm that Buckler was working for Sculthorpe. However, being a more resourceful woman than I realised, she found a way to follow him into the cathedral despite the tight security."

"Is that when Sculthorpe found her in the cloisters?"

"He wasn't meant to find the tract in her bag. I'd given Catherine one, to leave at the bakery, killing two birds with one stone as they say. I'm sorry she was caught like that. I had to adapt my plans, and do the job myself."

Why did I save this rat? He was as incompetent as he was heartless, a hollow fraud. Felde still did not seem to understand the gravity of what he had done.

"You should have looked after Catherine if she was working for you, and you didn't have to kill Buckler."

Surely, Felde would not try to plead ignorance nor avoid responsibility now. Although it was dark, I could see his hand was twitching, worrisomely close to his sword. He lifted his head and moved his stubby face closer, more like the Felde I knew from before.

"Don't pretend you're a saint, Baxby. The baker's death didn't trouble me like Catherine's. He spied for the Church as you did. Buckler shouldn't have argued back."

He knew more than I had realised. Felde could have killed me in Lincoln as he did Buckler. Thank God, I found the Martin Marprelates and burnt them straightaway. I did not deny or confirm his assertion though. Geoffrey had taught me to say nothing when challenged, always the best approach.

Felde chuckled, "What irony to be saved from death by one of Bancroft's spies. Life has a habit of surprising us. If I believed in God, I'd say he has a strange sense of humour."

It was heartless to laugh. Felde's explanation still did not satisfy me. Why had he printed Martin Marprelate tracts and disseminated them in Lincoln? There were easier ways to remove rivals. And what did he mean when he said 'kill two birds with one stone'?

"Why did you plant the Martins Felde? It's an unusual pastime even for you."

"To make Bancroft travel, of course."

"What do you mean?"

"I planted the Martin Marprelate tracts to make Bancroft leave London. Sculthorpe always followed procedures. It worked every time."

"Why?"

"Lincoln is the furthest diocese in the Canterbury province. Bancroft was away for days."

"No, why did you want to remove Bishop Bancroft from London?"

Felde stepped back, clearly shocked. Those who frequent the corridors of Whitehall, forget that the rest of us know little about its underhand methods.

"Back then, I worked on undercover assignments, assisting Cecil and his loyal band of lords. The Church interfered persistently, Bancroft being the worst offender. We needed to remove him from court when important decisions were being made, keep him away from the Queen for as long as possible."

Geoffrey had suspected Crespin of spying, but never Felde to my knowledge.

"It was never my intention to hurt Catherine," Felde re-iterated, "Some deaths are inevitable when national security's at stake. We couldn't allow Bancroft to prejudice those proceedings."

After waiting for so long, I had expected a nobler reason for Catherine's death. Crackleton and his children must never know.

PAYING IN BLOOD

She should have died for a higher cause, a kinder medicine. Our rivals' methods were as intolerable as our own, endangering ordinary people for factional advantage. Did anyone in Whitehall or Westminster care? Does political expediency always matter more than ordinary lives?

Felde added, "I had the good fortune to inherit land, in other respects we're the same. I was working for Cecil when you were working for the Church. We both followed orders and were rewarded financially. If I am guilty, then you are too. If you tell your friend Crackleton about my role, I will tell him about yours."

It was not easy to hear but true nevertheless. Over the years I had hurt people, deceived on a regular basis, with limited concern as to the true aims and consequences of my work. Joan still languished in York gaol.

People think spies know more than they do. In practice, each is given a brief, designed to motivate them. As this brief is seldom consistent with the official account or the truth, spies can become particularly confused and distrusting. However, that was not sufficient excuse. Felde and I were pawns on Cecil and Bancroft's chess-board, but that did not exonerate us from guilt. Catherine and Buckler had paid with their lives. Neither of us deserved to survive the storm, but we had.

Felde passed a blanket across and wrapped another round his shoulders. We stood on the deck as the sky filled with stars. I stayed behind when he went below to sleep.

76

Pastor Robinson joined me on the deck in the morning. As we admired the dawn-tinged clouds, he talked about his love for his missing wife and children.

"The Church can't hold them for long," I tried to re-assure him, assuming they had been captured at Bancroft's behest.

"Do you believe the sun will re-appear?" he asked, "Similarly, we must trust the Lord to act when the time is right."

"I don't think I could have that sort of faith."

"It is not for us to know the times and places. God uses every prayer, from people who have known Him many years, and those who scarcely know him at all."

We listened to the water lap the hull below, as we waited for the sun.

"I saw you with Sir Julian Felde," Robinson added.

"He knows why Catherine Crackleton died."

"You worked hard to discover the truth. Does it help to know?"

"Not as much as I anticipated. Catherine was squeezed between powerful foes, who scarcely saw she was there. I wanted her life to matter more."

"William Brewster and Thomas Helwys are great men of God, a new kind, not ordained. You have the potential to be the same."

He waited patiently for me to reply. I tried to explain, "You made big decisions which altered the course of your life. I feel others have always steered my ship."

"Everything happens by the grace of God."

"I fear other people have *controlled* me."

"Is it time to take the rudder yourself?"

"It is time."

"With God's help you can."

I wrenched my life from my spy-masters on that voyage.

He smiled, "God can deliver us from the storms inside as well as the storms at sea. You can cry out to God whenever you need help, Baxby."

Crackleton was not concerned about his bruises, "I can't believe we're going to live in Amsterdam. Whatever would Catherine think?"

"She wouldn't have given Felde any peace."

"I've kept away from him since we boarded the ship."

"I'm sorry, Crackleton."

"You didn't cause Catherine's death. I think it was inevitable. She never stood a chance against the Minster and Bail."

I was about to agree but stopped myself. Was this true? Given the rivalry between the Church and Cecil's faction, was Catherine's death inevitable? I did not want it to be so.

"Do you think you'll ever re-marry?" I asked instead.

"Who would have a one-legged fool like me? We should talk about your prospects."

"Thomas told me that Isobel was hoping to open a bread charity. Will she be interested in me? Her late husband was a rich alderman. She wore jewels, lived a different kind of life to yours and mine."

"Everything is possible in Amsterdam, I'm told."

I clasped his hand in mine.

Once the captain had navigated the straights into the Zuider Zee, we were safe from further storms. Tears welled as we saw our new homeland for the first time. The flat expanse on the starboard side swarmed with familiar sea birds and strange new ones.

"We're back in Lincolnshire!" little Anna exclaimed.

"No, this is the Dutch Republic," her father corrected, "It looks similar, but is safer for independent believers like us."

Windmills stood like pieces on a giant chessboard, stretching out beyond the sea wall, their sails marking circles in the air.

The Zuider Zee grew busier as we travelled further south, rocked in the wash of heavier ships converging on the port. Then we saw the line of masts, along the length of the harbour, with the twisted onion spire rising behind. My friends lined the edge of the deck, amazed at the sight. How strong the brick houses looked, compared with our homes in England. Mindful of what we had left behind, Pastor Robinson shouted a prayer.

A strange new world beckoned, freedom at last. Matthew, Agnes and Isobel had made new lives there already, perhaps I could too. We had reached our destination. Amsterdam, the greatest city in the world.

PAYING IN BLOOD

London 1613

77

Remembering the joy of his arrival, Baxby stops to smile. He did not escape forever, yet survived the storm and lived to tell his tale.

"I think you were right not to tell Crackleton why his wife died," the printer surmises.

"Catherine's death was tragic, but I don't think it was inevitable as Crackleton claimed."

"It was a terrible accident," the vicar responds.

"Like Piers'?" Baxby asks, "Did Catherine metaphorically fall into a dog-pit when she visited Lincoln? Did her folly seal her fate?"

The printer protests, "You can't blame Catherine. She was just a country girl who didn't know what the Church was like. Those clerics must bear responsibility. Sculthorpe imprisoned her and sent her to the castle where she died."

The vicar retaliates, "People always blame the Church. Those clergymen were just doing their job. They have a duty to protect their parishioners from harm."

"They are clearly failing in that respect."

"These are god-less days."

"What about God, is he blameless? Shouldn't an omnipotent God muzzle snarling dogs, not just count the bite marks afterwards?"

The vicar does not approve of the question, "This is what happens when people are allowed to read what they choose. Printers are guilty too."

"People need books to learn."

"They need bishops to explain them."

Baxby tries to intervene, "I don't think Catherine's death was pre-ordained. We see the ripples on the surface, deeper truths lie beneath. Thank you for listening to my story, telling it has helped me."

His two cell-mates argue into the night, without resolution. Baxby dreams of the seashore near his childhood home.

KAREN HADEN

Thursday

London 1613

78

The guards return with a blacksmith in the morning, announcing that it is time for the vicar to leave.

"What about the others? Will we all be released before the wedding festivities?"

Obeying orders and keen to return to their breakfast, the guards will not answer questions.

As they drag the vicar down, Leonard Redfern arranges two chairs behind a small table in the crypt, pleased with the location he has found. The tombs provide a suitably menacing backdrop for the interrogation. He remains unconvinced by Geoffrey's plan, but hides his scepticism when Baxby's former patron arrives.

Despite silvering hair, Geoffrey is still a handsome man, and his influence has not waned. The spy-masters discuss the latest drafts of the royal wedding itinerary and security arrangements, while waiting for the prisoner to arrive.

"Which one are you bringing down?" Geoffrey asks.

"The vicar. Are you certain Baxby will have talked in the cell?"

"They all do in the end."

After dropping the prisoner on the flags, one guard kicks his shins before retreating, to ensure he is sufficiently scared.

Geoffrey licks his lips and starts, "Thank you for joining us. We will return your cleric's licence once you've answered a few simple questions."

"You want me to inform?"

"I think the requirement is clear. We are grateful for your assistance."

The prisoner manages to raise himself on his elbows, despite the pain in his legs, to ask, "Who are you?"

"We need to know what Alexander Baxby told you."

The vicar's family will starve if he does not retrieve his licence. A guard kicks him again in case he is not convinced.

"What has Baxby told you?" Redfern growls.

"His life story, from the Battle of Nieuwpoort to his arrival in Amsterdam. He talked for days. I can't say everything."

"What about his crimes?"

"Baxby is a bastard, who never attends parish services."

"I think you must realise that we wouldn't go to all the trouble of bringing you here to talk about non-attendance at church. Did Baxby speak about more serious crimes? Insurrection, heresy, or dissent?"

"His Separatist-believer friends fled the country without a licence. However, I'm not clear what Baxby believes himself. He seems confused about religious matters. I'm tempted to blame his upbringing."

"Did he mention Catherine Crackleton?"

"Baxby became obsessed with her death, and tried to find out what happened when he was apprenticed in Lincoln."

"There were two letters when he returned from Nieuwpoort. Did he mention them or religious tracts?"

Geoffrey was the one who recruited the pick-pocket and arranged for the letters to be delivered in the same way, provoking Baxby's interest. He does not tell the vicar or Redfern that detail, only divulging what is necessary to accomplish his business.

The vicar adds, "I think Baxby had an illness in his mind, strange dreams and waking nightmares. God saved him from a storm while crossing to Amsterdam, though I fail to understand why."

"Did he associate with Thomas Helwys? Did they sail to Amsterdam together?"

"Helwys arranged the passage with a local man called Felde, who worked as a spy for Cecil."

"Sir Julian Felde?"

Nodding, the vicar explains how the official planted Martin Marprelate tracts to make Bancroft miss important meetings at court. Geoffrey smiles when he finishes, pleased to receive such useful intelligence.

He indicates for Redfern to leave. It should only take him a few days to find Felde and make him talk. How can Cecil protest? They have confidence in their source.

Geoffrey asks, "How is Baxby now?"

"He's eating more, and growing stronger each day."

"You must go back to find out more. We need names and places in Amsterdam. Those who harbour fugitives can't escape the Church, wherever they hide."

"But you said ..."

"We will find you a comfortable living afterwards, a rural parish with rich yeomen, free from financial concerns. Do you understand?"

"How will the church warden manage without me? I promised to take my family to see the fireworks too."

"There will be other royal weddings."

"Are you Geoffrey?"

Geoffrey neither confirms nor denies his identity as is his custom. He is delighted that his plan has worked, one needs patience in this job. His former pupil did well, although Geoffrey did not anticipate the flight to Amsterdam with a fanatical sect. Baxby discovered who planted the Martin Marprelate tracts, as he expected he would.

The guards haul the vicar out, calling for the blacksmith to accompany them back to the cell. Baxby looks away as they re-hammer the bolt. Informers are always listening, be careful what you say.

PAYING IN BLOOD

Author's Note

This is a fictional story, inspired by historical characters and events. The ideas are my own, prompted by interest in the way printing technology affected earlier generations.

Protestant exiles translated the first edition of the Geneva Bible in 1560, during Queen Mary's reign. Although never endorsed by the Church, it became the most popular English bible, and was widely used until the restoration of the monarchy in 1660. The pictures and explanations helped people understand the text.

Independent scholars John Smyth and John Robinson would not have relied on the Geneva, as they could read the original Hebrew and Greek. The translation benefited literate men, women and children with less education, influencing what would later be called the middle class.

William Brewster's group would have taken the Geneva with them when they left Scrooby. After release from Boston Guildhall, the men encountered a storm en route for Amsterdam. The women were held in York. Eventually, re-united in Leiden, they formed the core of the English Pilgrims who sailed on the Mayflower in 1620. Their covenant influenced the Mayflower Compact, and hence the Founding Fathers of the United States.

John Smyth and Thomas Helwys formed the first English Baptist Church in Amsterdam. Thomas returned to London with a group and petitioned the King for freedom for those of all faiths and none – the first such plea in the English language.

The fictional character Crackleton was inspired by the widower John Crackston (or Crackstone or Craxston). He lived in Leiden with his children, and was the twenty-fifth signatory of the Mayflower Compact. Little else is known about him, or his wife Catherine who died before he left England. There is no evidence that he only had one leg, nor that other historical characters in the novel suffered from particular medical conditions.

I would like to thank Ben and Zoe Haden for their invaluable support, along with those who read early drafts. Also, Roger

Nunn and Nigel G. Wright who kindled my interest in Scrooby and Gainsborough.

Finally, thank you to everyone who has read this far. Please connect with @kjhaden17 on X (formerly Twitter) and @kjhaden on Instagram.

There is more information about Christian beliefs at www.christianity.org.uk

Many Lincoln, Boston and Gainsborough sites can be visited today.